Tom Coleman
Horrors of the Night
Collectors' Edition

HORRORS OF THE NIGHT

COLLECTORS' EDITION

A Collection of Short Stories

TOM COLEMAN

Copyright

This is a work of fiction. Names, characters, places, and incidents either are products of the author's imagination or are used fictitiously. Any similarity to actual events or locales or persons, living or dead, is entirely coincidental.

BN Publishing

ISBN 978-8-6732-1512-9

ABOUT THE AUTHOR

"This book is horror redefined. Dark and with more twists than a labyrinth. I look forward to reading more from this author."
Amazon reader about Horrors Next Door collection

Since he was a child, he shared a great interest in riddles, mystery and the abnormal. He loved the thrill of having his mind puzzled and astonished by an enigma.

Today, he writes books for people who share his enthusiasm for scary and mystifying stories. If you love horror mystery you will love his books.

We are gathering all people with a passion for Horror/Mystery/Thrillers in our special group. If you want to be in and connect with us, join our group :)

Join here:

https://www.facebook.com/groups/541739063097831/

8

TOM COLEMAN

HORRORS OF THE NIGHT COLLECTORS' EDITION

9

TOM COLEMAN

TOM COLEMAN

BABYSITTER

11

TOM COLEMAN

TOM COLEMAN

CHAPTER ONE

Rachel walked out of class annoyed. She couldn't believe Mrs. Gertrude had chosen today of all days to give them homework. She already hated math, and she hated assignments, but to combine them on the day she had to babysit was almost unfair.

She groaned while walking in the hallway, filled with other disgruntled, excited, or passive teenagers.

"Why do you look like you're constipated?" her snarky best friend, Sally, asked with a smirk.

"Why do you think?" Rachel knew Sally was just teasing. It was a good opportunity for Rachel to get some nice cash as a babysitter, but the timing was absolutely wrong.

"Just do your homework after school so you can have time to babysit at night." Sally raised a reasonable point, but Rachel still looked at her friend like she was crazy.

"Who does their homework during the day? Besides, you and I both know how loaded the Graysons are. Babysitting tonight alone will get me more than I ever would on a per-day basis when I worked at Burger King."

"They are also super creepy—at least, that's what I hear."

"Not them—they're fine as far as I can tell—it's the kids who creep me out."

Sally laughed at her remark.

Rachel frowned. What was so funny about that statement?

"You know how weird it is for you to admit that ten- and eight-year-old kids are creepy and still want to babysit them?"

"How bad could it be? They're probably just entitled as all rich kids are. Also, they seem secluded, and they don't have many friends. It could be good for them to have me around."

Rachel's friend gave her a knowing look, causing her to break. "All right, fine." Rachel raised her hands. "I'm mainly doing this for the money, not because I give a damn about two rich kids. That being said, why can't I do both?"

"Fair enough. Just do your homework if you don't want to be given a zero tomorrow."

Rachel had a brilliant idea, but Sally beat her to it. "No," she said, "I'm not doing it for you."

Rachel frowned.

***

Later that night, she was finally ready to go. The young teen put on her best formal-yet-casual attire and headed downstairs. "Mom, Dad, I'm off."

14

TOM COLEMAN

"Make a good impression, sweetie," her mother, who was seated on the couch with her dad watching the news, said to her.

"Be on your best behavior," Dad added.

"Of course. When am I never on my best behavior?"

Both of her parents scoffed.

Rachel rolled her eyes.

***

Rachel didn't have to walk far to reach the Grayson mansion since she lived just a block away from the place. It was the largest building in town, and that was counting the school, hospital, and supermarket.

She reached the gate and saw the guard there. He was a fierce-looking man. "Hello, I…" she began, but before she could say any more, the man opened the gate. She looked at him awkwardly prior to rushing toward the mansion. Rachel liked the number of lights in the garden and the landscaping of the compound. There were a lot of red flowers, especially roses, and the lights were dim but varied. The distance from the gate to the main house felt almost as long as going from her house to the Graysons'.

Nobody knew much about the Graysons. They moved to town four years ago and seemed very rich, but they also seemed ominous. The patriarch of the household, Calvin

15

Grayson, was a handsome and charismatic man who was very good with people but always found a way to not reveal too much about himself—at least, that's what Rachel's dad always said. Caroline Grayson, his wife, was a regal woman who oozed exquisite taste and poise. She was always kind to Rachel, and her family, as far as the teen knew, and Rachel's mom liked her a lot. Her parents did, however, agree that she never talked about her personal life or the family's life before coming to Verdon.

The most peculiar thing about that family was, without a doubt, the kids, Jeremy and Maya. Jeremy was ten years old, and Maya was eight. Jeremy was the more forward of the two, and his diction was particularly impressive. You could tell he had gone to the best schools before moving to Verdon, but they insisted he'd been home-schooled. Maya was very reserved, but her ball-like eyes were pretty creepy if you asked Rachel.

She reached the door, frowning after the long walk. If she shouted for the gateman, would he even be able to hear?

Rachel knocked on the door, and it opened.

Young Jeremy stood opposite her, a smile on his face. "We've been waiting, Miss Rachel." There was something off-putting about his smile, but Rachel decided not to read too much into it. "Please, come on in."

"Hello, Jeremy," she greeted while walking into the large ante-room that looked more like a hallway, and she checked out that area of the house in awe. "Holy…" Rachel said, stopping herself from cursing in front of the kid.

TOM COLEMAN

Mr. and Mrs. Grayson came into the hallway with Maya, who hid behind them. Gosh, she looked scary.

"Ah, Rachel, you're here," Mr. Grayson said with excitement. "Thank you for coming. We'll just need you to watch over the kids until we return. Should be like an hour or two."

Mrs. Grayson whispered into Maya's ear. The girl seemed angry for some reason, and Rachel made a mental note to ask her about it later on.

"Did you hear me?" Mr. Grayson inquired.

"Oh, yes. Yes, sir," Rachel said, a bit flustered. The house was so bright and sparkly, with many glassy pieces of furniture like the huge chandelier at the center of the hall, a glass vase, sculptures, and other stuff.

"I know it's a bit much," the father said, referring to the conspicuous design, "but you'll get used to it."

"Please, take care of my children," Mrs. Grayson said to Rachel.

Rachel wondered why the woman was so tense, despite the fact that she was about to leave for a few hours.

"They are… special children who need special care. Just do everything they ask as long as it is within reason, and try to indulge their… eccentricities."

She nodded awkwardly at the woman who smiled.

"All right. We'll be going."

"Better be back soon, Father," Jeremy said with an odd smile, causing his dad to frown. Mr. Grayson opened the door for his wife to pass through.

"Don't do anything stupid," the father admonished

Though she thought it harsh, Rachel wasn't about to say anything. It was her chance to earn some good cash, and she would like for them to call her again.

"Sure, Father. When do I not follow your orders?"

Rachel sensed some tension between the father and son, and she had to remind herself that it wasn't her business. "Have a nice journey, Mr. and Mrs. Grayson," she said. They all waved before Rachel closed the door.

She turned to face the kids. They were a stark contrast to each other. Jeremy kept his chin up, and he had an upright posture. He looked confident... a bit too confident. There was something uneasy about the way he looked at her, as if there was something he knew that she did not.

Maya, however, was very reserved. Her shoulders were slouched, and she stared at the floor most times. Whenever she did look up at Rachel, Maya's eyes never blinked. Rachel knew it was not a good way to describe a kid, but she looked sinister.

"Okay, kids—let's do something fun while your parents are away." Rachel had planned to have some fun while making the kids believe they were having some fun, too. "Why don't you two show me around? I'd like to know more about you and this wonderful house, but it's too large..."

"Leave it to me," Jeremy offered. He grabbed her by the hand and dragged her along with him.

"W-wait—what about your sister?" she inquired, but Maya just glared at her as Jeremy pulled her away.

"She'll be fine. Trust me. Maya needs space to carry out her… experiments."

"Experiments?"

"Enough about her. Let me show you my room. After that, we'll check the green room where all the plants are grown. Then, the art study." Jeremy sounded too old for his age.

Rachel didn't want to upset the kids, so she went along with it.

They went to his room first. It looked like the room of a kid who was far too wise for his age. She saw more books than she ever expected to see in a ten-year-old's room. "Wow, you read," she said, flipping through the pages of some of the books.

Wait—what? She found some very… disturbing drawings on some of the pages. What were they—torture devices?

"The Middle Ages," Jeremy said from behind Rachel, startling her.

She whipped her head around to see him staring at her with a menacing glare and smile.

He turned his gaze to the book and ran his fingers over the pages. "They had the best torture devices back in those times. So many innovative weapons that struck fear into whoever witnessed it, let alone those who endured the torture."

Rachel focused on the kid's facial expressions as he talked. He seemed fascinated by the macabre devices.

"We should… get back to Maya," Rachel said, trying to ease whatever tension the boy's reaction had brought to the conversation. He looked almost hungry as he spoke about.

"If you say so," Jeremy remarked, "but we haven't finished our tour yet."

"But—"

"I *said* we haven't finished yet." Jeremy said this with a tone of finality, and he took her hand and led her out of the room and through the large, confusing hallways around the house to meet Maya in the green room, where she was playing with some animals.

Rachel was shocked to see the blood—was she experimenting with living animals?

"That's … interesting," Rachel said, trying to take an enthusiastic approach.

"Maya is interested in some darker things. My parents get worried, but I feel she should be allowed to explore."

"Huh—is that so?" Rachel was on the side of the parent this time. They were right to be worried about that kind of behavior, but whatever—she wasn't her kid. All Rachel needed was to collect the money and keep quiet.

20

"Will you keep this secret between us?" Jeremy asked with his typical weird but confident smile.

"Y-yeah." Rachel was a bit confused as to what, exactly, was happening.

When she was done, Maya washed up, and they had some fun playing board games like Monopoly and checkers. Maya seemed stressed and scared. She stayed close to Jeremy. They were siblings, after all, so that wasn't too surprising in and of itself.

***

Rachel's eyes fluttered open. The lights were off, but one of the lamps had been lit.

What had happened? She remembered they'd been playing board games, and that was the last of it. Rachel looked around. She could tell that she was in the sitting room, and she'd been sleeping. Where were the kids?

She wondered if they'd gone to bed. Rachel rubbed her eyes. She looked around, but the kids were nowhere in sight. "Shit! The Graysons are gonna be mad at me if they come home to see me like this and this place as a mess."

Rachel scurried about, arranging the place. She went to turn on the lights, wondering why the lights were even off in the first place. She guessed they'd turned them off for her sake when she'd fallen. Such nice kids.

21

That was when she slipped on something and fell on her back.

Rachel stood up and felt around to see what she'd fallen on. The light on the lamp was not overly bright, but it was still clear enough to show her exactly what she'd fallen on and what was on her hand.

"Blood," Rachel said in shock. She staggered backward and slipped in the pool of blood yet again. This time, she fell on a solid body.

Rachel turned quickly around, startled, her body covered in blood. She stepped away from what she'd landed on. "Oh, my God. Oh, my God," she said. "Oh, my God!" She couldn't believe what she was seeing. She stood up and promptly turned on the lights.

"Mr. and Mrs. Grayson… Oh, God."

They were back… and they were dead.

CHAPTER TWO

Rachel rushed to cover their bodies while looking for her phone to call 911. The cops needed to be there as quickly as possible. A murder had been committed. Rachel couldn't find her phone, but a thought occurred to her: what if the cops suspect her? She was in the pool of blood in the middle of a crime scene. The maids were not around, as far as she could tell, and the kids—yes, the kids! Maybe they knew what had happened.

"This fucking house is a goddamn maze," Rachel lamented. Her next best option was to call the guardsman, but even he might suspect and accuse her. She recalled the way he'd glared at her when she'd seen him at the gate. Rachel needed to go with the kids if she were to meet him, and the kids were nowhere to be found.

"Gotta find them. I hope they are okay," Rachel said. She first went to the visitor's bathroom near the living room to wash herself off. When she was done, Rachel started looking for them.

"Jeremy! Maya!" Rachel yelled. She tried to remember the route she had taken to Jeremy's room the last time. Why were all the goddamn lights turned off? The house gave her the creeps with the lights off. Add to that the dead bodies downstairs, and it was definitely not an ideal situation, nor was it what she had in mind when she'd gone there that night.

Where the hell was her phone, and where were those kids? How the hell had she gotten into that mess?

There was a sound, stopping her dead in her tracks. Every hallway had eight or so doors from what she could see. Was someone hiding behind of those doors? What the hell was going on?

"Is anyone there?" she asked, hearing nothing.

There were some sounds outside. They sounded like… raindrops? Was it raining? Rachel had to find the kids quickly, or she'd have a hard time explaining the situation to anyone. Nevertheless, she had the feeling she was being watched, and that made her uneasy.

Her heart beat fast, and she was worried that whoever had murdered the Graysons was in the house and following her. Maybe she should stop shouting for Jeremy and Maya.

Rachel walked quickly without looking back, taking as many turns as she could before entering one of the rooms and locking the door behind her.

The room was… weird. There were paintings on the walls of some hideous and unnerving things: a person having their intestines pulled out by some weird creatures, a woman being set on fire… who had drawn these things?

Rachel decided to leave the room—she couldn't keep hiding there all by herself. The kids might be in danger, and the murderer might be after them. She had to be courageous. The money no longer mattered. Shit was serious now, and she had to protect the lives of those poor kids while escaping from the killer.

"Shit! Shit, shit, shit, shit!" Rachel lamented her cursed situation as she left the room and ran as fast as she could. She heard footsteps behind her, causing her to run even faster. Was she really about to die? As she ran, she tried to turn on one of the lights to see who was behind her, but there was no one. Was it all in her mind?

Rachel walked around the mansion for about five more minutes before she heard footsteps coming her way. Was it the murderer again? Had he or she found her?

She didn't have a weapon, so she balled her hands into fists. In hindsight, she surmised that she should have picked up a knife from the kitchen. Speaking of knives, where was the murder weapon that had caused Mr. and Mrs. Grayson to shed so much blood?

"There you are."

The voice caused her to yelp and jump in the air.

Jeremy was standing in front of her, wearing a cocky smile. "I heard you calling my name, but I couldn't find you."

"And you couldn't yell back to let me know where you were?"

"Mother and Father said we shouldn't yell in the house," he answered. That reminded Rachel that the boy's parents were dead, and he didn't seem to know.

"Jeremy, I need to ask you something." She knelt on one knee so as to be at his eye level.

Jeremy nodded and waited for the question with a curious expression.

"After I slept, did anyone else come into the house?"

25

"No."

"Have you seen your parents tonight night?"

"No, I haven't. They probably spent the night forgetting that they'd left us at home. It's typical, Miss Rachel. Don't worry about it."

"I need to tell you something, Jeremy." Rachel did not know how to explain it to the young boy, but he did seem older than he looked, so coming clean was the best thing. "Your parents are dead."

"You're joking, right?" he asked with a smirk.

"I'm being one hundred percent serious." Rachel looked at him dead-on.

Slowly but surely, Jeremy's expression changed from relaxed to one of caution. He seemed deep thought, which was not the reaction Rachel had expected. Sure, the kid acted older than his age, but his parents were dead—why was he not freaking out? Had he already known about it? From his initial reaction, Rachel was sure Jeremy had been genuinely surprised at the news, but honestly, what did she know? She wasn't a lie detector, so she couldn't say for sure.

"Where is my sister?" Jeremy asked, looking very worried. It wasn't unexpected, given what he had just been told about his parents, but Rachel was more concerned with his reaction to his parents' demise.

"Why aren't you more surprised at your parents being dead?" she asked, curious as to how he remained so calm.

TOM COLEMAN

"All I care about is my sister, right now," the young boy replied. "So, do you know where she is, Miss Rachel?"

"I was looking for her, too. Where is she? I thought you two left after I fell asleep. You didn't hear when your parents got in?"

"This is a really big house, Miss Rachel. We don't see or hear a lot of things." The way he'd said it and the way this boy was acting… something was seriously off. For the time being, though, the best thing was to find Maya.

"We need to find Maya before the killer finds her. He or she might still be in the house, and I heard someone following me some minutes ago." A huge lightning strike outside reminded her it was still raining. In fact, it seemed to have gotten worse.

"Shit—we still need to call the police to report this."

"Language," Jeremy said, reminding her not to curse, but who the fuck cared about that just then? Rachel's main focus was to protect the kids and get out of the messy situation alive.

"Do you have a phone? Did you see my phone? I woke up and couldn't find it."

"Our parents don't give us phones. We are just kids, remember?"

It finally hit Rachel. "Wait! What about the landline?"

"Yeah, that's a good idea," Jeremy noted, "but first, I need to find my sister."

"Are you crazy? We need to call the goddamn police!"

TOM COLEMAN

"Not before I find my sister. What if the killer gets to her while we're heading for the phone?" Jeremy inquired. "I have to protect Maya, no matter what happens."

Rachel groaned in annoyance, and she placed her hands on her head. She could not fucking believe what was happening. Why was the kid so focused on his sister? Why was he not freaked out when he'd heard his parents were dead?

A thought crept into her mind. She did not want to believe it, but still, all the signs were there.

What if Jeremy Grayson had killed his parents?

CHAPTER THREE

Rachel did not know what to make of what was taking shape in her mind. She did not want to believe it, but everything going through her mind made sense so far. Jeremy had a weird affinity for killing and torture, which lined up with the brutal way his mother and father had been killed.

"Okay. We'll find your sister first." It seemed like the wise thing to do at the time. She had to try to find Maya to see what to make of the situation first. How did she even explain to the police—or anyone, for that matter—that a ten-year-old, mild-mannered boy had killed his parents? Even if they found the weird drawings in his room, would that be enough? Fuck, she should have paid more attention in civics class or read more about the law.

"Good. Let's check her room first," Jeremy said, and they both went. Rachel made sure to walk behind Jeremy as she watched him carefully. She found it hard to believe he could have done it, but it was possible. Rachel wondered if the Graysons had some sort of security cameras, but she did not consider it likely. A family that rich should have cameras, right? She hadn't noticed any cameras while walking around the compound, but then again, she hadn't been looking for cameras. She had been too in awe to notice anything like that. Nevertheless, wouldn't the kids know if there were cameras on the compound or in the house? They were eight and ten, so it was possible they hadn't been told. Rachel knew she was hoping for the extreme best, but it was an extreme situation.

29

TOM COLEMAN

"We're here," Jeremy said, opening the door to Maya's room.

Rachel entered. She noticed many pictures of animals, which wasn't that surprising, considering Maya's "experiments" in the green room.

Maya had covered herself with a blanket.

Jeremy went to meet her. Rachel was about to, but he signaled for her not to get too close. Was the little girl an angry sleeper or something?

"Maya," Jeremy said softly, "Miss Rachel is here. She just told me that Mom and Dad were killed."

Rachel was alarmed. Why had he just told her like that? She guessed that he knew his sister better than anyone, so maybe they had a different dynamic. Everything was abnormal about their situation.

Maya whispered something to her brother that Rachel did not get before she stood up. She rubbed her eyes, but Rachel couldn't tell if she was doing it because she was crying or because she had just woken up. What the hell was wrong with these children? One of them could be a killer, and the other was just weird.

"I'm so sorry, but your mom and dad are dead. Someone killed them, and the person might still be in this house," Rachel said to the girl. Her eyes looked so large and innocent, but they were still quite scary. Rachel had to look past that right now. The little girl had just lost two of the most important people in her life, and her brother could have done it.

"We have to leave this house and call the police as well." The moment Rachel said this, Maya looked scared. It was the first time Rachel had seen any real emotion coming from the young girl. Why had she not wanted the police there?

Maya's gaze turned to Jeremy, and he stepped quickly in.

"She's in shock. Can you let her rest, and then we can go downstairs?" It was evident that Jeremy had done something. Maya had known, and that was why she was scared of the police taking her and catching her brother.

"Let's go to the living room," Rachel said. "We aren't going to wait anymore. I'll go by myself if you two aren't coming." Rachel ruminated on whether Jeremy had taken her phone, as well. What had happened when she was asleep? A part of her was tempted to ask the kids if they knew of any cameras around the house—she didn't expect the surveillance cameras to be obvious, nor did she expect them to be in their bedrooms.

"Do you know if—" Rachel began, but before she could finish, something hard hit her at the back of her head, and she fell to the ground. Rachel was disoriented, but she was still conscious. She turned around, clutching the back of her head with her hand.

"What the hell? What is this, Jeremy?" she inquired.

The boy looked more scared than she had ever seen him. He was holding what looked like a wooden rod. "I'm… I'm sorry. I-I can't let you call the police."

"Huh? So, it was really you who killed your parents?"

31

"What? No!" He looked so disgusted by the fact that she would even think that, which made Rachel question if he had really done it.

"Jeremy, don't do it," Maya said in a soft voice, tugging on his shirt.

Rachel was grateful the girl was there to keep him in check.

"Listen to your sister, Jeremy. You don't want to kill anyone else." Rachel's head ached. She was also bleeding, but her adrenaline had taken over for the time being. Rachel needed to get out of there alive. Fuck! If she had known the kid was crazy enough to kill his parents, she would have gone straight to the guard.

"I'll do it, as always," Maya said, and Rachel was stunned. Was she saying that she had killed their parents?

"It wasn't you?"

The boy's reaction said it all. "You don't understand," he reasoned. "Maya is a… special girl. She needs me to keep protecting her from others whenever she has her episodes."

"Episodes? How many times has this happened?" Rachel scurried away from them while still on the floor. She was scared as hell.

"We had to move after Mom and Dad paid off the police whenever she killed someone. It's only happened twice. I thought we all had an understanding, but then Mom and Dad came back and told me they were taking Maya to a "special" home for special people. They felt guilty for what they had done for Maya in the past, and now they wanted to throw her away like a useless rag doll. Weren't they the ones who had brought her into the world this way? And they dare see her as defective? I already knew what that meant. I was not going to let them take her away." Jeremy handed the rod to his sister.

Rachel saw just how insane she had been. He might have an affinity for the macabre, but Rachel had been the one who had seen the pre-teen cutting up animals. She should have known better, but who the hell would ever suspect an eight-year-old of brutally murdering her parents?

"I confronted them about what they were doing. You were asleep then, when they returned, and in the midst of our argument, Maya took matters into her own hands."

Maya glared at Rachel as she came closer. That close to the murderer, Rachel could definitely tell the little girl was sick in the head and needed to be taken care of by any means necessary. Right then, though, she had to stay alive and protect herself from certain death. If she died there, the kids could frame the story anyway they wanted. In fact, she was sure that had been the original plan.

"You killed your own parents."

"They wanted to separate me from my brother... my protector... the only one who allows me to do as I wish."

Do as she wishes? She called murdering people and animals doing as she wished? Seriously—what *had* she gotten herself into?

"I was not going to let that happen."

33

TOM COLEMAN

"So, why didn't you kill me after that? You wanted to frame me for the murder, huh?"

"We were still trying to work out the kinks of our story when you woke up, so we had to improvise. I followed you for a while as you stumbled your way through the house, not knowing anything. It's a convenient story: kids kill the babysitter who killed their parents."

Rachel, however, was not going to let that happen. She might be seriously injured, but she was a teenager, and these were kids. There was no way she was going to jail because of this. There was a bigger reason she needed to end it there: the kids should not be allowed to live in normal society. They already seemed broken beyond repair. Had they been born that way?

Regardless, she did not care.

Maya swung, and Rachel lunged forward at the same moment, pushing the girl back. The siblings looked surprised that she still had that much strength and coherence left in her.

"You sick little bitch!" Rachel was filled with a primal instinct to survive and stop the manipulative children. The scariest and most unassuming killers in her mind were children, which was a nightmare brought to life.

Rachel punched the girl in the face with all her might, causing her to bleed. She felt a sharp pain in her waist and turned to see that Jeremy had stabbed her.

"You are not going to tear us apart," Jeremy yelled. "Maya needs me, and I need her. We are together forever."

Rachel grabbed his head and bashed it on the floor several times without stopping. "Then… you… should… be… together… in… hell!" She bashed his head after every word. He was dead before she'd finished speaking.

Maya screeched so loud, Rachel had to let go of Jeremy to hold her ears. She fell back.

"You killed him," the little sadistic girl screamed. She climbed on top of Rachel and tried to stab her with the knife Jeremy had used.

Rachel twisted the knife quickly away from Maya's hand and stabbed the girl. She stabbed her again, and one more time, just to be certain.

The little girl died with her sinister, owl-like glare fixed on Rachel.

The babysitter was injured. She knew she was about to die. Rachel slumped on the floor. She was ready to die. She knew no help was about to come.

Rachel glanced to her side. Her phone was under the table. Was that where they had hidden it?

She dialed 911, already knowing she would have a lot to explain.

"911. What's your emergency?"

"I'm at the Grayson Mansion in Verdon. Tell the county police to head over here immediately. There's been a series… ugh… a series of murders," she managed to say, enduring the pain before she cut the connection.

Just as her eyes were about to give way to the darkness, Rachel noticed what looked like a camera in the room. She smiled. It wasn't surprising that the parents, worried about their kid's uncanny behaviour, had placed cameras all around the house. She could rest easy now, knowing it had all been recorded… or had it?

(Based on the idea of my dear reader Constance)

36

TOM COLEMAN

DARK SIDE

37

TOM COLEMAN

"Good morning, sweetie." Selene's eyes opened to see her graceful and loving husband, Damien. She was awake, but she kept her eyes closed, knowing he was watching her. He did this often, and she loved it.

"Hey, handsome," Selene said to Damien.

He smiled and gave her a passionate kiss. As their tongues canoodled, she reflected on how great it was to have the love of your life next to you.

Selene Foster and Damien Richards had been together for two years, and they were happy. She definitely saw a future with the man. Recently, though, things had been different. Sure, Damien was still basically the perfect boyfriend—he was loyal, caring, rich, good in bed, and smart. That being said, Selene could not shake the feeling that something was wrong. He had been distant for the past few months, regularly going to his private room to work there. After a year of dating, Selene had moved in with him. Damien had only one rule: never go to the private room. She had respected that because he had time for her. Now, though, the time Damien spent with and on her had dwindled over the past couple of months, and it bothered her. Two days ago, he had spent twelve hours straight in the room. What the hell was he doing in there, she wondered.

"Hey, babe," Damien said. "I was thinking about inviting some of my friends over for a chill get-together."

"Oh, okay. When?" she inquired.

"Tomorrow. They'll be staying over for the next two or three days." That piqued Selene's interest. Why were they going to stay that long?

"What's this get-together really about?" She asked, giving him a suspicious look.

He simply laughed at her facial expression. "You're cute, hon," Damien said. He walked over to where she was standing by the bed. "It's just a get-together. You can ask Craig. It's nothing out of the ordinary. They're just a bit cramped at home, and I offered for Craig, Marcus, and Daniel to come and stay here for a few days so we can do guy stuff."

She squinted her eyes, analysing his face in search of falsehoods.

"Would you rather I go with them to a hotel for a few days until they feel better?" he asked, raising an eyebrow. "Think of it like this: you will be with us, and you can monitor us for as long as you'd like."

"You know I have work."

"Well, there's nothing I can do about that now, is there?" He made some solid points. Damien's friends meant a lot to him, so it wasn't unordinary for him to take care of them that way. They were also equally loyal to him, and they were all friends with her to some extent. Every girl has her insecurities, though. What if he brought girls to the house while she was away?

As if intuiting what she was thinking, Damien spoke: "You do realize that if I wanted to cheat on you, I could have done it any day, and I don't need my friends to do so." He gave her a knowing smile. Damien worked from home, and he was an artist, so he could manage his time as he liked, unlike Selene, who had a nine-to-five job in a corporate setting.

"Fine." She sighed.

Damien seemed surprised at her reticence. "Where is this... fear coming from?" he inquired. "Have I given you any reason not to trust me?"

She knew why. Selene had been getting more and more worried at Damien's secrecy. What the heck was in that bloody room? Damien was a man with whom she could see herself spending the rest of her life, but marriage comes with trust—could she fully trust him when he did not fully trust her?

"Come on—what is the problem?" Damien asked with worry in his eyes. "You can tell me. We are in this together. If you can't tell me, who else are you gonna tell?"

"What's in your private room?" There. She'd said it out loud. For twelve months, Selene had never questioned his decision not to let her know what was in the room, but now, she'd gone and blurted it out.

"It's where I express my art," Damien said. "I am sorry, but I am not ready to let anyone see it yet. I hope you can understand. Hopefully, in the future, when I am more comfortable, I will show it to you."

"Is it that you don't trust me?"

"No, no, no, Not at all. It's me. I'm not ready," he tried to assure her. "You know what? I will show it to you by the

40

end of this little get-together with my friends; how is that?" There was a piercing look in his black eyes as he smiled at her after delivering the proposal. There was something off about the way he'd proposed it, but she did not care. He was finally going to share the final part of his life with her. It was a great step toward their great future together.

"That would be great," she said with a smile. "To be honest, it has been bothering me for a while. I'm glad we're finally taking the next step."

"I am, too," he said, hugging her tightly before kissing her. She was so happy and so in love—why couldn't Selene let go of the pit in her stomach? What, exactly, was the problem?

The next day, Selene came home from work a bit early. She opened the door and went inside, and it was surprisingly quiet. Usually, Damien was playing some "Call of Duty," but instead, there was silence. She wanted to call his name and ask where he was, but she decided against it.

She made her way up the stairs, where she heard some weird noises from... the private room? Were those... screams? She was unsure. Selene had never seen the inside of the room, so she wouldn't know, but they sounded like screams. Was he watching a movie? The noise was not loud, but she could still hear it. What the hell is going on in there?

"What the hell?" she murmured, her curiosity piqued. For a second, Selene thought about just forcing the door open, using the fact that she'd heard screaming as an excuse.

"He isn't so stupid that he wouldn't know what I was doing," she said, presuming that the door was locked. Besides,

41

TOM COLEMAN

he was going to show her what was in there in just a few days—why couldn't she wait?

"Damien?" Selene said.

The screaming immediately stopped.

"Are you there? I came home early from work. I thought you'd be playing your video games right about now."

"Hey, welcome!" he said from inside without opening the door. This made Selene cautious.

"What was that screaming I heard?"

"I'm watching an audition for a role. I'll tell you about it later. I was trying to get into the mindset of a woman in fear 'cos I was about to draw on that." That sounded normal, to be honest. She had heard of artists doing even weirder things to get "in the zone.

"Okay, hon. I'm going to get changed," but even as she disrobed, something felt off. Was there a woman in there? It was doubtful, but Selene had the tendency to be insecure, and this ate at her. Could she wait a few more days to know what went on in that damn room?

***

It was the day Craig, Marcus, and Daniel were scheduled to come over. Selene thought that Damien would be more excited, but he kept his attention focused on his phone.

"Why are you so fixated on your phone?" she asked with a frown.

Damien smiled. "I'm chatting on Facebook."

"So? Shouldn't you be more excited that they are coming?"

"I am. Who do you think I've been chatting with?"

"Oh, that makes sense. Anyway, I'll go prepare something for them to eat."

"Don't worry—I'll make it. I need you to go to the store for me, though, to get some extra snacks and stuff."

"Sure." He handed her his credit card, and she went to the store. It was a Saturday, so she didn't have to go to work. By the time Selene had returned, all of his friends were in the house.

"Seleeeene!" Craig, Damien's wild thirty-four-year-old lifelong friend said. He ran over and hugged her tightly. Out of all of Damien's friends, she was closest to him, and they got along pretty well. "I'm sorry that we are coming to disturb you two like this."

"Aww. C'mon—it's fine. You guys have known each other for, like, forever," she responded with a smile.

The rest of the day was filled with fun activities for the guys down in the basement while Selene did her own thing in the living room. A couple of hours after they'd arrived, around seven o'clock, Selene heard the sound of someone coming from the basement. She turned around to see Damien looking stressed and tired. "You look like you've been lifting weights or something."

"I might as well have," he said with a weak smile. "Those guys have too much energy for me."

TOM COLEMAN

"I'll come down later to check up on you guys."

"No need. They're all fast asleep by now," he informed. "Apparently, Marcus had a big fight with his wife last night that lasted well into the early morning."

"I hoped they liked the meal you made for them, though."

He looked away from her.

Selene furrowed her brows in confusion.

"Yeah, they loved it," he answered, going up the stairs. "Anyway, I need to regain some energy now. I'm gonna have a shower, then go to the private room to draw a little."

"Okay." Selene knew something was off. He had been acting strange, and the mention of the private room always made her cautious, curious, and insecure.

After remaining seated for a few seconds, Selene made up her mind. She got up and tip-toed her way to their bedroom.

Damien had just gone into the shower, and she saw that his phone was still unlocked. Damien was a private man, and he'd never shared his password with her. This time, though, Selene was able to tap on the smartphone before it had gone off, allowing her to see his texts.

The first one that popped up read, "Make sure you do the sacrifice tonight."

Wait... what? was the first thought that ran through her mind. What sacrifice? Was it some kind of inside joke? She was thinking about asking him when her eyes trailed up to the top

TOM COLEMAN

of the chat group. The headline of the group read, "The Cult of the Diabolus."

"What the hell is this?" Selene whispered, keeping in mind the fact that her boyfriend was having a shower just a few meters from her. She read the remaining messages, and she was shocked. From what she could see, it was a legit call to kill people. The sacrifice was supposed to be the massacre of several people for "Diabolus," whatever that meant.

A part of Selene wanted to brush it off as nothing, but she continued to read, scrolling up to see the details of the plan. It was clear: the person chosen would get four people and sacrifice them in a gory, ritual massacre in an honorable offering to the deity they called Diabolus.

"Wait…" That was when it struck her. There were four of them in the house at the moment. Was it happening that day? What was in the private room? Who had been screaming before? She put the phone back exactly where she had found it, open to the Facebook group, left, and headed straight down to the basement.

Selene opened the door and went inside. The ominous feel of silence enveloping the basement as she walked down sent shivers down her spine. Why did she feel that way? Probably due to her new revelations. A part of her still wanted to believe that it was all some big, sick misunderstanding, but Selene knew she would have to be a fool to ignore the signs.

She swallowed her saliva. Her breathing was uneven. She reached the bottom of the stairs and saw all of Damien's friends sleeping. Were they sleeping, or were they dead? The group said there had to be some kind of ritual, so that meant they could not already be dead, but it was all speculation to her.

Selene sighed, gathered her thoughts, and summoned her courage before going over to where Craig laid. His eyes were weirdly open, and he could move them, but his body was still.

"Craig?" She was confused—was he paralyzed?

"He's fine," the all-too-familiar voice she knew as that of her boyfriend said from behind her.

Terror ran through her body, and she struggled to calm herself. Selene knew that if she looked back at him terrified, she was done for.

Three paralyzed bodies and one lady who was a potential victim were all there in the same room as their assailant—it was a worst-case scenario.

***

As she always did when she was nervous wanted to remain calm, Selene took a deep breath and bottled all of her fear inside before turning to face him. "Hey, is he okay?" Selene asked. She had to be smart. If she had not asked why their eyes were like that, it would only make Damien more suspicious of her actions. "He looks a bit weird."

"They just drank a bit too much," Damien said with a smile. "Now that you are here, why don't we watch a movie? I'll get you some of the pasta I made."

"Okay, sure." Selene did not know how to get out of her situation. She did, however, know that she had to get him to leave, and this was the fastest way.

"All right. Cool. I'll be right back." He left. It was what she had wanted. Selene went to meet Craig. She took out her phone to call 911, but she wanted to be absolutely sure that a crime was actually being committed.

"Craig, I'm gonna need your help, okay?" Selene said to him. "Were you drugged by Damien or not? If you were, look to the left. If you weren't, look to the right."

The man looked quickly to the left. That was all she needed. Selene quickly dialled 911.

"Hello, 911. What's your emergency?"

"My boyfriend is trying to kill me and three others. Please, come quickly," she said as boldly as she could without being too loud.

"Where are you right now, ma'am?"

"Twenty-four Newport Avenue. Please come qui—" She noticed Craig raising his eyes as if trying to tell her something, but before she was done with her call, the phone was yanked out of her hand.

Selene yelped and turned around to be met with a backhand slap across her face. It sent her staggering backward and falling to the floor. She wasn't sure if the police had gotten her address or not, which was not good.

"Stupid bitch," Damien said. The vein in the middle of his forehead popped out, and he frowned at her viciously.

47

TOM COLEMAN

Selene had never seen that side to him before. Was this the man with whom she'd been living all this time?

"You are trying to spoil my sacrifice. Do you know how long I have waited to do this?"

"Why are you doing this?"

"You know what? I am curious.

"How did you figure it out? Seriously." He seemed genuinely curious, and Selene felt it would be to her benefit to waste some time. Maybe the paralysis stuff would wear off, and they could all take him together, even though the guys would be much weaker, given their current state.

"Was that why you kept asking about the private room?"

That was when it struck her—the private room was a cult shrine or a place related to his cult. What the hell was in that room? Now, she really did not want to know.

"Ansa me, bitch!"

Selene was rattled by his shouting. "I just found out today when you went into the shower. Your phone was still on, so I peeked."

He chuckled as if impressed. "Not bad."

"Why are you in a cult? Why are you trying to kill your best friends and me, your girlfriend?"

"Because one must give up those whom they love the most to truly transcend into Diabolus's arms," Damien responded. The look on his face told Selene all she needed to know—he was a nut who had some strong beliefs. Sociopaths with convictions were the scariest kinds.

"You're crazy," she said. It seemed to hit a nerve with him.

"Crazy? For believing?" He pulled her hair and dragged her with him as he went up the stairs. "I'll show you freaking crazy! You wanna see the private room that badly? I'll show it to you."

Damien dragged her up the stairs to the private room, with Selene kicking and screaming every step of the way.

Once she was inside, it was a horror show. There were human skins and those of animals, as well. The room was colored red with some weird symbols drawn in black on all of the walls. There was a television and some weird, large pentagram drawn on the floor. Even the fluorescents were red. She also noticed some ropes and assumed they were meant to tie up his victims.

"Please, you have to—" A crushing punch hit her in the nose, disorienting her, sending her to the floor, and knocking her nearly unconscious. Selene could only see and hear things in fragments after that, but by the time Damien had brought the three other individuals to the room, her mind was clear as day.

Selene had taken a penknife that was next to Craig when she was in the basement, and now she played dead, or in this case, unconscious.

TOM COLEMAN

Damien took each individual to a different side of the pentagram except for Selene. He didn't seem too worried about her because she was a woman, and she did not have a weapon.

Well, he was wrong about that.

"*Aktar luvre, nessus...*" Damien chanted in some language or devilish tongue she did not understand while moving toward her. He stopped to check his phone—probably the Facebook group—and she saw her chance.

Selene sprung up and stabbed him in the torso, causing Damien to groan in pain. She pulled out the knife and attempted to stab him again, but he punched her in the neck. The poor lady coughed ferociously and clutched her neck as she moved backward.

The knife fell to the ground, and Damien was forced to go down on one knee. "Why can't you...ugh...why can't you understand?" he yelled at her. Was he seriously thinking of himself as the good one here? She could not believe it.

Marcus managed to jump on Damien from behind. The paralysis drug had worn off, but he was still weak. Marcus tried shoving his fingers deep into Damien's eye.

"Aaaarrrgh!" Damien screamed as he tried to stop his assailant from going any further. He felt his way to the knife, grabbed it, and stabbed Marcus in the eye.

"Oh, my God," Selene managed to say amid her coughs. He had just killed him!

Damien first dragged Marcus's lifeless body to his original spot on the pentagram. To Selene, it seemed like an

TOM COLEMAN

important part of the ritual; otherwise, he would have just come after her.

"Stupid ungrateful assholes," he said, finally turning his attention to her.

"Forgive us for not thanking you for killing us," she retorted.

Just as he was about to come after her, the other two men each grabbed one of his legs. In that split second, Selene ran at him and pushed him to the floor. She shoved her fingers into his earlier injury, causing Damien to scream in agony.

Daniel held onto the hand holding the knife while Craig held his other hand.

Selene's throat was injured, and her nose was broken and bleeding, but none of that mattered as long as she would finish what Marcus was trying to do.

Damien would not let go of the knife, no matter what, and the rest of them were weak, so she did the first thing that came to mind.

"Eat this," Selene said, looking into her lover's desperate eyes before shoving her thumbs right into them. Considering everything that had happened that day, perhaps calling him her ex-lover might be more apropos. She enjoyed his screams and wails as she bore her hands deep into his eye sockets. Blood squished out in spurts like water from a hose. Some of it splashed on her face, but she didn't care. Her fingers bore into his eyes, even after he stopped screaming, and she stared at the horrific face of the man she had loved for the past two years.

TOM COLEMAN

The police arrived a few minutes later to meet a gory and unimaginable scene. Everything was explained to them, and the rest of the details were taken from Damien's phone after it had been hacked.

At that moment, as she watched his dead body with her hands still in it, Selene wondered how things could have ended up that way. She knew how, of course, but still... what the hell was wrong with the world? What other mysteries and diabolical happenings lurked in the dark crevices of society? What was the dark side?

(Inspired by a true story that happened in USA some years ago.)

TOM COLEMAN

53

TOM COLEMAN

THE CURSE OF HERNANDEZ

54

TOM COLEMAN

55

TOM COLEMAN

CHAPTER ONE:
Welcome, Mr. and Mrs. Hernandez

Carlos and Christina Hernandez were happy. As they drove to their newly-purchased home, Christina squeezed her true love's hand.

Carlos smiled. This was the life he had dreamed of for years, ever since he was a kid. Now, at the age of thirty, the woman of his dreams by his side, Carlos was happy that he was going to see it manifest. He just wished *she* was there to see it.

"What's wrong, babe?" Christina said, noticing her man's changed facial expression.

"It's just… I wish *she* was here to share this moment with us."

Christina understood it was a sore spot for Carlos. "I understand, my love," Christina said, rubbing his hand. "I'm sure she is looking down on us from heaven with a smile. She is happy for us."

"Yeah, I hope so."

They drove for a little while before arriving at the home of their dreams, a four-bedroom apartment in a secluded area of El Paso. Carlos still could not believe he had come so

TOM COLEMAN

far, considering from where he'd started. He knew how hard he had fought his way from his lowly upbringing to reach where he was.

They got out of the car to look around. Carlos had never been one to care about neighbours, but the only reason he was initially sceptical about the place was the distance between houses. He was told that the area was undeveloped, and that was why it was cheaper. It would soon be overrun with neighbours, building their own houses, so he got a bargain.

Now, looking at the trees, bushes, and shrubs around him, the young man felt uneasy. There was something ominous about the place, but he couldn't quite put his finger on it. He was probably just being paranoid. More importantly, Christina loved the place.

He turned to see his wife smiling as she gazed around. She was happy, and if she was happy, so was he.

"This is great," she said. She walked over to him and kissed him. Christina didn't have the rough childhood Carlos had, but she had made many mistakes that still haunted her. Nevertheless, if someone like her could find love, anyone could. She had turned her life around after her teenage days and was now a newly-married twenty-six-year-old with a bright future ahead of her. Next would be kids, which was why they had bought the four-bedroom flat.

"Let's go inside our *home,*" he said, and she smiled.

Carlos felt something on the back of his neck as he walked away. It felt like a nail or something sharp had been pushed slowly into his flesh. He turned quickly but saw no one.

"What is it? Are you okay?"

"Yeah," he replied, though it sounded unconvincing, even to his own ears.

They went into the house. The lights were off. Carlos could have sworn he saw what looked like the silhouette of a large man standing at the end of the entrance when they opened the door and the light from the outside had momentarily pierced the darkness of the house. He blinked; there was no such figure.

He turned on the lights, and the house looked beautiful, as expected.

"Looks like the moving company has already brought in some of the other stuff," Christina mused, noticing the couch they'd had in their previous place. "Let's look around."

"We already looked around when we were appraising the house, Christina," he said, but he followed her nonetheless. Christina was a bundle of energy, and that was one of the things he absolutely loved about her.

They went to all the areas on the ground floor: the kitchen, the dining area, the living room, the store, and the guest room.

"Let's go upstairs," Christina said, dragging him yet again to the stairs.

TOM COLEMAN

Carlos wondered how she still had that much energy after running around as they went up the stairs and walked down the dark hallway.

"Where was the switch again?" Carlos inquired. Neither of them could remember. There was a window at the end of the hallway, though and some light shining through it, enabling them to see where they were going. The hallway had four doors and an attic door on the ceiling. One door, the last one on the left, led to the master bedroom. Opposite it was the bathroom. The two doors closer to the stairs were the other bedrooms.

Christina opened one of the bedroom doors, and Carlos felt some intense vibes coming from the room. No new furniture had been added to or taken away from the bedrooms except for the master, but he saw a doll in the middle of the room after Christina had opened the door. It had buttons for eyes and a sewn-on smile.

"Well, that's creepy," Christina noted. She went to pick up the doll. Carlos was a paranoid person—one had to be to survive the drugs and death-ridden childhood under which he had grown—but he was not superstitious. Still, that was one creepy-looking doll.

"Welcome," a whisper said from behind him. He turned back an instant later but saw nothing.

"My mind must be playing tricks on me today," Carlos muttered.

"Did you say something?"

TOM COLEMAN

"No, don't worry about it, darling." He did not want to scare her. As the man of the house, it was Carlos's responsibility to make his bride feel safe. If he was scared, she would be scared, too. He needed to suck up the growing pit in his stomach and be happy they had been able to get the house.

They went to the room opposite the one they'd just left. Carlos opened the door this time, and the moment he did, there was a sense of ease that came upon him. The room looked really nice. It just felt... fresh. "I like this room."

"Neat," Christina responded. She sounded happy that he was getting something out of the tour.

They checked the bathroom, too, before going to the bedroom. It was a nice, large space. All of their furniture had been positioned the way they'd wanted it, exactly as they'd instructed the moving company. Carlos heard footsteps. Not wanting to alert Christina, he walked back to the hallway, but he saw nothing. What the hell was going on?

Christina didn't seem worried about any of that. She removed her shoes and jumped onto the bed. Just seeing her happy alleviated any fear Carlos might have had. "Come on, honey," she beckoned to her husband. He went to meet her, and they kissed passionately.

"Why don't we really celebrate this occasion?" she purred. He knew precisely what she'd meant, and he kissed her some more. They had sex for the next two hours. Carlos was so happy. He felt so lucky to have Christina, and he knew she felt the same.

TOM COLEMAN

Later that night, Carlos decided to check the attic while his wife made dinner.

"Okay, honey. Be careful," she said, and he nodded. "Come to think of it, we never checked the attic when we scouted the house."

"Yeah, that's why I'm curious."

"Sure. Dinner will be ready soon, so don't take too long."

"All right, baby." He kissed her at the back of her head, a gesture she loved very much.

Carlos was tall enough to reach for the ceiling and open the attic. No sooner had he opened the trap door than a ladder came down, almost hitting him in the eye. Carlos was able to dodge it, but he fell to the floor.

"Is everything okay?" he heard his wife shout from downstairs.

"Yeah, just the ladder falling down," he called back.

"All right."

Carlos tried to play it down, but it had been close. Were ladders meant to abruptly drop from attics? He'd never had an attic in his house before, but still, it had been really surprising.

He climbed the ladder and poked his head in to see how the place looked. It was pitch-black, and a part of him wished he'd decided to check it out during the day. Wait— how could it be pitch black when the light from below should

TOM COLEMAN

have pierced through and into the area? He looked down to see the bulb was still working. Why had none of the light emanating from the bulb reach the area? Was it him? Did he lack that much of an understanding of physics or space?

Carlos heard footsteps in the attic, and he looked swiftly around. Shouldn't there be a window in the attic? He couldn't see shit.

"Is anyone here?" He could not believe he'd even thought to ask that, but the situation felt weird, to say the least. Strange things had been happening in the house since he and his wife had arrived, and it hadn't even been a full day yet.

Man up, he told himself. You've been through much worse. Stop acting like a little bitch. Carlos climbed up into the attic. He knew there had to be a window somewhere, so he tried feeling his way around.

He could hear some strange sounds, but they were faint. Probably his mind playing tricks on him again. Carlos felt the walls of the attic, looking to find the window. If he was right, the window was probably covered with paper or cloth. While feeling the walls, Carlos's hands felt some strange stuff. He could have sworn he touched something that felt like sand, but the moment he went back to the area, he felt nothing but wood. He also felt something sharp. He couldn't wait to light up the place so he could know what the hell was there.

Finally, Carlos found the window, covered in cloth. He tried pulling the cloth off only to discover that it had been nailed around the window to keep it covered. Why the hell would the previous owners of the place go to such great lengths to cover the window?

TOM COLEMAN

After pulling and pulling, Carlos finally tore down the piece of cloth, but immediately after doing so, he saw what looked like a grotesque, ghoulish face with an open mouth reflected on the window's surface.

"What the hell?" He staggered back. His legs stumbled on something, and he fell to the ground. Carlos quickly got into a seated position and looked around. There was nothing on the window, but the light from the moon refracted through the glass and into the attic. With the influx of light, Carlos could better see the room and its contents.

It was… empty?

Wait.

What?

How the hell was this room empty? He could have sworn he'd felt some of the contents when he'd searched the room. What was going on?"

It was then that Carlos noticed a suitcase in the middle of the room. "That's what tripped me?" He looked at the suitcase for a couple of seconds. Carlos tried to open it; it wasn't locked. Inside were things that looked business-like in nature. He couldn't see it clearly, so he decided to take the suitcase downstairs with him.

***

Christina hummed as she set the table, happy to be in her new dream home. She hadn't been too close with her family recently, but she was, nevertheless, happy to have a family of her own. She heard a giggle and turned around

63

TOM COLEMAN

quickly, scrunching her face in bemusement when she saw that no one was behind her.

"Carlos, is that you?" she asked, but there was no reply.

She continued with what she'd been doing when the lights began to flicker. "And they told me everything was in tip-top shape," she remarked, looking up at the flickering light bulb, disappointed. Christina decided to ignore it and keep on doing what she'd been doing… that is until she heard the same weird giggle again. It sounded like a little girl, but Christina knew that was impossible.

"Hey, babe!" she heard the familiar voice of her husband call to her when he entered the kitchen.

"I'm over here. In the dining room."

"Look what I found," he said, dropping the suitcase on the table.

"Did you hear anyone giggle?"she asked.

"What?" Carlos was confused.

"I could have sworn I heard a girl giggling."

Carlos's reaction changed immediately when she said that, causing her to be suspicious. His eyes widened and he clenched his jaw, a typical tell whenever he was hiding something. "What is it?"

"What is what?"

"You have that look you always do when you are hiding something."

TOM COLEMAN

"I don't know what you are talking about," Carlos deflected. "Let's talk about this." He opened the suitcase to reveal some papers.

"What is this?" Christina asked, perusing them. "They look like bank records or something."

"Yeah, and some other mundane stuff. It's written in a language I don't understand. I can't even recognize the letters," Carlos added, also going through the papers.

"That's strange," Christina said.

"What?"

"Our name is here."

"Huh?"

"Yeah. Take a look." Christina gave the sheet of paper to her husband to see for himself.

Carlos was confused when he read their names in perfect English. "Why the hell would someone write every other thing in a weird language but choose our names to be in English?"

"Probably because there is no equivalent for Hernandez in the language," Christina said, sounding nonchalant. "Don't overthink it."

It was his job to overthink things like that, though. He'd grown up in an environment where paranoia was encouraged, and that was hard to stop all of a sudden.

"Just burn it or throw it away tomorrow, honey. Let's eat."

"Okay," he said, though he sounded unconvincing, even to his own hears. He put all the papers back into the suitcase and set it to the side.

They sat down once Christina had brought out the food and made cheers to their new home.

"Our first meal in our new home," Carlos said, raising his glass of Champagne.

"May it be the first of many," Christina responded with a smile prior to clanking glasses.

Carlos was happy to be with the woman he loved— why was he so diffident?

The next morning, Carlos woke up early to throw the suitcase away. He normally got up early because he had work. Christina was a writer, so she worked from home and didn't need to wake up as early. He did not want to wake her, so he decided to do it on his own. The real estate agent had informed him that the trash came once a week, and anything should be disposed of in the large trash compartment opposite his house.

The moment Carlos had left the house, he almost felt something pass through him—had it been an out-of-body experience?

He dropped the suitcase and started panting. "What the hell is happening to me?" he asked himself. Carlos quickly surmised that he needed to get rid of the suitcase and be done with the attic and all of the old things that had been left in the house.

TOM COLEMAN

"This is my house! This is my house! This is my house!" he thought as he stomped outside. When, at last, he had reached the trash and threw the suitcase inside, it didn't seem like enough, so he went back in, came out with a box of matches, and retrieved the jerry can of fuel from the car.

Carlos walked back to the trash, angry at the suitcase but unsure as to why. He sprayed the suitcase with the fuel then lit the match, letting it fall on the suitcase before walking away.

"Enough of this weird crap," Carlos Hernandez said with finality.

Little did he know that this would be the catalyst for the horrors to come.

67

TOM COLEMAN

CHAPTER TWO
Dissonance

Christina's eyes fluttered open. She knew that Carlos had most likely already gone to work; she had prepared him his lunch the night before, as she always did. She checked the time on her phone: it was 8:30 am. That meant it hadn't been long since Carlos had left. Now, it was time for her to get to work.

"I'll call him later," she mused, getting up from the bed and heading to the bathroom.

"Free," something whispered to her as she opened the bathroom door, sending shivers down her spine. Christina did not look back because she dreaded what she might find.

"Freeeee," the little girl's voice whispered into her ear again. This time, Christina whipped her head around to see no one.

"What is happening to me?" she wondered.

Walking into the bathroom, she gazed into the mirror, thinking about the voice she'd heard in her mind. What had it been? What had it meant? Who was that girl?

Her mind drifted to her past. Hearing the little girl's voice had taken her back to that fateful day when she'd made the worst mistake of her life.

68

TOM COLEMAN

Christina's reflection in the mirror smiled slightly. She frowned, perplexed at how that was even possible, considering she did not smile, even a little. Just to be sure, Christina touched her cheeks and lips to see if she was unknowingly smiling.

An even bigger issue arose when her reflection didn't move her hands.

"What? Wh-what is this?" She staggered away from the mirror.

"Murderer!" Mirror Christina shouted loudly at her.

Christina could do nothing but stare in terror. Her breathing sped up, and her eyes grew so wide, she wondered how they hadn't fallen out of their sockets. She was terrified... petrified. It might be that she was reading too much into things, but Christina knew what that meant.

She flashbacked once more to her memories of that day.

"Breathe in... breathe out..." she said to herself, closing her eyes and trying to imagine a version of herself that was calm and not having a panic attack. This was her regular routine whenever she had an attack. It was all in her mind, and she needed to let the guilt go.

After a few calming breaths, Christina was okay. She opened her eyes and was, once more, met by her own reflection. She smiled. "You see?" she said herself, feeling relieved.

TOM COLEMAN

Christina opened the shower curtain, got into the shower, and turned on the water. "It's all in your head."

To her horror, instead of water falling onto her skin, blood did.

She screamed and fell backward, taking the shower curtains with her to the floor.

"Somebody, help me," Christina said, beckoning for aid, but she was too far from anybody's ears.

When she opened her eyes, there was nothing but water on her.

"What the… what is going on," she screamed at the walls.

Carlos was working at his job as the manager of the El Paso branch for the HomeGo shipping company, but he was unable to concentrate on his first day. He had been given a tour of the building by Greg, the assistant manager, which was funny because the assistant manager of where he used to work had also been named Greg.

Now, after the orientation was over, he was sitting in his office, going through the books, but he could not make sense of the numbers because his mind was not really at work; it was at home.

"Something is not right," he said to himself, and he didn't mean just at home. The building, the one he was in right then—something about it felt strange yet familiar. It was almost as if he had been there before. Even the people working

70

there all seemed familiar yet somehow different. Something was wrong with his head.

"I need to rest, man… or, at least, find a distraction." He picked up his phone, about to call his wife, when he heard a sound. The chatter outside his office continued as people packaged boxes, but the sound he hears was more musical, which was weird.

The sound hit again, and Carlos recognized it as the sound of a guitar string. Who playing the guitar? He looked around his office, but he was the only one there.

"We're free," a voice whispered to him. He tried to wave the voice away with his hand near his ear, and he got to his feet.

The string sound came again, this time louder than before. How could a sound for which he could not see the source be louder than the chatter and noise outside his office he *could* see? Nothing made any sense, but then again, nothing had made sense since he'd moved there.

He called his wife, and it rang a few times before she picked up the phone.

"H-hello?" Carlos immediately detected fear in her voice.

"Christina, what is wrong?"

"Nothing. Why w-why… why would you… think anything is wrong?"

"Tell me what is going on… now, Christina."

71

"I think... uhm... there is something wrong with me," she explained. "I don't want you to think I'm crazy, okay?"

"I won't. What is going on over there? I'm on my way." Carlos berated himself for leaving her there alone. Things were already weird—why would he leave her in that house alone? He was such an idiot for doing that, and he was going to make it right.

"No, you don't have to. It's just me having a panic attack. I'm seeing things and remembering some things, so... don't worry."

"No, honey, you are clearly not okay right now. I should be there for you."

"*No!* This is your first day on the job. We have to recoup the money we used to buy this house. If you get a reprimand or you're involved in some sort of issue on your first day, it will look bad on you. Seriously, just stay, and come home after work. I've got this. Let me fix my own mess." She seemed adamant that she was the one with the issues, but what if it was that bloody house? And what did she mean by remembering things? Christina was generally a cheerful person, even though she had panic attacks. She never did tell Carlos why they came. Was she finally ready to open up?

"We'll talk more when you get home, okay?"

"All right, sweetie. Take care of yourself."

She hummed in the affirmative.

"And if anything goes wrong... *anything* at all, call me. Call me... instantly."

"Sure. My knight in shining armour."

He smiled.

Carlos let out a heavy sigh after ending the call. He was worried... very worried, but she'd said she had it under control, so he'd just have to trust her. He had his own issues to worry about, besides. Something nefarious was going on in that place. Had it followed him from the house to work? What is it, even? Why did he acknowledge its existence?

"Get it together, dude," he tried to cool himself. "Don't let them sense fear in you. You're the fucking manager." Yes, he was, and if he wanted to stay that way, he'd better stop letting his mind mess him up.

Christina staring at her laptop, the blank space waited to be filled with written words, and stared at her. She'd positioned her chair and table in such a way that her back was against the wall. This was because she was scared to turn her back on anything that might be there. She had been staring at the screen for at least ten minutes since Carlos had called. It seemed like a good idea to write something to clear her head, but now, when she actually tried to write, she came up empty.

"Fuck," she yelled, lifting her eyes to the ceiling. That was when she noticed something imprinted on the ceiling... or was it just her imagination? There was a symbol there, right? It was not absolutely clear that anything was there, and she wondered if this were another case of her mind playing tricks on her.

"Murderer," the same little girl's voice said right into her ear, only this time, the voice screamed, prompting Christina to cover her ears with her hands.

She finally started putting the pieces together. "The girl… the word murderer… my past…" It donned on her, and the figure of a little girl became as clear as day to Christina. It was a face she recognized and dreaded. The girl looked no more than eight. She had pigtails and wore a pink floral dress stained with red.

"You." Christina pushed her table away and got up, transfixed by the girl in front of her.

"Me," the young girl retorted with a giggle.

"I'm… I'm so sorry," Christina said, her eyes watering. "I… I didn't mean it."

"Why did you do it?" the girl asked, her eyes growing bigger.

"I—"

"You got away with it. You got off, scot-free," the girl's shouted, her eyes growing abnormally large. They were as big as a cartoon character's now, and Christina could hardly believe what she was seeing. She remained transfixed on the girl, paralyzed by fear and guilt.

"You think you deserve to be loved after all you have done?" A stream of blood fell from the girl's immensely large eyes.

TOM COLEMAN

"What the fuck?" Christina's heartbeat skyrocketed, and she started breathing heavily. "What... w-what do you want from me!"

"This is all a dream, so you have to come. Play with me." The young girl's face was back to normal as she walked over to Christina and took her hand. "Come with me. Let's play tag."

By then, Christina was completely lulled into her spell, and she smiled at her. "I'll do whatever you need to show you how sorry I am."

"Good. I wanna play tag. I'll run, and you'll try to catch me," the girl proposed.

What a precocious young girl, Christina thought. "Sure. Let's play, Susan."

"Oh, you remember my name?"

"Of course. I see your face in my dreams before I sleep sometimes. I couldn't forget you that easily, not after what I did."

"Okay, I'll run, then. You count to ten," Susan instructed. "Oh, and there will be obstacles to stop you from catching me."

"What obstacles? What do you mean?"

"My friends. You'll see." Her smile turned maniacal, her grin so wide that her lips reached her cheekbones. This terrified Christina, but she was hellbent on gaining the little girl's forgiveness.

75

TOM COLEMAN

"All right. Start counting." The little girl giggled as she ran away.

"Ten… nine… eight… seven…" Christina had not gone halfway when she heard a rumble. She was afraid, but she had already assumed it was all a dream. If she died, she'd just wake up. She dreamed about Susan a lot.

"Six… five… four…"

Footsteps approached the door, but Susan remained steadfast and kept counting.

"Three… two… one." She ran from the master's bedroom despite the footsteps. It was most likely Susan, anyway. This was her chance to catch her.

Christina was met by a large silhouette of a man with no distinct features. The figure was entirely black, with his eyes the only color.

She screamed and fell to the floor.

The man opened his black mouth, and black liquid poured out onto Christina. It felt like acid.

Christina let out something that sounded like a gurgle. "Susan," she called, "help!" She screamed from the excruciating pain. Her skin seemed to melt before her eyes. The pain as the liquid ate through her skin and made its way to her organs was too much for her to bear. And still, she screamed out loud, begging for help.

It was all over in a flash, and Christina found herself in the attic.

TOM COLEMAN

"How did I get here?" she asked. She saw Susan through the open window, sitting on the roof outside on what looked like a concrete slab. Christina thought it weird, considering the architecture of the house and others in this area, but she was more focused on the young girl.

"Do you remember what you did to me?" Susan asked, looking sad.

"Yes," Christina said with regret.

"Do you think you deserve mercy?"

"No," she responded. "What I did to you was horrible. I should never have gotten away with it. I didn't mean to. It was an accident."

"And that is supposed to make it better?" Susan yelled, but it sounded more like a screech.

Christina had to cover her ears because the sound was too high-pitched. "I stopped talking to my parents because of that," Christina tried to explain. "I am a different person now, I promise."

"Did Susan have the chance to be different?"

"Why are you talking about yourself in the third person?" Christina asked, coming to her senses a bit.

"You remember the sight of my bleeding out? You *do* remember it, right? You remember what you did?" It was enough to cement the guilt back in Christina's mind. She was in tears. That had been the worst moment of her life, and now, she had to face her demons.

TOM COLEMAN

"You took the life of an innocent girl, and you got away with it. You are an evil person."

"I am… an evil person." Christina was near traumatized, hearing this from the very girl whose life she had taken.

"You don't deserve to be happy with your husband while Susan's family suffers in agony."

"I don't deserve to be happy with Carlos while Susan's family suffers." It was true. She did not deserve happiness after being such a horrible person. Susan let these dangerous thoughts fester in her mind.

Susan's figure Susan smiled. "Then, come," she said, holding her hands out to Christina. "We're playing tag, aren't we? You have to touch me."

"Will you forgive me if I catch you?" Christina hoped.

"Sure. You will be forgiven of all this and more. Just come outside."

Swayed by the false reality before her, Christina climbed through the window and placed her leg on the slab. The problem was that there had never been a concrete slab on the roof outside of the attic, and Christina Hernandez fell.

To be continued…

78

TOM COLEMAN

(This story is based on the idea of my dear reader Jennifer Williams and was a winning idea in "Write my next story challenge")

79

TOM COLEMAN

BLINK

81

TOM COLEMAN

82

TOM COLEMAN

"Sadie is sitting next to you, Jarred. Stop complaining." I rolled my eyes when my mother admonishes me and buckle up like I was told five minutes ago. This was going to be the longest car ride of my life, I swore it.

"I didn't want to move in the first place," I mumbled under my breath, picking at my jeans in boredom. I groaned. That was how it always started, wasn't it? Someone moved into a creepy, old house where an old man and his wife used to live along with their adopted stray cats. They passed away, and a stupid family—which happened to be mine by the way— decided it would be a great idea to go and live there, when all horror movies stated that something was bound to happen, like there would be a giant man-eating rat or a psychopath living next door. I mean, hadn't my parents ever read any horror stories or maybe watched a few movies?

I frowned when my mother kissed my head, and I slammed the car door without saying another word.

Guess not.

I sat back with my arms crossed, surrounded by little brats. I was in the back of the van, between my youngest sister, Sadie, and the second youngest, Sally. My dad was driving, and beside him was my mom. Behind both of them were my two older sisters, Sandie and Sabrina.

TOM COLEMAN

"All ready to go, girls?" my dad asked as my mom climbed into the front passenger's seat and did up her seatbelt. She clapped her hands excitedly, but no one responded as the van moved away from our old house.

I was sure the two younger ones wouldn't even remember it—they were like babies—but my older siblings and I would. It was where we had been raised from birth, after all, in a neighborhood that had nice old grandmas who handed out cookies to the children as they headed off to school each day. Our friends lived just around the corner, and we went to the park every night. Mr. Browne sometimes wore brown pants to school to make his class laugh because rainy days were the worst. There was nothing better than that neighborhood, nothing better than the friends and the cookies baked, but we drove away anyway, my eyes lingering on the house as it disappeared from view.

***

I set up my new room to look exactly like my old one. The walls were a different color, to my dismay and despair— boring old white—but it would do, I guess.

Dresser beside my bed, action figures on the dressers, and the bed beside the wall, with two pillows under my head.

TOM COLEMAN

There was a bookshelf near the closet, almost filled to the brim with novels, comics, and manga, and a closet burrowed into the wall with the extra boxes I didn't need piled inside.

"You made it look so… similar," was the first thing my dad said when he passed my room, holding Sadie in his arms as she sucked on her thumb. It was a habit of hers. He sounded surprised, but all the same, I guess he should have noticed, considering how distraught I was about moving. The oldest had called me a brat when she'd first seen it, and I'd called her an old woman since she'd already moved on.

I nodded. "Of course. I wanted there to be a little piece of home in this dump."

Dad paused, choosing his next words carefully. "Don't you think… well… uh… maybe a nice change might spruce things up?" he suggested, giving me the old dad grin.

I didn't answer, hanging up another shirt instead. I mean, maybe, I guess he could be right, but I liked my old room a lot more than the new one. No one had designed it but me, and it gave me a small bit of pride, knowing it was mine and only mine as long as I stuck to it.

85

TOM COLEMAN

"Well, little chap," he continued when I didn't answer, "get settled in. The whole family is going to be watching baseball down in the living room today if you want to join. Could be fun." These were his last words before he went off to get the baby her bottle down in the kitchen.

**

My dad had been a baseball fan ever since I was a kid, and even before that, I bet. Everyone who used to live around us knew that. Heck, sometimes we'd even have neighbors and friends over for the games. We'd have parties with chips, soda, and a lot of yelling and screaming for the tiny people on the screen to run even faster than headless chickens. I'd be on my mom's lap, hitting her knee as she bounced me up and down on it. She was always just as excited as my dad, face paint covering her cheeks and eyebrows, and her voice breaking, which made us laugh. I'd say she was the life of the party, always loud and tough, but this time, it was different.

Dad was mumbling to my mother at breakfast about a noise complaint from one of the new neighbors. The note said something about our family being too loud for the neighborhood. Supposedly, they could hear us from across the way.

TOM COLEMAN

My mom and dad just scoffed and said that the next time, they'd make sure to keep it down for the non-baseball fans out there. I didn't know why we had to be quiet, I mean, Dad always said we live in a free country, so we could do anything we wanted, but I guess he lied about that, too.

They both sat back down at the dinner table, continued eating, and hushed one of the babies who was crying.

***

"Time for school, little buddy," my dad said, flicking my light switch on.

It was a rude awakening, but I murmured an "Alrighty" as he went to go to make the babies' breakfast. This had become his routine: go around the house, wake everyone up, feed the babies their breakfast, then get to work.

I sat up and looked around the white room, maybe hoping I was back in the old house. I wasn't, but I went off to get ready. Showering, brushing my teeth, combing my hair—I made sure I didn't look like a complete mess. My mom would be the one to tell me if I did anyway. She was pretty nice about it, I guess, but sometimes she could also be a bit snooty and to the point.

87

TOM COLEMAN

Closing the bathroom door, I hopped down the stairs and eyed the basement door. For days now, I had been bugging my parents about it. I was convinced the old people didn't just up and die. I was convinced they'd been eaten by whatever was down there. Or maybe they'd even become zombies and now lived in the basement in the dark. Maybe they had sharp fangs and red eyes that lit up in the night.

"Didn't you see the claw marks," I'd exclaimed just before bed, but mom always said she was sure it was nothing.

"Jarred, sweetie, you're just confused with the move. Don't worry so much, my little monster," she'd say, and I'd sigh.

"Here, how about this—if you stop going on about it, we can get McDonald's later on today." That always shut me up for the night, but I was back at it the next day.

***

"Mama, what do you think might live downstairs if anything did?" I asked, kicking my feet while sitting in my chair. The kitchen chairs were so tall; I felt as if I could reach the clouds.

88

TOM COLEMAN

She looked back at me, rolled her eyes, and shrugged. "How about nothing? There's nothing in our basement, sweetie, and there won't be anything in the basement for a long time.

"Now, stop scaring your sisters and finish eating, okay?" she said, putting the dishes in the dishwasher.

We had just finished breakfast, and I guess she didn't want to answer because it was too early in the morning. I was still eating, though, 'cause I'd been babbling away. I frowned and pressed on. "So, you don't ever wonder if those old people didn't just die? Don't you ever wonder if it was something else?" I ask quietly, but she'd already moved on from the dishwasher and was wiping down the counters.

"Ma?" I said a little louder.

She hummed in response, and at that moment, I knew I had to prove my ma and pa wrong. I needed to show them that there was, indeed, something in the basement.

"Tomorrow night, I swear, I'm going to go and see if anything's down there. I'll prove you wrong, Mommy, I promise—unless you wanna try and stop me."

89

TOM COLEMAN

Watching her brush off my comment was like a wrecking ball to the face. It hurt, but then again, I accepted it for what it was. I'd promised her, I'd promised papa, and I sure as heck had promised myself.

If there was something in the basement, I'd find and catch it for the whole world to see.

***

"Sweetheart, I've checked downstairs. I've checked the attic." My mother sat next to me, caressing my hair with a steady hand as she looked around in the dark. It was silent, save for the wind gently hitting the windowpane.

Unlike my parents, I was still convinced that someone—or some*thing*—lived downstairs. Every night there were more and more claw marks at the base of the basement's door that I swore hadn't existed the day before. I swore it, but my parents disagreed. They said that maybe it was a rat or some sort of creature like a raccoon.

"I checked your closet, checked under your bed, checked the basement—what else do you want from me,

TOM COLEMAN

Jarred?" she asked in a pleading tone, but I didn't answer. I was quiet, peering at her from beneath my blankets.

With a sigh, she stood stiffly and kissed my forehead. "Try and get some sleep, my love." She left my door cracked open a bit, and I watched the light from the hallway flow in. Her figure disappeared around the corner, and I was alone again.

The wind howled.

***

I shone a flashlight down the hallway. All of the doors were closed except for my room and the babies', which was to the right and down the hall.

I sighed. Yes, I was doing it, and I was going to do it as intelligently as I could. Unlike my parents, I *had* watched horror movies and read books.

Was it a good idea to go after a monster in the basement? No.

TOM COLEMAN

That was probably my first mistake, but I thought nothing of it, swatting the thought away like I might a fly with the back of my hand.

I continued quickly on my way, soft steps creaking across the floor.

I made my way down the narrow hallway, creeping down the stairs as quietly as I could. I heard something off to the right of me when I was almost at the bottom. The sound wasn't loud, just barely audible above the annoying ring in my ear. It was a quiet, quiet sound, coming from down there in the darkness.

I shone the flashlight into the oil-colored hallway, narrowing my eyes so I could catch it if there was any movement.

The beam of light didn't reveal anything but the front door and the key table. I huffed and moved slowly around it, seeing if I could catch anything in the act, but I saw nothing. "Darn," I said, my voice low.

I headed further down, holding the railing beneath my trembling hand. It was cold and always left my palm smelling

TOM COLEMAN

of pinewood and bark. It was sometimes a soothing smell, but it could also hurt my head if I smelled it for too long.

I was finally down at the bottom. My foot met solid ground, and I turned in a circle, watching carefully for any sign of movement in the darkness—a flash, maybe a small flicker—but I saw nothing as I trotted forward.

It was almost too quiet, the wind seeming so far away despite the door being right behind me. The noise from before seemed to have stopped, and I walked alone in the darkness like some lone soul or ghost from a movie. The thought made me giggle, and I gripped the flashlight tighter.

Inch by inch, I shimmied forward with hesitant footing—inch by inch. Seconds went by, and I could hardly keep my breath steady. Inch by inch… and then a creak like a door was being opened, or a floorboard was crying under someone's weight.

I pointed the flashlight at the noise, but I was met with the basement door. It was slightly ajar, and by the looks of it, it wasn't by the wind—the claw marks were even more numerous here. I gulped. My hands grew cold as I glared at the scratches.

TOM COLEMAN

"You can do this," I said with confidence, taking a deep breath as I tried to calm my nerves and thoughts, which were going crazy. Horror movies were always like that, I was certain, so instead of heading toward the creepy thing, I turned to go the other way.

The light was a beat behind me as I spun on my heels, my eyes lingering on the scratches. My curiosity wasn't going to get to me, not even after I took another glance back, not even if my parents asked me what I'd found, and I'd have to hang my head in shame 'cause I was too much of a baby to check it out.

"Not today, Jarred. Not today. Today, you'll live," I told myself with a smile.

I headed back, and after a few steps toward the stairs, my eyes met a figure near the front door, standing so very, very still, as the wind crashed against the house. It was standing so still, with no movement other than the rise and fall of its chest, a smile etched into its pale, peachy skin.

I froze, legs trembling and refusing to move.

The smile widened the longer I stared, baring fangs too large to let the lips—if that's what they were—even close. It

94

TOM COLEMAN

was a smile with nothing nice to it, a bloody smile that seemed to have been carved into the flesh a few days before. The eyes of whatever it was were round, black orbs, round and black, and the longer you looked, the more they seemed not to exist. It was like looking into matte black car paint or the ebony sky; it was like a void.

My mouth slowly opened, and a word slipped quietly from my lips. It was a quiet, quiet word, and when I blinked, the thing was just a little bit closer. Inch by inch it seemed to come closer, yet it kept the same posture as before, like a statue being moved from one pedestal to another. It's limbs contorted to let the hands and feet rest on the ground. It was unnatural. It's limbs were twisted, and its twitching frown remained as it stood there, unblinking, unmoving.

I sad that word again, a quiet word, so quiet that no one could hear it: "Ma," but no one answered, I sure as heck kept my eyes open this time. They watered, twitching with each breath.

"Ma," I said in a shallow voice, and I took in a muffled breath. I could have yelled—maybe should have yelled—but my voice was stuck in that whispered tone. I tried again: "Ma."

Again, my eyes watered. They refused to blink. I was tired, so closing my eyes is what my mind wanted to do—get

TOM COLEMAN

some shut-eye, snuggled beneath my blankets. Maybe I should have stayed in bed. Maybe Ma and Pa were right. Maybe if I'd just stayed in bed, I'd be safe.

Blink.

Regret overtook me when I opened my eyes again; the creature stood not too far away, now. My body trembled, and my breathing followed suit. I was afraid to run.

Instead of both of its hands and feet on the ground like before, its position had shifted into a reaching hand—reaching for me.

Paralyzed with fear, I gasped for air and sputtered for my parents as real tears pricked my eyes. They clouded my vision, but I never blinked. I wouldn't blink. I couldn't blink.

My feet were glued to the ground, stuck in place, and trying to lift them was like pulling a thousand-pound weight up a mountain. I strained, tears flowed from my open eyes, my lips spluttered, and words came to my ears that were not my own: "Mama? Papa?" At that moment something take over my body. Some strange force.

TOM COLEMAN

A deep, deep voice came from the creature. Such a deep voice.

"Mama? Papa?" it repeated.

"Mama? Papa?" higher-pitched.

"Mama? Papa?" higher, and higher still.

"Mama? Papa?" higher, higher, higher, until it sounded exactly like my voice.

The creature smiled at me again, its frown disappearing.

My breath hitched in my throat, my hands shook, and my body trembled. The thing washed in and out of my blurry vision.

Like a nightmare, the creature's pale skin began shedding scales like those on a snake, but it remained still and didn't move. It stood on all threes, an arm outstretched to me, calmly breathing. Its black eyes fixed on me, on my every move and breath, and especially on my eyes. It waited.

TOM COLEMAN

Its skin fell off and crumpled to the floor, wrinkly and old. I sobbed but in silence. My nose picked up a stomach-twisting stench.

The creature's new flesh façade was blood red. It oozed pus that reeked of foot fungus and three-month-old trash. The smell made my eyes burn, but I still didn't blink. I mustn't.

One of my feet slipped across the floor as I tried to take a step. The beam of flashlight continued to tremble. My hand threatened to drop the flashlight, so I fixed my grip. My fingers were sore; my feet pulsated; the blood rang in my ears. My heart was bound to beat right through my chest. My eyes screamed, my ears continued to ring with sounds I hadn't heard before, and a small voice whispered in my head. My stomach swelled with the dinner I'd eaten a few hours before. I swore my parents should have been able to hear it, hear my voice and my heartbeat and my breathing. They were as loud as rock music in the darkened hall.

Blink, blink, blink, blink!

It was what my mind was telling me to do. My heart wanted to give in. Thoughts raced around my head. It was too much, too long, too fast, too much, too long, too fast, too much…

98

TOM COLEMAN

Blink.

***

99

The rain from the night before has stopped. There is bound to be a nice day ahead. The sun is shining through the curtains.

Jarred sits at the kitchen table, awaiting his dad to tell him his breakfast options. His fingers tap the surface of the kitchen table, and a grin makes its way onto his pale face. He blinks and then blinks again.

"Morning, Jarred. What do you want for breakfast, kiddo? Your dad can get you eggs with some bacon?" says his father. "You, okay? Ya seem a bit pale. That monster in the basement keep you up last night, Jarr?" he said smiling.

Black orbs watch them from behind normal-looking green eyes, and he smiles a toothy grin when the family isn't watching. Under his skin, it smells like death, but no one realizes. The baby gives a high-pitched wail. She slams her hands on the table, kicking her small feet at the baby chair. She wants out, and for a good reason.

The mother goes to pick up her child, hushes her, and takes her out of the room.

TOM COLEMAN

Suddenly a boy's voice answers the previously asked question as the older sister chow down: "I'll have everything in the room," Jarred says, licking his lips.

TOM COLEMAN

HALLOWEEN HOUSE

103

TOM COLEMAN

TOM COLEMAN

Heather was in no mood for parties. She didn't care about the same things as her friends. She wasn't big on texting, nor did she like makeup and the like. She knew that she was pretty enough, or so she believed since everybody kept telling her that. Maybe it was due to her looks that she had such a cool and diverse set of friends despite her snarky attitude.

It was getting late, and she knew what that meant: Halloween night.

Her phone rang while she was re-reading one of her favorite books, causing the teenage girl to groan. She already knew it was Mark. He was like the organizer of the group, the one who checked in on everyone and generally made plans. Some would say he was the leader, but he didn't see it that way.

"Yeah?" she said with obvious irritation in her tone after picking up the phone. She wanted him to know that she did not appreciate the interruption. Heather was an introvert, and she liked being left alone, but if someone were to contact her, it had better not be through a phone call. Texting or in-person meetings with her friends were better, in her opinion. Mark knew this, and he still called her. She was sure he did it just to annoy her. Fucking ass.

"You know that passive-aggressive shtick doesn't work on me, Heather," Mark said in his deep, soothing voice. Did that guy never get angry? Heather had tried everything to make him leave her alone when they'd first met, but he was hell-bent on being insulted. In the end, she'd reluctantly given in and became friends with him. To be honest? Her life had

TOM COLEMAN

been more exciting ever since he'd come into it, but Heather would never tell him this, of course.

"I know today is Halloween. Can't you just let me hide in peace, Mark?" Heather asked, frowning.

"I could, but it's always more fun to have your dry input when we go out together. Who will counterbalance Kelsey's uppity nature or John's jerk tendencies?" Heather rolled her eyes but smiled. Even if she liked being on her own, having a small group of friends was better than she thought it would be.

"Don't worry. I have a great night planned for us. You love scary books, don't you? This should be your favorite time of the year." He wasn't wrong. On paper, it should be her favorite day of the year. That being said, Heather was wary about going outside and being in crowds. It meant she would have to talk to people, and that was not what she wanted.

"Fine," she said. "I will be waiting for you guys."

"Great! We'll be there in thirty minutes." Mark sounded so excited.

Heather assumed her house was on the way to their destination. She'd already picked out her costume. She had chosen to dress as Valek from "The Nun." She bathed quickly, dressed, and did her makeup for the scary "Conjuring 2" villain. Her costume wasn't lavish or anything. She just wanted something that would not let people see her face or recognize her, but also something easy to wear. The doorbell rang as she was finishing up.

"Heather, your friends are here," her dad yelled from downstairs.

"I'm coming," she replied. She put on the finishing touches and went downstairs.

"What the fuck?" her father said, shocked to see her in full costume.

Heather chuckled at her father's reaction.

"Nice one, Sweetie," her mom said with a smirk. "Relax, Garry—it's Halloween, and you know how much she loves her horror."

Her dad sighed and sat down. "Have fun, pumpkin," he said, trying to hide his discomfort at the costume. They were Catholics, so Heather understood his iffy reaction to it, especially considering that he was the most religious in the family.

"I will, Dad," she said. "Bye."

"Bring my daughter back safely, Mark," her dad said sternly. "She's our only child." He always liked intimidating and making fun of Mark.

"Y-yes, sir," Mark managed to reply, trying to stay respectful.

John and Kelvin laughed from behind him.

"Hey," Heather said lifelessly after leaving the house and closing the door behind her.

"Ugh, Debbie Downer strikes already," John, the registered jerk of the group, did not hesitate to comment.

"Better to be a low-energy downer than a high-energy dick," Heather sniped back. Neither of them took it personally, though. They were used to each other, and they accepted themselves, flaws and all. Heather believed it was because of Mark. He was the glue that held their eclectic characters together in harmony. He could get along with anyone as long as he liked them.

"Ooh!" Kelvin said. He was a go-with-the-flow kinda guy, and Heather liked being around him. He didn't expect anything from her, and he took her nasty comments in stride. Kelvin was a good guy to vibe with, but that was probably the only benefit to being around him. He was not an ambitious guy by any stretch of the imagination. Heather wasn't either, but at least she thought about her future and how she wanted to end up; a huge part of that was due to Mark's influence.

"Shut up, loser," John barked at his friend with a frown.

"Enough, guys. This kind of talk is bad for your skin." Heather had wondered when Kelsey would speak. He was like the engine that kept on running. Heather was as superficial as it got when it came to how she looked, but she was also kind and caring. Kelsey and Mark were the closest in the group, and they got along well. They'd also known each other the longest. Heather always teased Mark that he and Kelsey were dating, but he denied it every time.

"All right, all right. C'mon—let's go, guys," Mark said, rallying the group as he always did.

"Where to this time?" John inquired.

TOM COLEMAN

Mark smirked mischievously. "It's a surprise, but trust me: it'll be scary," he assured.

They walked for a while until they'd reached the old house. Heather was confused. It was the old haunted house she had heard people went to. It was more of an amusement park kind of haunted house, but after some disturbing rumors had been spread, parents stopped sending their kids there. She heard a couple of teenagers had gone missing there as well, but the management denied it, and nothing could be proven due to there being zero evidence each time.

Now, the place was closing down. Her parents had warned her about the place, which wasn't surprising, considering how spiritual they were. It was located on the outskirts of town, too, but since they lived at the edge of town, it was closer to her house than the others'.

"Wait—is this the place?" Heather asked Mark.

Mark nodded. "We're gonna see what all the fuss is about this place," he said with confidence. "I'm sure our parents just wanted to scare us when they told us not to come here. They never brought me here, even when I was a kid." He continued enthusiastically: "They've already closed, but they haven't packed their stuff up yet. This will be our only chance to get a peek."

"Or maybe it is because of that kid that went missing when he went into that creepy place," John countered.

"Allegedly. Nobody knows what happened," Kesley noted.

109

TOM COLEMAN

"Although I am worried the cobwebs will get tangled in my hair." Heather shook her head. Was she really worried about her hair just then? It was a pretty renowned place in their town, and they were going inside on Halloween.

"Besides, if the kid really was lost in there, we can find the body and bring closure for his family," Kelvin added.

It was always hard for Heather to tell when he was being serious or not because he said things with such a lax expression. Nevertheless, she was not certain about going into the house. "I don't know," she said. Maybe it was a bad idea. Then again, if she was that scared, didn't that mean she should go inside to see exactly what was in there that was making her so scared? Maybe all she needed was to know there was nothing inside besides fun stuff to scare people with.

"Heather, do you trust me?" Mark inquired.

"Oh, here we go. The hero moment," John lamented. He was the only one against the idea other than her.

"Yeah," Heather said, nodding. She really did trust Mark.

"Then, trust me when I say that you have nothing to be really afraid of. Sure, the place is gloomy and weird, but that's just because of the lore surrounding the house, and that has put a psychological weight on us. It's also because that's how the haunted house had been designed to look. Aren't you the least bit curious as to what is in there? Wouldn't it feel good to just put everything to rest and know once and for all and to know the stories are bogus?" Damn, he was good at giving speeches as well as convincing people. It was probably because he

110

believed what he was saying wholeheartedly, which helped when making others believe, too.

"Fuck." Even John knew the speech was too convincing to say no. Besides, Mark had always been their planner, and they trusted him—why stop now?

"All right. Let's go," Heather agreed.

Mark and Kelsey high-fived.

"Okay. Here's how we're gonna enter," Mark explained. "We'll go through the back. I managed to pry open the back gate that leads to the house, and there is a clear footpath from there—cool?"

"Cool," they replied in unison.

TOM COLEMAN

Heather hadn't done anything that exciting before, and her heart was beating pretty fast. She had the feeling it was going to be a great night.

***

"Jeez," Kelsey had said what everyone was feeling, Heather included. From the moment she'd set foot on the compound, she'd felt a dour ambiance envelope her. Something was seriously abnormal about the place. A part of her wanted to go back, and she knew some of her friends felt the same way, but seeing Mark go forward gave her courage.

"Well, we're already deep into this, so we might as well go in and see if there is anything—ooooh—over there," John said, mimicking a scary ghost.

They got in through an unlocked window. The moment she passed through the window, Heather felt something change. Was the house really...haunted? Why did she feel that way?

"Did anyone else feel weird after entering this place?" Kelvin asked. Their facial reactions spoke volumes: they had all felt it.

"Now that we're in, we can go now, right?" Heather proposed, but everyone gave her a look that basically said, "Seriously, Heather."

TOM COLEMAN

"Let's start with the main hall, then work our way from there to the rest of the area," Mark said. "And we should stay together."

"I thought you were sure there was nothing to be afraid of, Mr. Fearless," John said.

"Yeah, but I'm not an idiot. People could get lost. We shouldn't try to put ourselves in a situation that allows for harmful things to happen."

"Says the guy who brought us here."

Mark sighed at John's comment.

"Dude, I just want us to have fun and do something with a bit of mischief. Can you please just try and enjoy yourself instead of spoiling it for oth—"

Something scurried near them. Mark went quiet. Kelsey shrieked. Heather was more scared by the scream than whatever roamed past them.

The teenagers looked at Kelsey; then they looked at each other. They smiled slowly and eventually laughed. The adrenaline that coursed through Heather when she'd heard the mix of whatever had gone past them—probably a rat—and Kelsey's scream. She'd never felt anything like that before. Now, she was starting to understand what Mark had wanted them to experience when he'd brought them there.

"Jesus, Kelsey," John noted. "Damn." He let out a nervous laugh.

"Sorry," Kelsey said. She laughed at herself for her intense reaction.

113

"Don't be," Mark interjected with a smile. "It's all part of the experience. You get scared a bit, but in the end, there's nothing to be scared of."

They were more relaxed after that incident. Heather enjoyed her time checking out the house with her friends. There were some scary sculptures but nothing really terrifying. She got more of a laugh out of Kelsey's reaction than to anything resembling or sounding like a ghost.

John, who couldn't help being the villain, purposely scared her a few times. "That was awesome," John yelled as they walked away from the house and onto the compound.

"Fuck you, Mathers," Kelsey said with annoyance, calling him by his last name.

Heather and Kelvin laughed, seeming to be enjoying the banter and the show they had just watched, with John tormenting Kelsey every chance he got.

"That's weird," Mark remarked.

"What is?" John asked.

"The back gate is open, but not the way I left it."

"Maybe the wind blew it open, or one of us forgot to close it," Kelsey said. "Don't overthink it. Let's just go."

They went out through the back. When the group had reached the street, it was very quiet, which wasn't really surprising, considering the location of the house was on the outskirts of town. Still, it felt a bit *too* quiet.

TOM COLEMAN

"Is it just me, or are there fewer streetlights than there were before?" Mark asked.

Now that he'd mentioned it, Heather remembered that it had been brighter when they'd arrived at the place. "Let's just go, please," she said, feeling a bit uneasy.

As they walked, it was as if the wind had taken a life of its own. The howling typical of wind bellowed in the streets. The more she walked, the less safe she felt. The sound of the wind was like loud whispers—if that even made sense. At times, it seemed to turn from loud whispers into something more nefarious.

"I really want to get home," Kelsey, who had been awfully quiet for a while, finally said, breaking their silence.

"Wait—who are they?" John asked, and they all stopped walking.

Heather looked up to notice seven people standing in their way. The unknown figures were a bit far from where she and her friends were standing, so it was impossible to make out any distinct features.

"Hey, wassup?" Kelvin said, walking ahead of them a bit.

"Kelvin, I don't think this is the right time to be carefree or whatever," Mark cautioned. He looked worried. "Things have been weird since we left the house. We should—"

"What is he doing?" Kelvin asked, turning back to look at Mark after one of them was winding up as if getting ready to throw something.

TOM COLEMAN

"I think we should run. They're about to stone us or something," Kelsey proposed.

"C'mon—they're probably some classmates trying to prank us or something." Kelvin seemed as unbothered as ever.

Now the other six individuals wound up as well, but there was nothing in their hands.

The first one executed his throwing motion.

"We are not scared, you idiots!" John had had enough.

"Let`s g—" said Kelvin. In that moment his head seemed to open up as if something had bored through it, and the blood splashed on Kelvin's friends' horrified faces.

Kelsey screamed in shock. Her hand shook as she brought it close to her face as if it were afraid to touch it.

Heather saw her friends screaming in horror and shock. She could not fully process what the hell was happening.

"What the fuck?" John yelled.

They watched as Kelvin staggered and fell to the floor. His head seemed to make a metallic clank when it made contact with the ground.

"Is that metal? Like a metal spear? Why can't I see it? What the fuck is going on?" John asked.

"I think it's whatever he threw," Mark said, dragging Heather along with him. "We have to get out of here. Whatever is happening, this is not normal. The others are about to throw more at us. Get Kelsey. I have Heather."

The strangers had begun their throwing motion. Heather saw this, but she could not bring herself to react because she was still trying to register what had happened. She was still hearing ringing in the background as they rambled on to each other. Slowly, the background sounds and voices faded to the periphery, and the sound of her heartbeat and breathing was all she could register. She was unable to breathe well, and her trachea felt blocked. Heather's larynx felt as if it was almost non-existent, leaving her with the illusion of being unable to speak.

Heather saw everything around her as her bulging eyes roamed from the lifeless body on the floor to her panicked friends to the menacing people after them. She knew the people after them would not going to stop, and if she didn't snap out of it, she would hold her friends back.

She calmed her breathing. When she did, the sounds came to the forefront, and she was able to hear what was going on around her.

The people threw, and thankfully, missed. As they hit the ground, it was clear that the weapons they were throwing were invisible.

"Where the hell are we?" John asked as he dragged Kelsey with him while thinking about Kelvin`s body which they left behind to save themselves. They entered the bush and rushed deep into it. Staying in the streets would not help their cause. "This must be some alternate universe or something."

"Shh," Mark said to him. "We have to be silent. I don't know who those people were, but we gotta lose them."

TOM COLEMAN

They ran deeper into the woods until they felt they had lost their attackers. All of them were breathing heavily. Heather still hadn't said a word. Even though she could breathe better now, her larynx still felt stricken by fear, and her heart was beating at two hundred beats per minute.

"Hey, Heather, are you with me?" Mark said, checking her eyes, probably to see if her pupils were dilated.

Heather was still having trouble coming to terms with what happened. "Kelvin... w-w... was..." she struggled to let out the words.

"Look at me, Heather." She did as Mark asked. "You need to breathe in and out, okay? Slowly...I am here with you. Follow my actions. Just like this, okay?" He guided her through the breathing process, and the frightened girl felt her muscles relax. The thing that had been clogging her throat seemed to fade away. Soon, she was calm and could speak fairly well.

"Kelvin, he's... he's dead," she said out loud, almost not believing it herself.

"What is going on? Where are we?"

"Shut the fuck up, Kelsey. Are you trying to get us killed?" John whispered.

"Hey, talking to her that way isn't going to help," Mark reprimanded his friend.

"Oh, yeah? And what's gonna help us—running? Running to where, huh?"

Mark looked to be in deep thought. "I have a theory," he said. He looked at John, then shifted his gaze to Heather and then to

Kelsey, who was rocking back and forth as if trying to comfort herself. Heather surmised it was her way of remaining sane. "This only began after we left the haunted house, so, if we—" He was sent to the ground from his squatting position when John punched him.

"So, it was you, huh? You're the fucking reason we are in this friggin' state? You killed Kelvin!"

"John, what is wrong with you?" Heather asked, but John was raging out. He had just seen one of his close friends die, and the killers were after them.

Mark tried to remain calm as he got to his feet and took a deep breath. "First, you need to stop shouting. Those things could still be searching for us, and they might be close since they saw where we ran to. We are just resting so we can gather up the energy to run some more. I call them things because they don't seem human. They can make things invisible, and we couldn't even make out anything about them other than that they were shaped like human beings. Second, you really believe that I would have brought you here if I knew this was going to happen? We have to get out of this alive first before—"

"You fucking bastard. Shouting is what you are worried about now?" John charged at Mark.

"John, stop!" Heather tried to keep it from escalating by getting between them, but Kelsey's scream pulled everyone's attention to her.

Her arm was outstretched, pointing to the distance. They followed her arm to see the seven baleful humanoid fiends charging at the hapless human teenagers. It was turning into a real fucking horror show.

***

TOM COLEMAN

"Oh, God. Everyone, run! Run for the haunted house. I have a plan." Mark said while starting to run.

Heather did not need to be told twice. Even though she did not know the route to the haunted house from where they currently were, she ran in the same direction as Mark. She was definitely not as fast as him, but she tried her best, and the adrenaline coursing through her body definitely helped.

John sprinted past her, catching up to Mark. Heather's biggest fear was that she would lose sight of them while running and get lost. She could hear Kelsey screaming behind her, which meant that her friend was still alive, but she could also hear the menacing, howling wind in the atmosphere.

Those things were after them. She did not get enough time to get a good look at the monster-like creatures, but she knew they did not look human despite having a human shape.

Where they zombies? No, they were sane enough to throw spears. They looked a bit like zombies. Whatever they were, they were also ominous, and that was enough for her to run away from them. Truthfully, she really didn't care about what they actually were.

To her discomfort, Heather's fear had come true, and she was separated from her friends. There was no path on which to run, so she just ran straight ahead and into the bush. Her hands and face were punctured and scratched as she ran ahead, and she had to bite her lip to avoid screaming.

After delving deep into the No Man's Land, Heather felt more afraid than ever. She had lost both Mark and John, and she didn't know the way to the haunted house. She also hadn't expected them to risk their lives at the possibility of finding her. What if they were searching for her, and they stumbled on the bad guys instead? The situation was bad on so many fronts. The thing she could hear now were Kelsey's incessant screams, meaning that she knew where her friend was and where the attackers were.

Heather was in deep thought. She had to think fast to come up with a solution that would help the four of them in their attempt to escape their uncanny hell.

"Got it," she said, having a light bulb moment. She got up and ran toward the screaming. Kelsey should have shut up a while ago, but she couldn't help screaming for help, and that would act like radar to drag John, Mark, and herself to their friend. Assuming the other two were planning to save Kelsey. Maybe they'd already assumed she was as good as dead. Heather could not blame them either way. To be honest, if she knew where the haunted house was, and she could get there, she might not come back for her friend. Then again, hearing those screams, Heather knew it would be hard for her not to at least try.

Heather finally met up with Kelsey as she ran. She had removed her shoes—when someone's life is on the line, they tend to forget their vanity. The things chasing them must not be very fast, considering she was able to outrun them. To Heather's disappointment, Mark and John were nowhere to be found.

"Oh, thank God," Kelsey said after seeing her friend. "You need to save me. They are coming after me."

TOM COLEMAN

"Me? What the heck am I gonna do? Come on—we've got to keep running."

"Where?"

Heather had no idea where to run. Her entire plan was predicated on meeting the guys. Mark knew where the house was, and the canopy trees were too tall for her to see anything like a house.

One of the gruesome-looking creatures suddenly ran at them. Did those paranormal creatures not feel fatigued or get tired?

"Run! Run!" Heather said, and she turned to run.

Kelsey was too tired, and she took a while to get to full running speed.

"Come on, Kelsey! You have to be qui—Jesus Christ!" Heather turned back right in time to witness Kelsey being split down the middle in one swift and horrifying motion. Her pieces fell to the sides of whatever invisible weapon had been used to kill her.

The creature had spit dripping from its mouth as it scowled at Heather, who was shocked as hell, but she knew she had to keep running.

John ran at the side at the monster with a huge piece of wood, and Heather breathed a sigh of relief. He jammed it right in the creature's face, causing it to stagger backward.

Mark then rushed out from behind him and rammed it with another huge weapon that Heather couldn't really make out. "C'mon!" he said, grabbing her by the hand as they ran away.

"That barely did shit," John lamented.

"You guys came back for me?"

"Technically, we came back for Kelsey since we didn't know where you were, but we assumed you would be with Kelsey," Mark explained. "We have to get to the haunted house. I think we entered an alternate haunted reality, and this town is haunted by…whatever those things are.

"I'm sorry I got us into this mess. It wasn't my intent…and who would have thought this was what was gonna happen? Anyway, if we get back to the house and come out again, the spell—or whatever witchcraft or juju this is—should be corrected, and we'll be back in our reality. I'm sure we all felt the force when we first entered the haunted house. That makes me believe this is gonna work. Besides, we don't have any better plan right now. The town looks deserted. They may have already killed everyone," Mark explained as quickly as he could.

"You know your way there, right?" asked John

"Sure." Mark replied.

"Thankfully, those things are slow compared to us," John remarked, "but they make up for it by being strong. I don't think our hits did much."

They ran until they got to the haunted house, went in through the back, and raced to the window they had used to leave the house.

TOM COLEMAN

"Go on—ladies first," Mark said.

"No, you should go," Heather said.

"Enough. I'm tired of this crap," John interrupted, fed up with the courtesy. He climbed through the window. "It seems like the two of you have forgotten that monsters are chasing us." He got inside, and Mark told Heather to go next. She heard the wind howl, which meant those things were close. Had they killed every other person in that reality, or was she overthinking things?

"I caused this, whether I meant to or not, so you must go first. I couldn't forgive myself if anything happened to you," he pressured.

She caved and climbed through the window. Heather heard a sound, Mark groaned, and then something grabbed her leg. Heather was too scared to turn to see what it was, so she tried to push through. Half of her body was already inside. She realized that the monsters' powers were not as potent as they were on the other side of the veil.

"Go, Heather!" She turned around after hearing Mark's voice to see him push the monster to get her away from its grip, but the others had caught up with them, and one of them ripped off Mark's face with its clawed hands.

Heather screamed as she fell into the house. She felt a change in being the moment she fully entered the house, but Heather didn't care about that. She would never recover from this.

TOM COLEMAN

"What happened? Where the fuck is Mark? Why are you screaming?" John kept asking her questions, but all she could do was stare at the window, half-hoping Mark would appear within it. The fact that she could not see the fiends on the other side of the window meant that Mark was right, and they would go back to their own reality.

"Oh, God, no. I said it was his fault, and that was why he felt guilty. I'm such a fucking asshole." Now that Mark was gone, John felt responsible, but Heather knew it wasn't his fault. She was too weak to do anything but cry. The stark contrast between John, who was angry and shouting, and Heather, who was quiet and crying Heather seemed to fill the house. A place that had been meant for fun and joy had given them the worst experience of their lives, a pitiable, menacing ordeal that would live long in the minds and hearts of Heather Crawford and John Mathers.

(This story was inspired by an idea from my dear reader William Wimpee)

128

TOM COLEMAN

THE CURSE OF HERNANDEZ
PART TWO

129

TOM COLEMAN

TOM COLEMAN

CHAPTER THREE:
House of horrors

Carlos had decided to pretend he was sick and use the opportunity to go home. He was driving his way, hearing that guitar noise all the while. "This is starting to get irritating," he murmured. No sooner had he finished speaking than sand began pouring from the air conditioning vents.

"What is this? What the hell!" The sand poured out so fast that Carlos had to veer to the side of the road and get out of the car as quickly as possible. When he turned around, it was to see an empty car. Where did the sand go?

"What is happening?" He wondered if he were going crazy. He checked to see if there were any onlookers, but the street was empty. The road seemed shockingly similar to the one near his former place in Florida. Why did everything look so familiar? Was it the town?

"No, no. That's just crazy," he said. He had to think rationally if he were to understand what the hell was going on. The problem, however, was that the things happening to him were not rational. Maybe he needed to see a therapist or something.

The man took a deep breath and sighed. Irrespective of his personal troubles, he had to get home to his wife. She had sounded worried, and that made him worried.

131

TOM COLEMAN

Carlos got back into his car and started to drive. He kept hearing the guitar, but he could not quite place where he'd heard it before. The sound was starting to get to him by the time he'd reached his neighbourhood. It bothered him that he hadn't seen any neighbours since they'd officially took possession of the house. For a moment, he considered stopping by one of the houses to talk to the neighbours, but he chose to talk with Christina about it first. He'd be more comfortable if they went to see the neighbours together. Carlos was not generally a neighbourly person, but this was a unique situation. He needed information about the neighbourhood, and the neighbours were the fastest and best way to get it.

Upon arriving home, he noticed the attic window was open. Who had opened it? Had Christina been cleaning and chosen to let some air in?

"That place is weird. She shouldn't have gone up there," he said. He should have told her about his experience there. Things looked all right despite that, so he got out of the car and hurried to get inside the house.

"Carlos," Christina said. Her accent… her voice… the way she'd pronounced his name…

Carlos knew it was impossible. He was not sure if turning around was the best option. What if he turned and was disappointed? How would that turn out for him? Carlos knew his mind was fragile when it came to her, so he did not want to lose it.

"Aren't you going to look at me?" Her voice as she spoke again was enough to cement Carlos's resolve. He turned

132

TOM COLEMAN

around slowly and was stunned to see her standing there, frowning at him.

"Rosa?" he said, spluttering the name of his sister.

There she stood in the flesh. Her typical scowl and the mean look that hid her kind heart... she looked as if she hadn't aged a day since she'd died. She looked just as he'd remembered her.

"It took you that long to look at me?" she complained.

"How are you here?" he asked with a wide smile. "Is this my imagination or something?"

"I don't know. Anyway, why are you living here?"

Carlos was confused. What was that supposed to mean? He knew one thing: the fact that Rosa did not know how she was there meant that she was a projection of his imagination, but since when did he have the power to project stuff like that? Something wasn't right, but things had been seriously off ever since he'd moved into that damn house.

"What are you?"

He must've finally asked the right question because Rosa looked at him with amusement. She scoffed, then giggled, then laughed. "Thank you for setting us free."

"Huh?"

"We will thank you by feeding on your fears." Her face started to melt away.

Carlos did not have the mental capacity to process what was happening before his eyes. It was as if his brain had

133

shut down the moment he'd witnessed his sister's face melt away like ice cream.

"We will feed on your guilt. We will you to replenish us, our hate, our pain." The creature— whom Carlos would definitely no longer refer to as his sister—spoke cryptically.

" This isn't even real. Snap out of it." Carlos tried dragging himself back to reality, but the morphed entity just laughed.

"You will both know our gratitude."

"Both?" Carlos finally remembered that he was worried about Christina. He looked up and saw Christina trying to climb out of the window. What the fuck was she doing?

"Christina, no!" he called.

She looked out of it as if she were in a trance or had some sort of spell cast on her, and she looked about ready to fall.

"Christina, stop! What are you doing?" He could not believe it. Carlos knew he could not reach the attic in time to stop her from jumping, so he had only one option. He ran over to where his wife would fall to as fast as he could. Carlos checked to see if the thing would try to stop him, but it was not there anymore.

He knew there was no room for error. Christina was going to fall, and there was nothing he could do about it. Still, he tried persuading her against it. "What are you doing,

TOM COLEMAN

Christina? Are you trying to throw away your life? Snap out of it!"

Carlos prayed to anyone who might hear: God, nature, somebody, the wind, luck—anything that might offer some assistance. "Please, help me save the life of this woman." They had just started their lives together. It would be too cruel a fate to strip him of her now. He'd planned a future with her, and there was no way he was ready to live in that sick house alone.

Christina fell, and it was as if time had stopped for him. Everything happened in less than two seconds.

Carlos got there in time and ran into her before she hit the ground, causing them to tumble together a number of times. He was able to shield her head from the worst of it, and he hit his head quite badly as a consequence. Before he passed out, Carlos wondered why the hell they'd chosen that goddamn house. They needed to leave it, and immediately so.

***

"Ugh," Carlos grunted, blinking. He was awake, and the last thing he remembered was pushing Christina out of the way, saving her from death. He looked around to see that he was in the master's bedroom, which he did not like. Where was Christina?

Carlos got up and saw Christina seated on a chair, writing. Why was she acting as if nothing had happened? Was she okay?

135

TOM COLEMAN

"Christina?" he called to her.

When she saw he was awake, she seemed happy, which was eerie to him. "Hey, you're awake." She got up from her chair and jumped onto the bed, hugging him.

"What… happened?"

"I was gonna ask you the same thing, silly," she said. "Last thing I remember, I was in the attic, then I woke up and saw you by my side. You were all bruised, and so was I. Your head was cut, too, but I patched you up nicely." Did she really not know what happened? He felt the side of his head and noticed that she had applied some nice first aid on him.

"Christina, I think we need to leave this house now."

***

Christina did not want to leave. She had purposely left out the part about the little Susan in her explanation of what she remembered. The last thing she remembered was reaching out to Susan after going through the window, but it all got fuzzy from there. Was she in denial? Or did she just need Susan's forgiveness? Yes, that was it: forgiveness. Christina had never told Carlos about what she had done or the root of her issues with her family, and now was the worst possible time she could think of to come clean. Her mind was unstable at the moment—maybe she needed to see a therapist.

"What do you mean that we have to leave the house?"

136

TOM COLEMAN

"Something is seriously wrong with this place." Carlos tried to explain the dangers of staying in that deadly place. "I saw my sister, my fucking sister who died almost seventeen years ago. That isn't normal. I keep getting a bad vibe and seeing things that are not there."

"What?" she looked at him, shocked. She had also been seeing things and thought it was just her imagination and guilt.

"Let's go... now!"

"Wait—we need to pack. We can't just lea—"

"Yes, we fucking can!"

***

"Yes, we fucking can!" Carlos was not kidding. He took her hand and yanked her off the bed with him. "Being alive is better than anything else. This house is fucking crazy!" Carlos was going to have a word with the realtor once he'd left, and by "word," he meant beating the shit out of him.

"Wait. Wai—"

Both of them shut up. Carlos had just opened the door, and they were stricken with fear by the dark silhouette facing them.

"Oh, God—no," she said, and she started backing up.

All of Carlos's spirit and vigor were drained in an instant from the sight of such a menacing figure. His firm grip

137

on Christina had loosened, and she pulled her hand away as she backed away in fear. The putrid aura and smell emanating from its being were enough to make them cough.

The humanoid-looking entity was as tall as the door, and it wore a menacing smile.

"You don't want us to leave? Why?" Carlos asked, confused as to why and how all of this was happening.

Black mucus ran from its nose, spraying Carlos and Christina.

Carlos groaned in pain, screaming—what was that black semi-liquid?

"Fuck!" he screamed.

Carlos heard Christina wail, and his pain became secondary as he turned to help her. She seemed as if she were being roasted alive.

He ran to her to try to stop her from burning, but to his shock and horror, maggots started burrowing out of his skin. The pain and fear of feeling and seeing maggots make their way through his skin were horrifying. "Wh... what is happening?" he cried as the pain was growing too much to bear. Besides, watching his skin turn to maggots was... not fun. Carlos had to remember that it was all in his mind... or was it? He was getting less and less sure about what was real and what was fiction.

***

TOM COLEMAN

Christina seemed sold that it was reality. Having your skin being set on fire due to some black mucus will do that to a person. She was told that immolation was the worst way to die based on pain received, and she definitely was not questioning that now. The crunching sound of her skin being conflagrated was enough to send her into near-madness. She had to keep her head in check, but it was hard to do so when this much pain was being instilled in her. Christina couldn't take it anymore. Her mind was getting fuzzy, and her eyes were about to close to black; that was when Carlos held her hand and dragged her out of her own psychological nightmare, closing the door to the Master Bedroom on the Silhouette Man's face.

"Are you okay? Are you okay, baby?"

"Do I look okay?" she lashed out. He guessed that she was trying to cope with her pain and fear.

"I understand, honey." He pulled her into his arms while she sobbed. "I am here for you. We'll get through this together."

Her hands and every other part of her body that had burned were healing at an exponential rate.

"That thing won't let us leave. We have to find a way to make our minds sturdy enough to realize that everything happening to us isn't real," he explained to his wife. "That was how I got over the maggots."

"Maggots? What do you mean?"

"My skin was being opened up by maggots from the inside."

TOM COLEMAN

"Jesus."

"Yeah, tell me about it." Carlos sighed. Seeing her husband look so confused was… disconcerting. He knew the house was somehow attacking them psychologically, but the problem was that he did not know the how or why. There had to be a rule to it and how the ghosts worked.

"The ghost of my sister—or a ghost taking the form of my sister—said something about us setting them free," Carlos said.

"How? Did we set them free just by moving in?"

"No, I don't think so." Carlos thought hard. "We must have done something to make them feel free. It was not this bad when we first moved in."

A light bulb seemed to light in Christina's head. "True. Was it the suitcase we burned?"

"Yeah, it had to be," Carlos concurred. "The attacks only got worse when I entered that gloomy attic and burned the suitcase."

"We have to find a way to get to that suitcase and put it back where we saw it."

"But that would involve us leaving the which, at the current moment, will be hard to do. We may even die."

"Yeah."

They sat on the bed in silence, save the sound of Christina's light sobs and sniffles.

"Carlos, I—"

TOM COLEMAN

"Shh…" he said, rocking his wife's body slowly and steadily. "I just want to savor this moment. If anything happens, no matter what, I got to have this single moment with my beautiful wife." He pushed away from her to get a clear look at her.

Christina looked up at her husband. He looked at her with so much love. Would he feel the same way if she told him what she did to that little girl? Marriages should be built on trust, but she was not trusting him enough to divulge the truth to him. What does that make her?

"What did you see?" he asked.

"Huh?"

"I saw something from my past—what did you see?"

"We're not safe, even in this room, you know?"

"Wait—we're not? How do you know that?"

"Because I came to play with her here," a little girl said from behind them, causing them both to fall from the bed.

Christina yelped.

"Who are you?" Carlos asked, shielding his wife from the little girl who was covered in paint… or was it blood? He couldn't tell.

"Why don't you ask your wife? This is her guilt."

Carlos glanced at his wife before focusing back on the ghost. From the look on Christina's face, it was clear that she knew the ghost. "Christina, what is going on?"

TOM COLEMAN

The room distorted. The Hernandez's saw strange shapes of disorienting sizes. Carlos tried to close his eyes and remain calm even if the warping confused his sense of balance.

"Carlos!" Christina yelped. She held on to him for dear life while Susan laughed maniacally. Her voice had turned into that of a man, and it was fucked up.

"This isn't real. This isn't real. Once you know this, it can't hurt you," Carlos kept whispering as everything went to shit around him. The atmosphere surrounding him felt worse and worse... but after a short while, it stopped.

Carlos slowly opened his eyes, happy it had stopped but also to check if the room was back to normal.

The doll from the other room was seated in front of him.

"Oh, hell no!" Carlos had always found dolls creepy. He grabbed his wife and went running out of the room. There was no way he'd let the doll near him. Upon opening the door, however, he saw that the Silhouette Man was still there. His hulking and menacing figure shook Carlos and Christina to their very cores. That was how bad things had devolved. They had to choose between a shadow creature who spat black goo and a creepy doll. Who knew what other demonic entities lurked around there? Carlos had no idea what they were. Demons? Ghosts? Something else? All of them at once?

"Close the door," Christina said with a tone of finality that he was not about to question. He knew why—she did not want to go through what she had with that man again.

TOM COLEMAN

The Silhouette Man opened his mouth, and they could tell another bout of the weird black stuff was going to come out again. These entities really did not want them to leave the house.

Carlos reached for the door just as the wraith spurted out the liquid. Thankfully, he was able to close the door in time, but some of the substance had touched his hand.

"Carlos!" Christina yelled, worry in her eyes.

The liquid seeped into Carlos's skin, and a few seconds later, he saw what was, perhaps, the worst thing he had ever seen in his life.

Miniature baby heads, each of them crying, birthed from Carlos's skin. He was mentally strong, but this was something else. Carlos screamed like a maniac while looking at his hand, with Christina staring in horror. And that wasn't the worst of it.

***

With Carlos in his own psychological nightmare, there was no one to protect Christina, and before she knew it, Mrs. Hernandez found herself in a graveyard.

"What the fuck?" She was perplexed. How had she ended up there? Christina noticed the doll atop a grave. She did not want to get closer to the creepy-looking doll, but it was the only familiar thing she knew in the apparent graveyard, so against her better judgment, she walking closer to the grave, and she was able to read the inscription on the tombstone.

"'Esther Carrey,'" she read, and to her distress and shock, a skeletal hand burst from of the grave and took hold of the doll.

Christina screamed. She careened backward and stumbling over her own feet. She backed up, still screaming, and watching in terror at the part skeletal, part muscular limb, protruding from the grave. The thing even had blonde hair and petted the doll as if it were its own.

A hand held on to Christina's from her side, making her yell in fear. She turned to see another weird hybrid of skeleton and muscle, only this one took hold of her. All of the dead creatures in the cemetery had awoken, and they were about to consume her. The dread that brought to her entire being was unfathomable, and she felt herself reaching a peak level of trepidation unlike ever before. Was this the end?

As the countless number of hands crawled out and onto every part of her body, from her face to her legs, she could only cry and wish to be saved, and something broke mentally.

As always, his hand reached out to her, pulled her out of the amalgamation of skeletons cascading over her body, and Christina was finally back to reality. She looked around to see that they were in the bathroom.

"Are you okay?" Carlos said. "Christina—look at me!"

TOM COLEMAN

CHAPTER FOUR:
Confession

"Christina!" Carlos had to know she was all right. She seemed a bit dazed, which worried him a lot. They both had to stay sane if they were going to get out of that horror show alive. These ghosts must be feeding off of their fears and guilt or something—why did Carlos have the feeling there was something even more sinister behind the creatures' attacks?

"I'm fine," she said, looking blue.

"You don't look fine."

"What the hell is happening, Carlos?" She finally broke down. "Why are we being attacked by things from our past… by ghosts we don't even have any relationship with… by a house that seems hellbent on making us go mad or worse… kill us?"

He had no answer to her inquiries, but at least she'd confirmed she had been seeing things as well.

"And how are you so good at combating it while I… I'm just a burden for you, like always."

"Why would you say that, a burden?" He was confused that she would see herself like that. Carlos believed that he was the one lucky enough to have her in his life. She was a girl from a rich family who could have had anyone, and yet she chose to be with him, a rugged guy from the slums.

As for her main point, he knew why she had been targeted the most and easily prone to the emotional and psychological attacks.

Carlos's mother had told him about superstition many times before since she was a very spiritual person. He had never been one to believe in God or any of that stuff, but considering what was happening to them, he definitely was reconsidering that stance. She had told him that when an evil spirit, curse, or demonic entity was trying to latch on to a group of people in a particular space, they generally went for the one who was more gullible or emotionally vulnerable. Even though he was paranoid, he was not as emotionally susceptible as his wife. He didn't have any panic attacks, and he was more suspicious of things, which meant he took more caution where his emotions were concerned.

But… how could he tell her that? He had to find a better way to explain it to her without making her feel weak or broken. "I think it is because you are nicer and more open to things. Considering where I came from, I'm much harder to deceive," he said, the best way he knew how.

"It's because I'm weak." She admitted, causing him to frown.

"Don't say that. This is what the house wants, for us to begin doubting ourselves."

"Well, it's working." Christina looked tired… really tired. It seemed like she had no fight left in her, and this worried Carlos. The house wasn't attacking them at that particular moment; maybe it was because they weren't trying to leave. Would the house have any power to stop them from going out the door? It attacked the mind, not the body, and it only gave the illusion of the body being attacked, but Christina could have died that time in the attic. That hadn't been the house inflicting physical damage, though. That sick place had led her close to death without touching her physically.

"The girl's name is Susan," Christina said.

"Huh?"

"That little girl; she is a manifestation of my memories." Was that what she did had not wanted to tell him, Carlos wondered.

"Who is she?"

"You mean was. Who *was* she?" she clarified. Carlos felt he should have known that, considering the girl had been covered in blood and ghost. He didn't know it could manifest living people.

"This house. It feeds on our guilt… our insecurities. Whatever feelings and regrets we have deep inside, it takes that and poisons it until it manifests the worst of the worst. I think the longer we stay here, the more it will adapt and learn our weaknesses. It's already done this much—who knows what it'll be like if we are forced to stay here for two more days?" She sighed and looked down at the tiled floor.

"No matter what it is, Christina, we will get through it together."

"I hope so. I really do." Carlos had never seen his wife's eyes so deadpan. "Maybe I deserve to die."

147

TOM COLEMAN

"What the hell is wrong with you, Christina?" His yelling had startled her, but Carlos did not care. He was not going to lose the woman he loved before they had even begun to live their lives together. "Stop this. I don't like it when you talk like that."

"You don't know what I've done, Carlos." He did, however, know it had something to do with the little girl.

"What happened?"

"Well, since we could die at any moment, I might as well tell you." She sat up beside her husband. "I was sixteen years old and still a brat. My parents are rich, as you know, so I grew up in a very… entitled childhood."

"Yeah."

"One evening, I was driving while partly drunk." Carlos finally got where this was going, and he did not like it.

"I was driving so fast that I did not notice the red light. I was going to hit a car, but I veered off and ran into a house. The little girl was playing with her skipping rope when I crashed into their yard and hit her."

"Wow." Carlos did not know what else to say. Needless to say, he was shocked.

"That isn't the worst part."

"What do you mean?" There's more?

"What really… really broke me was what came after," she said. "My parents, being the horrible people they are, worried more about their image than morality. I wasn't

TOM COLEMAN

eighteen, so I would go to juvie and be out in a few years, but they didn't like how that would look, and they threatened the family of the girl until they were forced to accept a settlement."

"Oh, my God." Carlos had always known that Christina's parents were assholes, but this was next-level.

"And I agreed to it."

"What?" Carlos immediately wished he hadn't said that. He knew it might make her feel judged.

"Yeah." Christina didn't seem to mind, though. She seemed to have almost expected it. There was no way he could not be surprised, considering the version of her he knew now.

"I was fine with it... for a while. Then, I couldn't sleep. I got away with manslaughter... and I had this dark cloud hovering over me all the time. I turned to drugs and alcohol, which didn't work. Eventually, I realized I needed to take accountability for my actions, and I severed all ties with my family and went back to find Susan's parents, only to discover the mother had committed suicide."

"Jesus."

"Imagine putting a price on your daughter's life. That's what she and her husband felt they did when they accepted the check from my parents. It's harsh, but that's the reality. Susan's father, Mr. Cole, said they felt guilty ever since the day they accepted the check. Mrs. Cole more so than him."

"So, that's why this has such a stronghold over you," Carlos noted.

149

"And the reason why I have panic attacks. Every now and then, I feel that dark cloud over me, and I get anxious, like the poor little girl is coming for her revenge."

"You could have told me, you know? I would still have loved you."

"I'm sorry for keeping this a secret. I just did not want you to see me differently. I wanted you to continue looking at me as that bundle of joy you always said I was." Carlos cupped his wife's cheeks and looked into her dark brown eyes. He wanted her to know that and that it would never change.

"I will always love you, Christina. I would do anything for you. Who you were back then and who you are now are two different people. I did not fall in love with the sixteen-year-old brat who would be fine getting away scot-free after something like that. I fell for the woman who could not sleep at night and had to cut her family completely off, the woman who went to the family and tried to make amends, and still, you still feel guilty. That is precisely what makes you a good person, Christina. You will always be my light."

She could not bear hearing such kind words from the person whose opinion mattered most to her in the world. For so long, Christina was afraid of what would happen if he had found out about what she had done, but Carlos had brushed it off like it was nothing.

"That thing out there is not the little girl you killed. That is a monster taking advantage of our goodness to try to poison us from the inside out. We have to find it and defeat it in a battle of wills."

TOM COLEMAN

"I can't." She shook her head to indicate she did not want to go back inside after everything she'd witnessed.

"You can, my love. It's just a leap of faith." Even Carlos sensed the dark aura coming from the other side of the bathroom door. He knew they were in for pain, but at least now they were in it together, and they knew a bit about what they were up against.

"Take my hand."

Christina hesitated, after looking at him, caved in. "Okay," she said, finally taking Carlos's hand, and they opened the door together, running headfirst into the void of illusion and pain.

And then all hell broke loose, and the screaming began.

To be continued…

151

TOM COLEMAN

TOM COLEMAN

THE OTHER SIDE

153

TOM COLEMAN

154

TOM COLEMAN

<u>Chapter 1</u>

"It is my great pride to give you the graduates of Carlton Boarding High," said Principal Coleman with a smile. The tall, grey-haired principal stood back as the hall filled with the deafening sound of celebration. Parents, friends, students, staff members, and school visitors clapped and cheered in unison as the youngsters trooped onto the podium in the school's hall. This was it--the moment Joe Phillips had dreamed of since he'd started Carlton Boarding High.

Joe scanned the crowd, grinning from ear to ear. His little sister jumped excitedly where she stood. His mom and dad had their hands busy with applause. Mom was teary-eyed and flashing a tooth-glistening smile. Dad, on the other hand, wore a small smile.

"Thank you," Joe said under his breath.

His father nodded amidst the unending applause as though he'd heard his near-silent words of gratitude.

Joe would have continued staring at his family through the rest of the graduation program had his best friend, Kyle, not pulled him by the neck.

"This is it, bro," he said into Joe's ear. His voice was raised so Joe could hear him. Kyle took off his graduation cap and waited for the signal.

TOM COLEMAN

Realizing what he'd nearly missed, Joe hurriedly removed his graduation cap just in time to throw it into the air alongside his mates. It was official: they were finally high school graduates.

***

The rest of the graduation ceremony was a breeze of teary-eyed goodbyes, the exchange of numbers, and loads of promises to keep in touch. It was how things were supposed to be, and Joe enjoyed every moment of it.

After a few more moments of excitement, Joe was in his family's minivan. Dad was driving, and that meant his mom had the four hours' drive time to herself. There was no better way for her to spend the four hours save chatting excitedly with her son about his graduation and probably chip in one or two hints about college. That was her trademark. She wasn't as reserved as her husband. Although Joe was tired from the ceremony, he didn't mind the chitchat.

"So, I spoke to--"

"Come on, Liz, let the boy rest. You've been going on for the last two hours," Mr. Phillips said, finally. They were his first words since the journey had begun.

"But hon--" his wife began to protest.

"No buts, Liz. I'm sure Joe's had more than enough talk for today. Let the young man rest his head and dream about his

156

TOM COLEMAN

friends," Mr. Phillips said, cutting off his wife. "Am I right, Joe?" He glanced at his son via the rearview mirror.

Joe gave him a weak smile in response. While he didn't want to hurt his mom's feelings, he definitely needed to rest his head.

"Oh," Liz started, her voice low, "guess you should rest your head now, dear." Joe's mom adjusted herself in her seat and remained quiet.

Joe stared for a while, wondering whether to spark another conversation with his mom. He knew she'd been hurt by being told to keep quiet, no matter how little. He hadn't liked that bit, even though he knew that his dad meant well, and he desperately needed to rest his head. Jeanne, his little sister, was fast asleep with her head on his shoulder--sleeping was hardly a problem for a ten-year-old.

"Guess I'll be joining Jeanne, then," he said under his breath. He adjusted himself, snuggling into the seat, and allowing his eyes to drift shut. No sooner had he done this than he was off to sleep and faster than he'd expected.

***

"Well, well--look who's finished high school," said a voice much like Joe's.

"Huh? What?" Joe muttered. His eyelids fluttered.

"Oh, no, you don't," the voice said.

TOM COLEMAN

Joe felt a breeze brush over his eyes, and his eyelids felt like lead. "Who's there?" Joe asked, turning his face from side to side. Try as hard as he could he could not open his eyes.

"Relax, Joe, " the voice said again.

Joe's head was forced to a standstill. Dread filled him as he wondered where he was and who was holding him captive. He couldn't feel anything touching him, yet he was heavily restrained.

"I'm a friend, Joe. I just came to give my hearty congratulations," the voice said after a moment of silence. "You don't know me, but I know you, Joe. I know everything about you.

"Let's just say that I'm that friend who's always been there, but you never really cared to know," it said. "I figured that if I'd said congratulations while you were busy with your other friends, you'd hardly hear me, so I decided to wait, at least until I knew we were alone and you'd hear me.

"Anyway, congratulations, Joe. I hope you had fun," the voice said. "Not to be a bother or anything, but I'm here fo you. You and I are going to have so much fun soon." It chuckled.

A few minutes passed. Joe slowly felt himself regain control of his body. He felt as if the environment around him was slowing down. Once he could control his eyelids, Joe opened his eyes and jerked upright.

"Wow, easy there, mister, " Mr. Phillips said to his son, who had nearly jumped out of his seat.

TOM COLEMAN

"We just got home," he said.

"Oh, okay," Joe said. He took in a loud breath, rubbed his eyes, and looked at his mom, whose brows were frowned; she looked concerned.

"It's nothing, Mom. I just had a weird dream, that's all," Joe said, stretching slightly. Although something didn't feel right about what he'd experienced, it was better not to give Mom something else to worry about. He knew how overprotective she could be when there was something to worry about, and he didn't want that kind of attention, besides. At least, not at that moment.

"Hmm. Guess you're starting to miss your friends back at school," Mr. Phillips said.

Joe smiled slightly as if to say, "Maybe."

"Anyway, you only just left them four hours ago. I'm sure you'll be just fine after a week or two. Didn't you get a few cards and phone numbers?" Mr. Phillips queried with an arched brow.

Joe nodded and mumbled something along the lines of, "I guess I could place a few calls."

"It's settled, then, " Mr. Phillips said, getting out of his side of the minivan. "Come--help me with some of the stuff in the trunk."

"But John, " Liz protested, stepping out of the minivan.

"Don't worry, mom. I'm fully rested. I can take the stuff out of the trunk," Joe offered, and he stepped out of the car, as well.

TOM COLEMAN

"No, you can't," Liz said sharply. Her eyes did not leave her husband, who was trying to stifle his laughter. "It's your big day today, and I intend for you to enjoy it fully," she added, her voice turning sweet.

"Come on, Mom. Taking some of my stuff out of the trunk won't make a difference. It's just normal stuff," Joe said with a shrug.

"Jeanne?" she called.

Her daughter, who'd been watching her family from inside the minivan, peeked out her head.

"Come with me. Let's leave the men to do their thing," she said sweetly.

"Okay, Mom," Jeanne replied, and she made her way promptly out of the minivan, skipped a little, took her mom's outstretched hand, and walked in-step with her.

"I'm sure you agree that I'm right, " Liz said to her daughter as they made their way into the house. They lived in a quiet neighborhood with rows of houses on either side of the road. Each house had a neatly mowed lawn secured with a low fence. It was the perfect setup for mild chitchats with the neighbors, but at that moment, none of the neighbors were in sight. It was just them, having arrived a little past five pm without fanfare or inquiries from nosey neighbors.

***

The kitchen and dining arrangements were Liz's turf, and she did exactly as she pleased. First, it started by banning Joe and his father from the kitchen while she sorted out dinner preparations. By the time she was out of the kitchen and had set the round dining table, there were two steaming bowls sitting in the middle of the dining table, one with spaghetti and another with chicken. A third bowl held mouthwatering salad.

Mr. Phillips whistled when he saw the dished laid out before him. "Now, this is the real celebration," he said, smacking his lips.

The first bit of the feast went without a hassle until Mr. Phillips decided to help himself to more.

Liz acted fast, her fork intercepting that of her husband just before he could pick up a piece of chicken. "The latest graduates get to pick first," she said with a wink.

Her husband stared. When he recovered himself, Mr. Phillips tried outsmarting his wife by pretending to remove his fork, but she was ready for him. No sooner had he tried to sink his fork back into the bowl than she was there to intercept it.

"Come on, Liz," Mr. Phillips whined. "He's not even done with his plate."

"Oh, well. Guess we'll have to wait for him, then," his wife replied sweetly, her fork still deflecting that of her husband's.

Joe looked at his parents, who were hunched over the dining table in a battle of forks. It was as silly as it was endearing. This was the part about home he'd missed terribly while he'd been in school. It wasn't as though school was all that bad, but it definitely didn't compare to home.

TOM COLEMAN

Joe's mind flooded with loving memories of the past, and a streak of tears fell down his cheek. It was enough to break the battle between his mom and dad, who turned to look at him. "I... I love you guys," Joe said with a shaky voice.

Mr. Phillips stretched a hand to Joe and rubbed his head.

His wife ambled over to her son and buried him in a hug.

"We love you, too, son," Mr. Phillips said in response. "I am proud of you," he added.

Jeanne had quietly joined in the hug alongside her mom.

For a while, it seemed as though dinner might end with the hug. But Mr. Phillips saw his chance, went for the bowl of chicken, and took off with it.

"John," his wife screamed. She broke the hug to chase after him.

Mr. Phillips laughed as he evaded his wife, and Joe and his little sister joined in. It was, indeed, one of those days.

***

The night wore on smoothly, and it was finally time for Joe to retire. With all the excitement he'd had, his body needed all the rest it could get.

Joe slumped onto his bed and gave a sigh of relief. It had been a great day. Memories of his friends at school came rushing in, and he took his time savoring each one. The pranks, the tests, the difficult times, the games, the hangouts... he replayed every moment dear to him. Kyle, his best friend, had pulled through on many occasions for him, and it was with a mix of regret that he realized it was all over. At least, their high school years were over, and the likelihood of going to the same college was bleak.

Just then, it hit him: he hadn't called any of his friends, especially not Kyle, whom he'd promised to call once he arrived home.

"Well, then, let's see what he's up to," he muttered. Joe turned over on his side and slid his hands over to his bedside dresser, where his phone laid on the edge, switched off.

He picked up his phone, switched it on, and waited for the phone to complete its booting process. Not too long after it was done booting, a string of notifications sounded. Text messages. Not just from Kyle but from a ton of others.

"Guess I'm a little late," he said with a smirk, and he opened the first message from Kyle.

It read: "Hey, man--how's home? Nothing out of the ordinary happening here. A few words from my old man and that's all. PS, the gang's hanging out next Saturday. I'll send the details later."

Joe smiled, and his mind drifted to what Kyle had said concerning his dad. It was always a few words that were said between them. He was the only son of a single father, and his dad never joked about Kyle's career path. For what it was worth, his dad had plans to get him into one of the top colleges. His dad was unlike Joe's, who had a good sense of

TOM COLEMAN

humor despite being reserved. While a good sense of humor could calm some tense moments, it wasn't always enough. Bills still had to be paid, and Joe knew how much he had to work to earn a scholarship to ease the burden on his parents. It had paid off with a partial scholarship, but the depressing thought of why things weren't better than they currently were always hung out in the back of his mind.

"No time for that now," Joe muttered, shaking himself out of his thoughts. He needed to call Kyle.

Joe switched to his dialer, flexed his finger over his phone's screen, and tapped out the number off the top of his head. Without crosschecking that he'd dialed correctly, he hit the dial button and brought the phone to his ear.

For a moment, there was no ring, which prompted Joe to check his phone. The silence was odd. Joe checked his phone, puzzled at the silly mistake he'd made: he'd unconsciously dialed his own phone number. That explained why there was no ring; it couldn't connect.

He smiled lazily and moved his finger toward the red button to disconnect. In the few seconds it took for his finger to press the red button, the call connected.

"Hello, Joe," an eerily familiar voice said.

<u>Chapter 2</u>

"H-hello?" Joe stuttered. "Who is this?"

"Ha-ha--don't you know already?" the speaker asked. There was an unsettling feeling in those words.

"What? I don't know you," Joe said, steeling his voice, so it didn't sound frightened. The other speaker sounded all too familiar to ignore, and it made his skin crawl.

"Come on, Joe--don't tell me you've forgotten so quickly. Or didn't I make that much of an impression the first time?" the voice retorted.

"Look," Joe said firmly, "whatever game this is, I don't want any part in it. I don't know you, and I don't know what kind of hack got you into my phone number."

"Oh, strong words, " the voice said with a chuckle. "Maybe I should cut to the chase then."

"Yes, quit stalling and answer my question," Joe demanded, his initial fear turning to a mild annoyance. He was much too tired to continue the conversation with the strange voice on the other end of the call.

Silence reigned between the duo for what felt like hours. Joe, who couldn't take it anymore, sighed and was about to hang up when the voice spoke once more.

"I am you, Joe Phillips," it said.

TOM COLEMAN

A chill ran down Joe's spine at the words. Despite his room being mildly warm, he felt eerily cold. There was something about that voice that screamed terror. "Ex-excuse me?" Joe finally said, but there was no response. "He-hello?" Joe queried after a few seconds passed in silence, but there was still no response.

He drew his phone away from his ear and glanced at the screen. The call timer blinked steadily, displaying "00:00."

"That's not possible," Joe muttered, feeling confused by the display on his phone's screen. Just then, the call dropped.

Joe stared at his phone. The screen had long turned off due to inactivity. His tired mind reeled with unease. He'd heard of people dialing their own phone numbers for fun, but he'd never heard of calls like that going through. It was odd that his had gone through, not to mention the creepy turn it had taken when the person on the other end had claimed to be him. As much as he wanted to write it off as a prankster who had hacked into his phone number, there was something about it that made him shiver. He'd heard that voice before. It was the same voice as he'd heard in his dream when he'd taken a short nap on the way home.

Unsure as to what to do, Joe double-tapped on the screen of his phone. It came on, and as expected, his number was the first on the call log. He stared, his finger too hesitant to redial. He didn't feel so sleepy anymore.

Joe steeled himself, closed his eyes, and let his finger drift to the redial button. A few minutes passed in silence, prompting Joe to take a peek at his phone screen. No sooner

TOM COLEMAN

did he do this than the screen lit up with the call timer, which read "00:00."

"H-hello?" Joe stuttered

"Hello, Joe. Guess you finally decided to call again," the voice replied.

Joe gulped. "Tell me again: who are you?" he asked, trying to maintain as much control over his voice as possible. To an observer, it would seem as if he were having a normal conversation, but on the inside, he was shaking.

"I am you, Joe," the voice said.

"But that doesn't make any sense," Joe responded.

The voice chuckled and said, "Maybe. Aren't you the owner of this phone number?"

Joe replied in the affirmative.

"Since you're the owner, aren't you supposed to be the one who receives calls on this number?" it queried.

"Yes, but that's not the point," Joe retorted. "I *am* the owner, and I *am* the one to receive the calls. I am me," he said, his voice rising.

"Yes. I agree, " the voice said flatly.

"Y-you do?" Joe was taken aback by the response.

"Yes, indeed, Joe. You're you... and *I* am *you*," the voice said

TOM COLEMAN

"But how? It's not possible that when I call my line, I answer my own call to my own line, if that makes any sense at all," Joe said. His frustration was starting to show.

"Ha-ha. Don't think too deeply on this, Joe." The voice chuckled.

Joe grumbled. "if you claim to be me, then you must know what I know--"

"Like what you like, and hate what you hate?" the voice said, completing Joe's line of thought.

"Wait--how did you?" Joe asked in disbelief. He hadn't expected the voice to steal into his thoughts and complete his sentence.

"Guess that helps convince you a little, doesn't it?" The voice chuckled.

"You know, it's already late, " Joe started, "Mom and Dad are probably asleep--"

"That's not what's on your mind, is it Joe?" the voice retorted.

Joe kept quiet, fishing desperately for an answer in his head.

"Kyle is fine, and he isn't all that bothered about you not calling," it added.

"Shit," Joe exclaimed. He'd been fishing in his head for an excuse to end the call, and the voice had picked up on it.

"I understand this is a little confusing for you, Joe, but it is what it is; I am you," it said.

TOM COLEMAN

Unsure of what to say, Joe kept quiet. The voice didn't seem to mind the silence. The duo remained like that until Joe felt himself drift off to sleep.

"You know, it's not exactly smart to sleep while on the phone," the voice said.

Joe's eyes shot open. His phone was still by his ear, but the statement hadn't come from his phone--he'd heard it in his head.

Alarmed, he tapped the red button on his phone's screen to end the call but nothing happened. The call timer kept blinking, meaning he was still on the call. He tried a few more frustrated taps, but Joe couldn't get the call to end.

"You know, instead of trying to run, how about you ask me all you want to know?" the voice said amidst Joe's incessant tapping. That got a reaction from Joe, who paused as though considering the offer. Creepy as it was, Joe needed to know who he was dealing with. First, it seemed like he was dealing with a top-notch hacker, but that didn't explain how the voice was able to enter his head.

"Fine," Joe said finally. His shoulders dropped in an unconscious shrug. "Since you don't plan on letting me off the call, tell me who you are again?"

"We've already gone through this, Joe: I am you. Your other half, the part that exists between here and there," it retorted.

"What does that me--"

"It's not yet time for you to know that," the voice said, its tone dark and foreboding.

"Oh," Joe said. "So, how does this you being me work?"

"Well, I know all about you. I was there at each point of memory," the voice replied. "I can help you recall any memory, and I can pretty much help you get into someone else's mind," it added.

The latter comment caught Joe's attention, but just as he was about to ask for clarification, the voice took his cue and said, "Yes, I can share your thoughts with another. Make said person see and hear thoughts as though you're speaking to them directly."

"Wait--are you saying that you can connect me telepathically to another person? Like read and talk to minds?" Joe asked, his interest piqued.

"Well, if that's how you understand it, then yes," the voice replied.

"Wow," Joe said. There was nothing more he could think of to utter.

"But wait--how, exactly, are you able to do that?" he asked after a while.

"Let's just say I am your un-tethered self. Your other side," it replied.

"Hmm," Joe muttered as his mind processed what he'd heard.

"Just so you know, you're not the first," the voice quipped. "There have been others before you, and there are others like you."

"You mean there are others who can call their phone lines and link to strange voices that claim to be them and talk about stuff that's never been heard before?" Joe retorted. This didn't seem to sit well with the voice, who kept quiet at his remark.

"Hello?" Joe called, but there was no response. After waiting a few minutes without a response, Joe tried disconnecting the call once more.

"Careful, Joe, you may hurt yourself," the voice finally said. At this, the call dropped by itself, leaving Joe staring uneasily at his phone's screen.

It had been a crazy night for Joe, who had kept going back and forth between being creeped out and intrigued. The talk about mind reading had piqued his interest, and he'd already thought of a few people he'd like to try it on, but his mind had also been thrown into unease at the last words he'd heard, which were foreboding.

Joe sighed heavily, dropped his phone on his bedside table, and got comfortable in the bed. His mind was intrigued, confused, and scared at the same time. He just couldn't understand how something could be both creepy and fascinating. For what it was worth, he was done for the day, and he could finally rest.

***

TOM COLEMAN

"Please, don't do this--please," Joe pleaded desperately, clambering for the support of the wall behind him. Five lanky figures loomed over him, their faces obscured by darkness. He was cornered.

"You know what time it is, Joe?" one of the figures queried. A pale hand dropped heavily onto his shoulder. The weight forced him harshly to the ground. There was a splash as Joe fell to the water-laden tile floor. He was locked in the bathroom. Worse off, it was flooded.

"It's teatime," the same figure said and burst out laughing. The five lanky frames shook eerily as they burst into maniacal bouts of laughter.

"Please! I'll do what you asked. I'll fix your notes... homework... anything," Joe cried.

"Too late, little man. First, you drink, then you fix our mistakes," the lead figure said. In a swift motion, Joe felt himself being hoisted onto his feet by two powerful hands. The force with which they'd lifted him sent him crashing into the wall. He grunted as pain shot through his body; screaming was futile.

Without giving him a moment's breath, he was lifted high into the air. Four pairs of arms held him firmly on both arms and legs, so firmly he had very little wiggle-room.

The chant of "Teatime" continued as they dragged him through the flooded bathroom passage. A stall at the far end of the passage gleamed an ominous shade of red. That was his judgment room, and he knew what was coming.

TOM COLEMAN

A kick sent the door of the stall flying open. Almost immediately, he was thrown to the floor, his head barely missing the decrepit ceramic toilet tank.

Joe raised a weak palm to his nose as the stench from the toilet slammed heavily into his nostrils. Not that it mattered, though. It was only a matter of seconds before he would be in the toilet, head first.

"Not so tough now, are you?" one of the figures queried Joe as he was yanked to his feet.

With his eyes shut, Joe gulped as he felt himself being raised by his legs. In a matter of seconds, he was dangling above the toilet. In the last moments before he was dropped into it, Joe felt himself recoil. Something had stirred in him. Was it disgust at his weakness? Hatred for his oppressors?

Just then, he heard, "All this time, Joe, you've ignored me."

***

Joe jerked out of his sleep, panting and sweating. He darted his eyes from left to right, glancing around his darkened room. It was an act designed to reassure him that he was safe, that all he'd seen and all he'd felt had been nothing but a dream.

He heaved a sigh but remained seated in the dark, and his eyes began to play tricks on him. The shadows seemed to

TOM COLEMAN

move in the periphery of his vision, but each time he turned to look, nothing was there.

"Not tonight," he said under his breath, and he reached for his phone. There was a wave of peace when he switched on the phone's torch app, which he used to scan around the room to make sure there were no figures hidden in the corners. Once he was satisfied he was alone, he dragged himself off the bed and walked groggily out of his room.

Joe made his way to the fridge in the kitchen and pulled out a can of soda. He downed the entire contents in a single gulp, wiped his mouth with the back of his hand, and sighed. It wasn't the first time he'd had that nightmare. As a matter of fact, it was one of five recurring nightmares, and at the end of each one, he heard the same voice saying the same words.

He tossed the can into the recycling bin by the kitchen door and went off toward his room, but just as he got to his door, he made a U-turn. He definitely wasn't going to get any more sleep after the nightmare, so there was no point lying in the darkness in which his mind would only unleash a new chapter of unease.

Joe retraced his steps, went into the living room, picked up the TV remote, and sank into the sofa. After a few clicks, he found a channel airing a documentary on animals. He glanced at his phone's screen. The time read one o'clock am.

"Guess I won't fall asleep till a little past two, then," he muttered to himself and dropped the phone beside him.

TOM COLEMAN

Watching TV so late at night turned out to be the best option for Joe because he didn't realize when he'd dozed off. It wasn't until the TV suddenly blared static that he jerked up from the sofa and blinked to settle his eyes to the environment.

He sighed, went groggily to the TV, and switched it off. He rubbed his eyes and stared at the dark screen for a while. After a few minutes passed with him standing and staring, he sighed once more and turned to go to his room, but as he did, he heard some movement outside. Someone was out on the lawn.

Chapter 3

Joe's nerves twitched as he listened. The hairs on his arms stood on end, and he couldn't help the sudden chill around him. There was someone on the lawn.

Unsure of what to do, Joe crept quietly into the living room. He wasn't a fighter, so there was no way he could exchange blows with a home intruder. At best, he could keep his hands firmly on the door to resist it being forced open.

Standing in front of the door, Joe peered through the door's peephole. While the view wasn't great at night, it would help him catch a glimpse of the intruder. It was pitch-black outside, save the flickering overhead bulb on the porch. Its shine hardly cast a few inches down on the lawn.

The footsteps grew a little louder as Joe peered through the peephole. He could hardly see, but the sound of footsteps told him the intruder was approaching the main entrance. Joe swallowed, took his gaze from the peephole, and glanced around, looking for a weapon—anything he could use at all—but there was nothing. Resigned, he gulped and took another peek out.

Joe jerked back from the peephole, nearly tumbling backward as he did.

A lone figure had appeared on the porch, its head bowed in the flickering light. Panic had set in fully, and Joe was about to take flight to his room. Just then, he paused and

TOM COLEMAN

turned back to the peephole. Something seemed familiar about the figure standing on the porch.

Joe was hesitant, but he steeled himself and took another peek. Just then, a wave of shock and relief washed through him—the figure had on clothes he'd seen on several nights at home: Jeanne's pajamas. He had the presence of mind to wonder what she was doing out in the dark, and then he got his answer.

The figure stirred, lifted its head slightly, and revealed a placid face, its eyes shut.

"Jeanne?" Joe said once he'd recognized the face. He grumbled, scolding himself for being afraid. Jeanne was a sleepwalker. He should have known she was likely to have an episode.

Relieved he wasn't dealing with an intruder, Joe opened the door and stepped onto the porch. It was chilly outside.

He took Jeanne by the hand, led her in, and shut the door quickly behind them. There was an unsettling feeling in the pit of his stomach that wasn't really about the chill outside.

Jeanne was still fast asleep despite being on her feet.

A little smile crept on his face as he watched his little sister sleep without a care as to what might happen to her. He let out a sigh and lifted his sister into his arms, cradling her like a baby. With her head resting against his shoulder, he took off toward her room, careful not to make any sudden moves that might disturb her sleep.

TOM COLEMAN

Jeanne hardly stirred on the trip from the living room to her room. It wasn't until Joe had placed her in her bed and covered her with a blanket that she stirred to snuggle into the bed for warmth.

Joe smiled at the sight and left her room quietly. Not only did he shut the door quietly, but he locked her in.

He reflected that Jeanne's sleepwalking episode was nothing special for him, and he went back to the living room and dropped back onto the sofa as his phone chimed with a message notification.

"Good job, big bro," the text said.

As simple as it sounded, Joe's sleepy eyes glared widely at the message. The unsettling feeling in his gut increased when he took note of the sender to see that it had come from his own phone number.

Angry yet uneasy, Joe turned off his phone and willed for sleep to take him. He was better off sleeping on the sofa than having to put up with the shadowy corners of his room.

***

Joe's eyes twitched when the sun's rays persisted, intruding on his sleep. He grumbled, and his eyes opened slowly to stare directly above him. Joe blinked, his eyes darting around, taking note of his environment. He remembered sleeping it off on the sofa, yet there he was, in his room. He shrugged it off, reasoning that his mom or dad had probably had a hand in it.

"Morning, Mom," Joe greeted his mom, who was fixing breakfast when he walked into the kitchen. She was focused on the eggs she was frying. A plate of toast sat on the kitchen counter, and Joe reached for a slice.

He took a bite and asked, "Mom, did you help me to my room last night?"

His mom didn't take her eyes off the eggs while replying.

"No, honey. I didn't step out of my room last night. Why—did something happen?"

Joe shook his head. He watched his mother in silence as she continued preparing breakfast—toast and eggs hit the spot—and he had a flash of the night before: the conversation with the strange voice, Jeanne's episode, the nightmare, and him waking up in bed. Joe shook his head, shut his eyes tightly, and willed the images away.

"Are you all right?" came his father's voice.

Joe opened his eyes and looked at his dad, confused.

His father nodded at Joe's hands, which were gripping the side of the table firmly.

Joe got the message and loosened his grip.

"Yeah, I'm fine. Just had a little flash, that's all."

TOM COLEMAN

"You slept well?" his dad queried, to which Joe nodded. His hands twitched, but he clasped them quickly together.

Joe asked his dad about the night before, but his dad shrugged in response. Just then, Jeanne stepped into the kitchen, rubbing her eyes; she'd just woken up.

"Well, the sleeper's finally awake," Joe said. He laughed.

Jeanne looked blankly at him and turned to her dad.

"You were sleepwalking last night, little one, and I helped you to your room, remember?" Joe said.

"No, I don't think I walked last night," Jeanne replied with a little pout.

"Oh yeah? Then how come I carried you back to your room like a baby and locked the door?"

"Daddy, Joe's mocking me," Jeanne whined, pulling at their dad's trousers.

Joe laughed and recounted the episode to their parents, but in the end, neither Mom nor Dad was laughing.

"Am I missing something?" Joe asked, looking from his mom to his dad.

Jeanne didn't find it funny either. She kept protesting that she hadn't sleepwalked the night before.

"Are you sure you slept well, Joe?" his dad queried with a raised brow.

TOM COLEMAN

"Jeanne hasn't sleepwalked for about three months now. It's why we no longer lock her door at night," his mom added.

Joe was perplexed. If his little sister no longer sleepwalked, then who had he seen outside the night before? Worse, who had he brought into the house and placed in the same room as his sister?

He darted out of the kitchen and hurried straight to Jeanne's room. His dad went after him.

Joe threw the blanket off frantically, crouched low, and checked beneath the bed, but there was nothing out of the ordinary.

"Whoa, whoa, whoa—slow down, young man," his dad said, but Joe was past hearing as he upturned Jeanne's boxes and ransacked her closet.

His dad stood there as if too dumbstruck to act.

***

It was silent inside the minivan. Joe – their son stared out through the window for most of the drive. Nobody said anything, not even Liz - his mom, who seemed greatly discomfited by the silence. Whatever had happened at home, they had all settled on an unspoken agreement to say nothing, at least until Joe decided to.

181

TOM COLEMAN

Mr. and Mrs. Phillips knew their son dealt with depression that tended toward manic bursts. They knew the bullying he experienced at school didn't help matters, but they had no real options when it came to changing schools. Joe had promised he would be fine, and for a while, he seemed to have kept his promise. His brief holidays hardly experienced incidents of mania or silent depression, but they always saw the sorrow masked in Joe's smile when he was to return to school. Thought they called as often as they could, they couldn't really tell if he was, indeed, doing fine in school.

Now, two years since his last outburst, Joe had had another episode. From recounting an old memory of his sister sleepwalking to making a sudden dash for his sister's room, an old fear had been rekindled.

Whenever Joe drifted into silence, there was no telling when or what would get him back to speaking as lively as he normally did. Since the episode, he hadn't uttered a word, and he hadn't resisted his parents' offer to take a drive to clear his head.

***

"Can I get a new SIM for my phone?" Joe asked quietly. His sudden query after being silent since that morning's episode startled his parents.

"Just feel like changing it since I'm done with school," Joe explained

182

"Yes... I guess," his mom said uncertainly, looking at her husband for approval. Mr. Phillips nodded without taking his eyes off the road. Whenever Joe was in the throes of one of his bouts, their best option was to give in to his requests. Though the SIM didn't need replacing, it was more about Joe, probably trying to cope.

"Well, we could take you to the service center now, if you don't mind," his mom offered.

Joe shrugged and continued staring out the window. He knew what the others thought about him. His mom, dad, and even some of his neighborhood friends knew about his stained history, but to him, he was pretty much normal, along with his share of life's misgivings.

With what had happened earlier, he knew just who was to blame: the voice that had been messing with him. The calls, the text, and worse off, the intrusions into his mind, had all come from the voice. He'd probably dreamed the whole sleepwalking episode. It was just like one of his post nightmare dreams, where he would wake up from a nightmare, still asleep and dreaming. Whenever such a thing happened, he could hardly separate his dreams from reality until he finally woke up. Just like that morning, he would end up speaking to someone about what seemed to have happened but never did. Kyle knew about these post dream occurrences, and it made it easier for him to clear his head, but his parents were in the dark about it all, and he wasn't keen on telling them just yet.

Talking to his parents about the voice didn't seem like a good idea, either. They'd only freak out and decide it was time to see a therapist, but he didn't want that. Instead, he

183

TOM COLEMAN

decided to pretend he was fine. If he spoke and acted as though nothing had happened, they would feel a little relieved, and their relief was his chance to figure things out. For starters, he would block the voice from reaching him.

***

Switching his SIM was pretty easy. Joe made a mental note never to try dialing his own number. He placed a few calls to some friends to inform them about his change of phone number. Kyle was the first he'd called, and the duo spent ample time on the phone, chatting about their plans, particularly the list of fun things they had to do before getting worked up over admission into their respective colleges. As it turned out, Kyle had gotten tickets for them to an after-grad house party, and it was only seven days away.

"Just a minute," Joe said over the phone. He turned to his parents—who were, once more, overshadowed by silence on the drive home—and asked if he could make the trip to the house party slated for the following weekend.

"Well, if it's Kyle, then it shouldn't be a problem," his mom said. His dad nodded in agreement.

Upon receipt of their assent, Joe switched back to Kyle and said, "I'll be there, man."

***

184

TOM COLEMAN

Ever since Joe had changed his SIM, he felt a little more at peace. There had been no voices intruding his mind in weeks, and he relaxed into his environment, checking in with old friends and neighbors. Kyle had come visiting twice, and it had been a blast reliving hilarious memories from their school days.

"Tell me again why you switched your SIM—what happened to the old one?" Kyle asked during one of their conversations.

Joe flinched slightly. "Nothing really, I discovered it was allocated to someone else." Joe said evasively.

"That's odd. You've been using that SIM for a couple of years, and it's all of a sudden allocated to someone else?" Kyle said thoughtfully.

Joe shrugged and said, "Don't look at me—I don't know how it works. I only know that someone else is allocated to my phone number, and I only just discovered it after graduation."

"Oh, well, if you say so. For a moment, it seemed like you wanted to bail on the rest of us." Kyle said jokingly.

Joe scowled and said, "That wouldn't be all that bad. Ha-ha"

The conversation with Kyle dragged on for most of Joe's day until it was time for him to return home, but just as Kyle waved him off after getting into his cab, that old, unsettled feeling crept in once more. While he'd evaded most

185

TOM COLEMAN

questions from his friends about the change in phone numbers, Kyle's query had left him uneasy. It reminded him that he hadn't heard the voice in over a month. While disconnecting from the voice had been a relief, he couldn't shake the unease in the pit of his stomach.

"It's nothing. I'm not being traced. There's no one out to get me," Joe reassured himself, shaking off his thoughts of fear.

For every sin, there is a temptation. That was the case with Joe, who couldn't take his eyes off of his phone's screen. It was nighttime, and he dialed out his phone number for the third time that night. He just couldn't shake the feeling of his fingers itching to press the buttons. It was all he could do to resist, by hovering his finger above the dial button. But it was only a matter of time before he went through with it and dialed.

Joe, who kept reminding himself not to press the dial button, found that his fingers no longer yielded to his will. Like an addict falling into a relapse, Joe's thumb finally tapped the dial button, and he shut his eyes.

TOM COLEMAN

Chapter 4

"Hello, Joe—how was your little break? I've been waiting for you," the voice responded. The call timer remained steady at 00:00.

At the sound of the eerie voice, Joe pressed the red button in a bid to disconnect the call, but the timer remained active.

The voice chuckled at his futile act. "You should know by now, Joe, that you can't get rid of me. I am you, your untethered self, your other half. We are one and the same, two sides of a coin," it said eerily.

"What do you want? Why are you monitoring me?" Joe asked, his voice heavy with fear and resentment.

"It's really simple, Joe: I want you. I want every bit of you—your life, your bonds, your time, your friends... even your enemies."

"This doesn't make any sense. Why would anyone want—" Joe's protest ended when the voice cut him off.

"There is so much you do not know, Joe. So much you could do, so much I could help you achieve, but here you are, resisting," the voice snapped.

"Be careful, Joe," it said quietly. "I always get what and who I want."

No sooner had the voice uttered these words than the line went dead.

Joe remained seated on his bed, staring at his phone's screen for hours on end. He was genuinely afraid, his body shivering despite the mild room temperature.

That night, time passed slowly for Joe. While the others slept, he stared at the phone until the batterie run out.

***

Drip... drip... drip!

The sound of water drops rang through the empty canvas. It was silent save for the echo of the drops.

"Hello? Anybody here?" Joe heard himself call. It was pitch-black all around him. He felt his way around until he stumbled into a body of water.

He got hurriedly back to his feet. Joe inched slowly forward, feeling as though he was walking deeper into the water. What had previously only covered his ankle had risen to his waist and continued to rise the more he moved forward in the darkness.

"This way," a voice said. There was a strong echo, making it sound ominous.

"A... Are you sure? Is there an exit there? Please, I don't know where I am," Joe pleaded. His eyes darted from left to right, but there was nothing but darkness.

TOM COLEMAN

"Over here, Joe. We're waiting, " a much different voice called, carried by the same echo. Though grim, Joe followed the voices, walking deeper into the water that soon threatened to cover his head.

Walking blindly with only echoes as his guide, Joe missed a footing and sunk momentarily into the water around him. Though alarmed, he held his breath and swung his arms desperately around in a bid to reach the surface.

Then came the laughter.

Bubbles floated around Joe, each of them bursting to release the trapped air inside along with the sound of maniacal laughter. Afraid for his life, Joe struggled against the bubbles and insistent pressure preventing him from reaching the surface. Eventually, his will gained dominance, and his head finally bobbed above the water, breathing heavily.

"Had fun?" a voice queried.

Joe blinked, then rubbed his eyes clear. Five shadowy figures stood in an arc around him. He looked up at their faces, and his breath caught in his throat. Pale white faces resembling his glared down at him. Each face had a grin reaching from ear to ear and pitch black eyes. These were his tormentors, and he knew what came after their grin.

"No, no, no... no, please!" Joe screamed as the faces inched closer to his until there was nothing left. It was pitch black.

***

TOM COLEMAN

Joe jerked out of his nightmare and flicked his head from side to side. His heart thumped speedily in his chest. His eyes slowly adjusted to the darkness, and he breathed heavily when he realized he was in the safety of his room.

Joe sighed, stepped gingerly out of bed, and took a walk to the bathroom. His intent was simple: wash his face and return to the living room.

He switched on the tap on the bathroom's lone sink, dipped his hand into the pool of water, and shut his eyes. The feel of the water on his skin was soothing.

Joe cupped a little into his hands, splashed the cold water onto his face, and rubbed gently. His eyes stung delightfully and the cold soothed his frayed nerves. Time quietly passed as Joe savored the calm and soothing feeling.

He relaxed and splashed his face again before opening his eyes. Just as he did, his breath nearly left him at the sight before him. Staring back at Joe in the mirror was his own reflection, but rather than his usual reflection, his was a living reflection that wore a smirk and had cold, dark eyes.

"Hello, Joe. I thought I might show myself a little," the voice said. Panic drove Joe before his brain could restrain him. In one swift motion, his fist connected with the mirror, and there was a loud crack.

***

The sound of glass shattering drove Mr. Phillips from his sleep. Alarmed and alert, he scurried to his feet and tiptoed

190

TOM COLEMAN

to his door. He felt his way around for the baseball bat beside the door, picked it up, and slipped out.

He walked lightly on his feet to avoid creaks that might alert the home intruder, searching the length and breadth of his house, listening for telltale sounds and sights, but there was nothing.

From the kitchen to the living room, Mr. Phillips checked every corner until he reached his son and daughter's adjoining rooms. First, he peered quietly into his daughter's room, but there was nothing out of the ordinary. Relieved, Mr. Phillips turned to his son's room. It was then he noticed the door was unlocked. A tinge of panic swept over him as he peeked into the open room.

There was no one in sight; no one there to answer when he called out his son's name.

Uneasy, Mr. Phillips glanced down the corridor of his three-bedroom apartment. Joe and Jeanne's rooms were separated from that of his and his wife's by the bathroom in the middle. That was when he realized he had omitted the bathroom in his security check.

He went to the bathroom where he met the door ajar. It was dark inside. Worried, Mr. Phillips pushed the door further open and stepped in. His left hand reflexively felt around the wall for the light switch. The light went on with a flick.

In the middle of the bathroom, his head hung in between his legs, was his son. A stir of emotion sent Mr. Phillips down onto his knees. "Joe... son, what's wrong?"

"It's nothing, Dad... it's nothing," Joe replied, hardly lifting his head.

Mr. Phillips inched closer to his son and wrapped his arms around him. He pulled his son into an embrace, with the latter breaking into a sob..

"I know you've been going through stuff. I know you've been trying to settle it on your own, son, but you don't have to. I'm here. Your mother and I are here for you," he said quietly, occasionally running his hands over Joe's hair.

"I wish I could, Dad, but I can't." Joe whimpered. "I wish I could tell you both, but you won't understand. I can't explain it, but it keeps disturbing me... stalking me." He sniffed back some tears.

His son's words stung him, but Mr. Phillips shrugged the hurt off and listened. In moments like that, when Joe was overwhelmed, he knew that the best way to help was to listen quietly, and that was what he did.

***

"I... I keep hearing voices. I keep having these nightmares. I keep seeing things that are not real, things that never happened... or maybe they did, I don't even know. I don't know what's wrong with me," Joe protested.

"I know you wanted to ask, that you felt it would help me heal, but then you didn't bother. It's fine. I'll tell you.

192

TOM COLEMAN

"I didn't change my SIM because I needed to forget my friends in school. There's no special package or plan for the SIM. I just needed it to... to escape," Joe said

"There's something—no, some*one*—stalking me," he said. He let out a huge sigh.

His dad stared silently, as if battling for the right words to say.

Joe forced a smile and kept speaking: "He claims to *be* me, claims to know all I know and feel everything I feel. He claims he's my... other half... an untethered soul or something, but he scares me, Dad.

"He's in my head, and he's in my phone. He makes me relive each nightmare every night, and that's why you find me awake at two a.m. every single day.

"I keep asking who he is and what he wants, but he keeps talking about being me and wanting me, and then some vague nonsense about things to do and achieve, as though he's trying to draw me into some cult," Joe added, and he sniffed to clear his nose.

"That's all there is, Dad. That's all," he said, and he let out a heavy sigh.

His dad kept silent, watching him. After what felt like hours, his father chuckled. "Guess you're really a weak one, Joe," he said, his voice sounding eerily like the one Joe had been hearing. Shocked, Joe jerked away from his dad and stared. The image of his dad's face slowly shifted into the cold, dark face he'd seen in the mirror.

TOM COLEMAN

"You like my new look?" the voice queried, morphing its face back to that of his dad.

"Get away from me. Leave me alone… please!" Joe screamed, scurrying away from his "dad." His fingers stumbled on a big shard of glass, and they curled around it. He pointed the sharp end at his father, and in a dark, threatening tone, he repeated the words, "Leave me alone."

***

Mr. Phillips was taken aback by his son's sudden jerk backward. Even worse was when he picked up a threatening shard of glass and pointed it at him. Afraid Joe might hurt himself, he tried shifting closer to his son, who not only glowered at him but tried slashing him with the glass shard. That was more than enough warning for him to maintain his distance.

The racket from the bathroom drew out his wife, she looked flustered from the disturbance.

"Honey, what's going on?" she queried. No sooner had she taken in the scene than her hands clasped to her mouth in shock. Tears welled up her eyes and fell down her cheeks. Not long after, she sank to her knees beside her husband, who held on to her lest she act on impulse. For all he knew, she might reach out to embrace her son, but in Joe's current state, that was too dangerous.

"Son, I know you're in a state right now, but you don't have to do anything. Look, we're only sitting here. We won't disturb you. We won't hurt you. Relax, son," Mr. Phillips said, raising his hands in surrender to calm to strained figure that was his son.

"Don't hurt yourself. Just relax, and let's stay here together. You'll get through this, and we'll help you through it all," he added.

His wife had slumped her head against his shoulders and was sobbing quietly as she stared at her son. Just like the episodes before, there was nothing much they could do other than wait out the mania and keep encouraging him with their words and presence.

***

Joe remained huddled in the corner, with the hand holding the glass shard stretched out before him. Although he felt tired and weak, he couldn't afford to sleep it off. A second tormentor had appeared, and this one had taken the face of his mother. He felt sickened by it. "I'm done with your games. I won't let you hurt me anymore," he'd said, spitting in their direction.

Neither of them moved, and he was grateful for that. He knew they would eventually carry out their usual torment. His life would flash before his eyes moments before he was swallowed up in pitch blackness to repeat the whole nightmare again. Though horrible, he wished they would get it over with. He needed to wake up. At least, he could feel a semblance of love and peace during the daytime when he wasn't asleep, and his tormentors no longer had a hold on him.

TOM COLEMAN

Joe's eyes blinked from the stress. His eyelids were heavy; they desperately wished for him to give in. He needed all the rest he could get, but then his fear was far more palpable than the need for sleep. In a moment of weakness, his eyes closed against his will. His tormentors moved as his vision blurred, and that was all.

***

Beep! Beep! Beep!

Joe heard the sound, faint at first, then a little clearer. Stirring, he felt his eyes drift open to a world of white lights. He blinked to focus and realized he was staring into an array of fluorescent bulbs overhead. He brought his gaze down to see that he was on a white bed with leather straps on his arms. His hands were covered in bandages, and there was a thin tube attached to a vein in his left arm. Joe glanced around to find a lone figure, sleeping quietly in a seat beside his bed.

"Mom?" he called.

Her eyes flew open, and she drew her seat closer to him. "I'm here, dear. I'm here," she said. Her hand reached out to touch his forehead.

"Can I get a doctor in here? Phil," she called, then turned her gaze to her son.

"Mom, I'm sorry, " Joe blurted. His emotions raged, and he wasn't sure which one he felt more. "I'm sorry I couldn't be strong. I couldn't fight them off. I don't even know

196

TOM COLEMAN

if I can fight anymore. I don't want to anymore." His tears fell freely as he spoke.

"Don't worry, honey, it's fine. I'm here. We'll get through this," she said, her voice quaking.

"We've been through this before. We can still push through. The doctors are saying something about meditating with local experts, that it'll be good for your mind and all that.

"You don't have to worry, son. You'll be fine. Your dad and I are with you through it all; just please, don't give up. Don't let go, swee—" It was as if she couldn't find the strength to go on. Joe knew he wasn't fine, and she was only trying to keep hope alive. He knew she could tell that he was afraid, there was no masking his emotions at that point. It was only a matter of time before he couldn't fight his demons anymore.

Chapter 5

"So what are you saying, Doctor? My son's crazy?" Mrs. Phillips asked. The thought of her son's condition forced her into another bout of tears and sniffling. Her husband, who was seated next to her, reflexively placed her hand in his and gave her a consoling squeeze.

"It's not every day we get patients like your son, Mr. and Mrs. Phillips. While the symptoms of dementia are clear, there are a few things that do not add up, Things we might need to take some time to monitor," said the doctor, slowly. He sounded as though he didn't want to aggravate the situation.

"Doctor," Mr. Phillips said.

"Joe staying a few more days or weeks in the hospital isn't a problem for us."

"But is there a chance Joe will be fine, no matter how little, Doctor?" queried Mr. Phillips.

His query left the doctor short of words, and both men were left staring at one another for way too long. Eventually, the doctor gave in and shut his eyes briefly. His action told more than the words he could muster. "As you know, Mr. Phillips, we're always committed to doing our best. We can take care of your son in the meantime—"

"Until there is nothing left to care for, right?" Mr. Phillips asked. His voice was hard.

TOM COLEMAN

Silence—punctuated by Mrs. Phillips' sobs—reigned in the doctor's office for what felt like hours.

"Thanks for your time, Doctor, but I don't think Joe will appreciate staying here. It might be best if we do the monitoring from home and give you a call should there be changes," Mr. Phillips said with a sigh. Joe had spent a week in the hospital with hardly any change, desperately begging that he be sent home. While the doctor was right about needing to keep an eye on Joe, the hospital just wasn't the right place for him.

"It's not a problem, Mr. Phillips. I understand how hard this must be for your family, and I'm willing to work with you on this," the doctor said, rising to his feet as he spoke.

"I'll have one of the nurses give you the prescription tabs for Joe. The suppressant tabs will keep Joe calm, while the pain meds will help curb his headaches. As for the insomnia, give him the sleep tabs in the prescribed dosage, and he won't have to worry about waking up for at least seven hours," the doctor explained.

Mr. Phillips nodded and stretched out his hand, to which the doctor extended his own.

Mrs. Phillips rose quietly beside her husband and wiped her tears with a hanky she pulled from her handbag.

The couple stepped carefully out of the office with the doctor, who led them to one of his standby nurses, gave a few instructions, and sent them off to the pharmacy.

TOM COLEMAN

***

Joe's eyes lit up at the news of leaving the hospital. He was the one to break the news. From changing out of his hospital gown into his own clothes and finally getting into the car for the drive back home, Joe felt a sense of relief wash over him. Being at the hospital hadn't been the best option for him. Rather, it had left him vulnerable. The voice had kept taunting him with its sinister laughter, reinforcing his nightmares.

Although he wasn't utterly safe from the voice at home, he knew he was better off there. At the very least, he would find strength and hope there, compared to the hospital that seemed confining, with its white walls, sterile smell, and routine nurses whose smiles were no less reassuring. He never saw them for their smiles; he saw his tormentors instead.

The drive back home was quiet and uneventful, and he was glad for the silence. Once they'd made it up the driveway, he sighed, looked over at his parents, and said, "Thank you." No further words were exchanged as they got out of the car and made their way indoors. As far as he was concerned, his bed was calling him.

***

"Well, well, look who decided to wake up," Joe's dad said jokingly. The rest of the family was seated in the living

200

TOM COLEMAN

room with the TV on when Joe stepped groggily from his room. It was a few minutes before eight pm, and that meant Joe had missed dinner. For what it was worth, he was relieved to see his son so relaxed.

"There's nothing like a good sleep, I can tell," he added, to which Joe smiled. It had seemed genuine, with no trace of weakness or fear.

"Come here, Joe. Come sit with me," his wife beckoned to their son.

Mr. Phillips protested, saying, "Don't be selfish, hon—"

"Come sit with us," his mom said, turning to Joe. The little drama kept Joe's smile intact as he scuttled over to the couch and sat on the rug between his parents.

The three of them sat in silence as they flipped through the channels and settled on a show. After an hour-plus of TV, Mrs. Phillips' eyes closed, and she was soon fast asleep, her head leaning on her husband's shoulders. Joe was left with his father in the night's silence.

"How are you feeling?" his dad asked quietly.

"I feel better. Guess all I needed was a proper sleep," he said. He chuckled at the end.

"That's good, Joe, that's good," his dad replied.

Joe took a moment to turn to his dad. His dad had a smile on his face.

***

201

Daylight came, and Joe found himself sprawled on his bed. The night had been without the usual nightmares, and for that, he was relieved. He did, however, feel odd in the far edge of his gut, as though he anticipated something sinister.

Since he'd left the hospital about two weeks before, he hadn't had to deal with his nightmares. His cellphone was well within reach, but he hardly touched it. He was mostly uninterested in his phone than afraid. His parents, who'd suggested keeping it from him, seemed to relax when they noticed he had barely touched the phone since he'd returned. Anytime they'd spoken to him about it, he usually shrugged and said he just wasn't into his phone anymore.

"Besides, it's not like I have a thousand people calling me or who I have to call," he often added to justify his break from his phone. So far, he only had one person he could call, and he'd resorted to using either of his parents' cellphones when he felt like it. Kyle, having received calls from two different numbers, had grown used to his friend's new means of reaching out.

Now that he thought of it, his gaze fell to his phone and lingered there a little more than he'd wished.

"Not today," he muttered, shrugging his lingering gaze.

He took off to the bathroom and made quick work of brushing his teeth, followed by his routine face washing. With the tap running, he scooped water to his face and pressed his hands to his eyes; the water was soothing.

TOM COLEMAN

Joe exhaled and brought a few more handfuls of water to his face, and let it trickle slowly down his cheeks. He opened his eyes. His reflection in the bathroom mirror caught his attention—it was wearing a smirk, but Joe wasn't.

Joe blinked. The smirk on the reflection relaxed, and it displayed the same curious gaze as Joe. He blinked again and followed it with a wave of his hand to ease his fear. He could have sworn his reflection had taken on an expression of its own. Joe shut his eyes and let his mind relax.

Upon returning to his room, Joe's eyes drifted to the top of his bedside table where his phone laid idle. He turned to leave his room but no sooner had he taken a step out than he flipped back into his room.

He muttered about the experience as he snatched the phone from his bedside table—it had turned on. A few seconds later, and his phone was fully booted. In no time, he was on his dialer, tapping out a phone number. "Here we go. " He sighed and made the call.

Silence.

After a few more tries, Joe finally gave up. Deep down, he felt a stir of hope. Maybe he was finally free of his demons.

TOM COLEMAN

Chapter 6

"Well, well, you're looking good, Joe," he said to himself as he examined his reflection in the bathroom mirror. The tap was running endlessly in the sink, and the light bulb hanging above his head flickered at his every word. It was a little past midnight.

"Nothing like a good wash to clear the head," he said, splashing a handful of water on his face.

"So, what's it going to be tonight? Hm—maybe a little TV?" The water trickled down his face in tiny drops. Without a second thought to wipe his face, Joe turned for the bathroom door.

Upon getting to the living room, he crashed on the couch and picked up the TV's remote. A few clicks afterward, he settled on an off-air station. "Ahh, yes—midnight classic it is," he said with a little clap.

"What are you doing?" a low, sleepy voice queried.

Joe's eyes darted in the direction of the voice.

Jeanne was staring at him, a puzzled expression on her face. It was as though she couldn't decide whether to yield to the lure of sleep or query the sight before her.

"Ah, Jeanne—Guess you finally decided to come join me. I was waiting," Joe said happily. He beckoned her with a

TOM COLEMAN

hand gesture and said, "Come on—come, join your big brother."

Jeanne yawned in response, made her way groggily to the couch, and huddled close to Joe. She rested her head on his shoulder and wrapped her arm around his. "What are we watching?" she asked.

Joe looked at her sweetly and said, "Take a guess."

Jeanne rubbed her eyes and looked at the TV screen. A frown slowly crept onto her face. As though frightened by what she saw, she turned to Joe. "I don't like this movie," she said, her voice conveying fear.

"Really?" Joe asked brightly. "But I watch it every night." He added, "Come on—it's not that bad, Jeannie."

"But he's scared. They'll do bad things to him," Jeanne said apprehensively.

"Hmm, maybe you're right. Maybe they'll do bad things to him, but it's pretty fun," Joe replied. "Oh, here's my favorite part: the chants." Joe turned his gaze back to the static on the TV screen.

As though responding to Joe's expectations, the TV screen flickered. The white noise of the static changed to a more discernible sound. The chant of "Teatime," repeated through the TV's speakers, growing louder with each passing second.

Joe looked on with glee while his younger sister cowered where she sat, squeezing closer to him.

"Make it stop," Jeanne pleaded, tugging at Joe's arm.

TOM COLEMAN

He turned to look at her wearing a wide, unnatural grin. "Is Jeannie scared?" he whispered.

She nodded, her face buried into his arm.

"Don't worry, Jeannie—your big brother's here. It'll be over soon," he said, planted a kiss on her head.

***

"Good morning, Mom—what's for breakfast?" Joe asked once he'd stepped into the kitchen.

His mom was washing dirty dishes.

Jeanne was standing at the counter next to her, but the moment she saw him, she scurried into the corner.

"Jeanne, no running in the kitchen," Mrs. Phillips said, turning to her youngest child, who was trying to make herself scarce.

"Sorry," Jeanne said from her hiding spot. "Joe is scary," she added.

Joe and his mom exchanged perplexed glances at her words. Joe felt even more confused. "But I didn't do anything," he said, raising his hands.

His mom stopped tending to the dishes, went over to Jeanne, and said sweetly, "Come on, Jeannie—you love your big brother, don't you?"

"Yes," she replied quietly, "but he's scaring me."

TOM COLEMAN

"How?" Joe said aloud.

His mom held up a finger. "Talk to me, sweetie. What did Joe do?"

"He was watching a scary show on TV. They were doing bad things to him on TV," she said, playing with her fingers as she spoke.

"The show was really scary, huh?" their mom queried.

Jeanne nodded.

"So, it's the show that's scary, and not Joe, right?" she asked again.

Jeanne nodded her head, but she glanced quickly at Joe and shook her head. "Joe is scary. He was looking at me in a bad way," she mumbled.

"Oh, really?" their mom said. "When did he look at you in a bad way?"

"Last night, " she said quietly.

Mrs. Phillips stared at her daughter for a while and then sighed. "Don't worry about it, okay, Jeannie?" she offered. "He was just playing, and I'll ground him for that, okay?" she said. Her voice rose a little at the latter part of the sentence so he would know she meant business, and it wasn't an empty threat.

Jeanne nodded and reluctantly allowed her mom to pull her away from her hiding spot. She avoided looking directly at Joe until he'd left the kitchen with a bottle of water.

TOM COLEMAN

***

Mrs. Phillips knew that Joe had no idea about what his younger sister was talking about in the kitchen. He'd played it according to his usual script of saying nothing and waiting for her to resolve whatever misunderstanding what going on between him and his younger sister. This mostly happened after she'd succeeded in coaxing Jeanne to speak about whatever was wrong, but on that day, Jeanne had hardly budged. Apart from what she'd said in the kitchen, she wasn't forthcoming with the full story of what Joe had done.

Nightfall came, and there was still nothing from Jeanne concerning what she'd said about Joe. For most of the day, Jeanne had avoided him totally. She'd even gone as far as staying cooped up in her room.

"Relax, hon—she'll be fine, " her husband had said when it was time to go to sleep, but she couldn't shake the fear she'd seen in her daughter's eyes. It wasn't like the other times Joe had pranked her. It was much darker. As though there was, indeed, something in Joe that scared her.

***

A lone chime sounded in Joe's room. Joe's cellphone screen lit up. The time read 00:00.

Another chime and Joe's screen flickered. A message popped up in the notifications tray that read, "Wake up, Joe. "

208

TOM COLEMAN

Joe's body sat up in the bed as if on instinct. His eyes stirred, and he opened them slowly. They were dark and foreboding. He craned his neck slowly toward his phone. His hand followed his gaze, and it hovered slightly above the phone. The lone light from the phone's screen cast an eerie glow on his open palm.

He picked up the phone and clicked on the new message. The sender was none other than his phone number. A smile crept over his face.

Joe rose to his feet and left his room. Though he had no destination in mind, he wound up in the kitchen and sat on a tall stool by the kitchen counter. Joe looked around, but he settled on staring directly ahead. His fingers tapped on the countertop in unison to the sound of the wall clock on the kitchen wall.

He stayed that way for ten full minutes, staring ahead and tapping away before breaking out of his reverie. His gaze drifted to the knife block. His body followed his gaze, and within seconds, he was standing before the rack, his eyes roaming from knife to knife.

"Clean and simple, that's all you need," he muttered. His fingers wrapped around a carving knife, and he pulled it slowly from the block. There was a flash before his eyes, a picture of the knife being pulled from the block covered in fresh bloodstains.

Joe smiled at the thought.

He raised the knife to his face and trailed a finger across the knife's edge, feeling its sharpness.

209

TOM COLEMAN

Joe nodded, took a few steps back, turned, and walked out of the kitchen. He made his way to the foyer, between to house's three rooms. He moved towards his parents room, and stopped at their door. There, he let out a sigh.

He placed his left hand on the doorknob, turned, and heard, "Joe?" coming from behind him.

Joe tucked the knife into the shorts he'd worn to sleep, draped his shirt over it carefully, and straightened his posture. Then, he turned to his little sister and smiled. "How are you, princess?" he asked.

Jeanne took a step back and muttered, "Fine."

Joe noticed her retreat and said, "Shh. Don't worry, Jeannie. I'm your big brother. I'm not going to hurt you."

"But... but you're scary," Jeanne said.

"That's why you didn't play with me yesterday, huh? You couldn't even look at me?" Joe asked.

Jeanne nodded.

"It's okay. I'm sorry I scared you. I didn't mean to," Joe said, taking a step closer.

Jeanne looked hesitant, but she waited till he came within her reach.

Joe crouched low to her eye level, shut his eyes for a moment, and then opened them again. "See? It's still me, your big brother," he said, looking at her.

Jeanne stared at him with a worried look on her face. She sighed and said, "Yeah, I guess it's you."

TOM COLEMAN

"Of course, it's me, Jeannie. And I'm here if you need me," he offered. "So, do you want to talk about it?" he asked after a few moments had passed in silence.

Jeanne nodded.

At this, he sat down on the floor and leaned against the wall. He indicated that Jeanne should do the same, and he put an arm around her after she'd complied.

"I know you weren't lying. About me walking," Jeanne started.

Joe's mind traveled to the time he'd returned from school: the sleepwalking episode.

"I was dreaming, and then I saw you bring me in and tuck me in, but—"

"But what?" Joe asked.

"You... you came back and stood in my room. You were looking at me like the other night," she said.

Joe kept quiet and allowed her to continue speaking.

"Then, you left, and you left my door open. I was afraid, so I didn't want to get out of bed," she explained.

Joe recalled her denial about sleepwalking, but the part about him returning to her room escaped him. He had no memory of doing such a thing. Neither was he aware of a second night on which he'd stared at her. "But you said you didn't, " Joe said uncertainly.

Jeanne said, "No, I thought I was dreaming."

"Oh," Joe said thoughtfully. "It happens like that all the time, huh? You dream about walking, and then you actually do?"

Jeanne nodded. "But then I forget," she added after a while.

"Huh?"

"When I wake up, I don't remember dreaming or walking," she explained.

Joe nodded. He understood what she was talking about.

While Jeanne kept talking about her sleepwalking episodes, he felt an unsettling stir in the pit of his stomach. His hands twitched at intervals, and for a moment, he swore the knife hidden in his shorts was getting hot enough to burn his skin.

"That's why I was afraid of you yesterday. Because I know I wasn't dreaming, and it wasn't you," Jeanne said.

Joe, who'd been focused on restraining the unsettling feeling in his gut, snapped back to reality. "What did you say?" he queried.

"The other night. I had a bad dream, and then I woke up," Jeanne said.

Joe made a hand gesture, encouraging her to keep talking.

"I went to the bathroom, then I heard the TV, so I came out to check. I thought that maybe, I'd see dad or mom, but I saw you, instead," Jeanne explained. "But... but then, it wasn't you. It looked like you, but it wasn't you. It was a bad person. A very bad and scary you," Jeanne said.

Joe's breath caught in his throat as Jeanne explained what had transpired the night before. He had no memory of what had happened, but as she spoke, images began forming in his head: his reflection in the mirror; the trickling of water off his face; the static from the TV; the chant.

Jeanne had been there, but that wasn't what had sent him jumping up to his feet and racing to his room. Visions of him waking up at midnight poured in. Realization dawned on him in flashes. He had been sleeping too well for weeks, and that was why he felt uneasy. The silence hadn't been what he'd hoped. It hadn't been because he was finally free of the voice, the one who'd claimed to be his other-self.

Joe gasped for air as his mind pieced the influx of thoughts together. He had been waking up at midnight since he'd returned from the hospital, but it hadn't been him who was conscious during those moments at midnight. It had been his other-self. The untethered being that had been speaking in his head and through his phone number.

Joe stumbled from the floor to his feet and on to his room. He pulled out the red hot knife and threw it as far as he could. His hand reached for his cellphone, and he dialed quickly.

Call not connected.

"Come on," Joe exclaimed as he tried redialing his phone number to no avail. Three more unconnected redials, and his phone flung from his hand. But the crash of the phone

TOM COLEMAN

into the far wall hardly registered in his mind when he noticed Jeanne standing in his doorway, open-mouthed and confused.

"Wh... what's wrong?" she asked.

Unsure of how to answer, Joe shook his head. "Something's really wrong Jeanne," he started, "but I'm going to find out what, and I'm going to fix it." He sighed, and took a few careful steps toward her, took her hand, and led her out of his room.

***

While Joe did his best to distract himself from the eerie feeling in his gut, his mind kept replaying Jeanne's words and the images of each night he'd been awake but not in control of his consciousness. That night would likely have followed the same pattern with a lethal result if Jeanne had not woken when she did. For all he knew, the knife hadn't been for fun, and he definitely hadn't planned on entering his parents' room for a midnight chat. He hadn't thought much about it, but now that he did, his other side hadn't been joking about getting what and who he wanted. He'd sounded dark and threatening, and now Joe understood those words for what they'd meant. Joe was dealing with a malevolent entity who could turn him into a monster and ruin his home, but he had no idea why.

Joe sat beside Jeanne's bed, waiting for her to fall asleep as she eyed him through concerned, sleepy eyes. At different times, he noticed her staring at him, but in the end, sleep won out.

TOM COLEMAN

Although Joe had no idea about how to handle the situation, he felt a nagging feeling that he needed to contact his darker self and maybe strike a deal. Giving the numbness he'd felt in his mind since he'd gone on the meds, the calls no longer connecting, and his phone totally smashed, he was at a loss.

"The mirror," he realized. While he had discarded the last experience with the mirror as his mind playing tricks on him, he understood it was his only option, so Joe made his way to the bathroom, turned on the tap, and carried out his routine wash.

***

"Well, well, look who's decided to call me," the sinister voice said with a chuckle.

Joe stared at his reflection in the mirror. The only difference was in their eyes—Joe looked weary and fearful, while his untethered self had a threatening aura.

Joe swallowed. "Why are you doing this?" he asked quietly.

"Is there ever a reason for what we do?" the voice replied.

Joe gritted his teeth at the evasive response.

"But I'll humor you," it added. "Free will is either taken, or it is given. There is more to you than you realize, but

TOM COLEMAN

you have failed to yield. It is only wise that I take what is mine—"

"I don't belong to you," Joe muttered.

His reflection arched an eyebrow.

Joe said even louder, "You don't own me!"

His other self looked perplexed for a split second before it burst out laughing.

Enraged, Joe threw a fist at the mirror. Its impact caused a sizeable crack on the mirror's surface.

His other self wore a clear expression of shock at the sudden move. "Joe," it started. The mirror cracked further. With each word it tried to say, the mirror cracked further until the pieces shattered and crumbled into the sink.

Exhausted, Joe crumpled to his knees on the bathroom floor.

Hurried footsteps approached the bathroom, and for a moment before his eyes closed, he saw his mom and dad rush in.

***

Ever since his previous encounter in the bathroom, Joe had burned his SIM card and thrown his phone thrown in the trashcan. With his phone, SIM, and bathroom mirror gone, and his meds ensuring he no longer woke up during the night, Joe felt peace. When he was ready, he told his parents what he'd been battling with. Although the looks on their faces said they'd found it his story hard to believe, they agreed not to replace the bathroom's mirror.

Days turned into weeks and weeks into months with no unsettling feelings in the pit of his stomach. Although Joe had told his parents that all was well, they had gone the extra mile to bring a priest into the house. After a few uncomfortable conversations, the priest blessed the entire house by sprinkling Holy Water. Joe was offered communion bread and wine and given a few scripture verses to say aloud before going to sleep. Joe obliged his parents and the priest and soon found that he could sleep without the meds on which he'd heavily relied. The scriptures were working, and he relayed that message to the priest, who congratulated him on being free of the demons that had troubled him.

"But remember, Joe—demons are jealous beings who stop at nothing to regain what they have lost. Be careful not to let your mind wander. Avoid thinking of your past or the voice you once heard, lest you call to him and be taken back into bondage," the priest had instructed Joe. True to the man's words, when Joe found his mind wandering, he began to feel uneasy. And that reminded him to restrain his thoughts and let go of the past.

***

217

TOM COLEMAN

Joe remained safely at home, gradually forgetting about the horrors of the past, but his untethered self remained very much present. Though separate from Joe due to measures put in place by the priest and the young man himself, the other side of Joe watched and waited, growing more vengeful as the months passed.

Time passed rather swiftly, and Joe was on to the next phase of his life: college. He reconnected with Kyle via a new SIM he'd taken to the priest to bless. Together, he and Kyle applied to a list of colleges and kept their fingers crossed for updates. Their admissions in sync, the young men looked forward to a bout of joy. There was, however, someone else biding his time, counting on their joy.

***

Drip...drip...drip.

Water trickled down Joe's face. His eyes were closed, his breathing even.

"We meet again, Joe," an uncanny voice said.

Joe's eyes darted opened to meet those of his reflection in the mirror. His other self stared at him, dead in the eyes. Unlike the last time, its eyes were pitch black. Dark veins extended from his eyes across his face.

"You've been a very stubborn one, Joe," it said.

TOM COLEMAN

Joe reacted quickly, and he launched a fist into the mirror. Before his fist connected, he felt an unimaginable force restrain it, inches away from the mirror.

"No, no, you don't get to do that again," his darker self retorted.

Joe pulled his hands from the force of the mirror and turned to escape. He took a step toward the bathroom door and felt a force lift him off the ground.

"You should have listened," he heard his untethered self say. In one swift motion, he was slammed into the ground, and his head crashed through the ceramic sink.

There was silence.

Drip...drip...drip.

Joe felt the familiar sensation of water, only it wasn't the water it had been in his dreams; it was his blood.

***

The news of the boy that had been found dead in the college bathroom traveled fast. Joe Phillips's body was found in a flooded bathroom with a sizeable crater beneath it. The autopsy report attributed the cause of death to a domestic accident. The medical examiner had theorized that Joe had fallen and broken not just his head but the bathroom sink.

What neither the police nor the autopsy experts could not understand was what had formed the crater beneath him. It

TOM COLEMAN

looked as if Joe Phillips had been thrown high and smashed into the floor by an inexplicable force, only they could not determine what might have had enough force to do that.

"He was my friend. My best friend, " Kyle reported when giving an interview on behalf of the grieving family. "We went to school, studied, and graduated together. The things we went through together… and now he's gone, just like that." Kyle's voice broke. His tears flowed freely.

"There's something dark out there, something the cops aren't telling. I know it because Joe kept trying to run from it. He told me about it. First, it was in his dreams, and then the calls, and then the hallucinations. " He figured he'd said enough. Though others might guess that his grief had silenced him, the truth was that Kyle's tongue had frozen against his will. It hadn't been grief, but something else, something that didn't want him to say all he knew. It was the same thing he'd once told Joe had been nothing more than his thoughts gone wild.

Kyle kept quiet. He was there to grieve with Joe's family, and that was what he did.

When it was time to return to his parents, Mr. Phillips offered to drive him home. "It's the least I can do," Mr. Phillips had said.

Kyle accepted the offer, and the duo drove in silence until Kyle was home. As Mr. Phillips drove out of sight, Kyle felt a buzz in his trouser pockets. He pulled out his phone and blinked twice; it was his own phone number calling him.

TOM COLEMAN

THE CURSE OF HERNANDEZ PART THREE

221

TOM COLEMAN

TOM COLEMAN

CHAPTER FIVE: PAIN

For Christina, the first wave came in the form of pins and needles. She looked at her skin and saw needles all over, but she managed to hold her scream. It didn't hurt that much, and she was grateful for that. The problem started when it legit began to hurt.

"Carlos, you said it was just in our m—" but Carlos was no place to be found. Had the house been able to separate them so quickly? It was as if the house sucked on their fears and guilt even faster than before. It was unreal.

"How are they doing this? What is happening?" Christina's brain could no longer function optimally by then due to the excruciating pain. She knew she had to overcome this by herself. Hiding behind Carlos would get her nowhere. It was a sickening scenario unlike any other, and Carlos had his own demons to fight, some of which she did not even know about. She had to get out of this mental hell on her own.

"They're just needles…they're just needles. Keep it together," Christina repeated to herself. With each needle prick she felt, Christina reminded herself that her pain was in her mind.

"Look at what you did to me," Susan said, standing with her head in her hand. Christina could not believe the sight before her. It was too much.

TOM COLEMAN

"That wasn't what happened." She was letting her emotions get in the way again, luring her deeper into the mindfuck. "My God."

"God isn't yours, and he isn't going to save you."

"So? Would it have made a difference?" Susan inquired.

Her decapitated head rested on her hands as it spoke in the most disturbing of ways. It wasn't real… none of it was real. Christina knew it, but it was still a scary and unnerving sight to behold. How could that thing do this to the poor girl's memory?

"Why are you doing this? Susan does not deserve this." Christina was confused. Was it the house or the ghosts instead? She and Carlos needed to get to the suitcase as quickly as possible before they were consumed by the creatures' nefarious attacks.

The entity masquerading as Susan walked closer to Christina, but she backed up. Christina could practically feel the terror on her face.

As the ghost came closer, it grew more disfigured but maintained Susan's general shape.

"Once, there was a woman. A beautiful, strong woman." The headless body kept growing, as did the head. "She bought a house thinking it was a bargain. Little did she know he would come to watch her sleep. Who, you say? The pitch-black man who came again and again. It got so bad, Heather could only weep." By then, the ghoul was right in front of a petrified Christina. The head continued to grow in

224

TOM COLEMAN

size as the mouth spoke. Christina was hanging onto her sanity for dear life, but it wasn't working at the moment. Her fear covered any coherence her mind might have like a blanket.

The pitch-black man? That big, huge monster that could not get into the room but lurked right outside? Who was he, and what was this story she was being told? Christina could barely take in all the information she was being told. Who could and be expected to retain it when they were that scared and in pain? The needles were still incredibly painful, but there was something even more unnerving and creepy about the headless demon holding the head of the girl she'd killed that made the needle pain subside a little.

The fiendish creature raised the head of what still looked partly like Susan up to Christina's face, positioning it to face her. "Do you know what happened to Heather?" the head inquired.

Christina just stared fearfully. There was nothing more she could do than look at it and try to calm down. She had to get her mind under control, but it wasn't working.

"As things got harder, she retreated deeper into the room. He couldn't get in, and that was enough for her to remain inside."

"What... what kind of... what are you saying?" Christina said to the head. The fact she was being talked to and responding to a giant head was ridiculous, but it was her reality. Wait... no. Christina cautioned herself—it was not real. There was no reality. Everything was a simulation in her mind, a metaphysical creation emanating from the house's ability to see her memories and weaknesses.

TOM COLEMAN

"I wonder where Heather is right now?" the head said, looking to the corner as if trying to remember.

"Please, just let us go," Christina pleaded.

The head laughed after hearing that. "Heather used to say that. It didn't do anything, though, and it won't do anything for you, either."

The needles continued boring into her skin, leading Christina to scream in agony. She yelled as loud as she could, reacting to the immeasurable hurt coming from her pain. "Why… why are you doing this? What is this house?"

"You will know soon enough about our tragic fate."

She could only hear the voice of the fiend. The pain had caused her to fall to the ground and face the floor, so she couldn't see it. Was this the end, the way her life and dreams would come crashing down? Christina thought about a lot of things at that moment. Could she have reconciled or made the relationship better with her parents? Would she ever know the experience and joy of motherhood? More importantly, Christina would lose the chance to share her love with the man of her dreams.

"*No*," the determined woman yelled, enduring the pain and getting to her feet. "I will not let you win. I won't let this sick house prevail. You won't have me, and you won't have my husband, either." She looked up, but the apparition was no longer before her.

The needles still pricked her skin. Even breathing was painful, and every step she took felt like a wild animal bite. She knew it was not real, and all she needed to do was to stand

226

TOM COLEMAN

her ground and be steadfast. To Christina's surprise, the more she held onto the belief that everything happening was not real, the less painful the needle pricks.

"I will get through this and reach my husband. You are in my way. *Get out!*" There was such gumption in her words that it actually helped to clear the darkness a bit, and Christina spotted a figure ahead of her. It could be a lot of things, but she chose the best option.

"Carlos," she called, and she noticed the pain from the needles was gone. She smiled and scoffed, relieved her mind had been strong enough to fight back and win.

When she looked back up, a needle inserted itself into her eye. "AARRRRRRRRRGGHH!" she cried.

Carlos didn't know where Christina had gone, but the worst possible thing that could happen right then—especially for Christina—was for them to be separated. She was mentally fragile, and he needed to be there for her. The familiar sound of the guitar reverberated through the dark space, and Carlos finally remembered where it was from.

"So, that's what it is, huh?" he said, facing his sister. Carlos, however, knew the thing on the chair facing him and holding the guitar was not his sister.

"Yes."

"That sound was the note Rosa kept playing when she learned how to play the guitar," Carlos said, and the demon nodded. Just remembering how she had failed at her early lessons made Carlos smile. He never liked to remember much about his sister due to how painful it was, but this memory brought a smile to his face. Rosa had played the same old note, bothering him. Oh, what he'd give to go back to those glorious days. Sure, there were many other problems—like the crime and the lack of basic amenities—but it didn't matter because he'd had her, and she'd had him.

"You think this will do… what? Make me break down and cry? I already know this is not real, so why don't you just let me go?"

The entity laughed out loud, its mouth widening abnormally. Carlos stared at her in confusion. He was surprised at not being tortured, but he knew he had to be on guard. Anything could happen in that blasted house.

"You honestly believe you can escape?" The voice had changed, becoming less like his sister's and more sinister. "Why do you feel so guilty about Rosa?"

"Stop it." Carlos felt himself grow agitated, which was the last thing he wanted.

The ghost smiled, finally having found an entry into his strongly fortified mind. "Let's see, shall we?"

Carlos was suddenly standing in his childhood home. It was bad. It was really bad. The sounds of multiple gunshots went off outside, and he knew what that meant. In the room, Carlos saw him and his sister hugging each other under the bed.

"Mom wasn't around, was she?" the ghost said from behind him.

TOM COLEMAN

He turned to see a hellish-looking ghoul floating in the air.

Carlos dropped to the ground in fear.

The ghoul completely ignored him and focused on Carlos's past. "Of course, she wasn't around," it said. "She had to work twice as hard to put food on the table for the two of you."

"Stop this," Carlos warned sternly, but he was surely in no position to warn anyone or anything.

"And we can't forget the humiliating beatings you received from your drunken father." The setting changed to another from Carlos's childhood, one he remembered all too well. He had come back at night to find his father beating his mother. Rosa could only beg him to stop from a distance— who knew what he might do to her if she intervened?

"Rosa couldn't do anything," Carlos said, transfixed to the scenery before him, lulled deeper into the clutches of the nefarious house. Past guilt and trauma were always better forms of pain to manipulate an individual than present and physical ones.

"Yes… yes," the ghoul spurred him on as he watched his mother being kicked. "You had to intervene, didn't you?"

"Yes. I ran and pushed him off her with all my strength." As he said it, the scene unfolded in front of him.

Carlos's dad frowned at the young boy with so much anger, it brought Carlos back to that moment in his head, and he relived the fear that had coursed through him back then.

229

"And your father beat you until you were near death for that, didn't he?"

Carlos watched his mother and sister cry as they watched him getting beaten… until his sister crashed a large vase on their father's head.

"He wasn't going to stop," Carlos said, trying to explain why it had not been her fault. "I was almost unconscious. I might have died. She had always been a great sister, and she looked out for me. There was no way Rosa was going to let me die."

"Then why did you let *her* die?"

The question hit him hard. He did not want to have that conversation. Carlos rarely talked about it.

The setting changed to another time in his life, when he had come back from what looked like a brawl, his knuckles partially bloodied.

"As you grew older, you wanted to help your mother out, is that it?" It kept speaking into his ear.

Carlos was breaking down mentally. It was not what he'd wanted. He hadn't wanted to bring his mother any pain or sorrow. He'd just been a young kid, trying to be the man of the house after they'd killed for him and saved his life.

"They reported it to the police as self-defense, which it was," Carlos responded without blinking, fully immersed in the illusion before him because it felt like reality. The adult man watched his younger self treat his mother and sister badly. Carlos knew why he'd done it—he'd wanted to prove himself

230

TOM COLEMAN

so badly it took him to dark places, and when his mom had talked to him about it, he'd dismissed her harshly and said it was all for them to survive.

"You beat people up, stole, lied, and did all other horrible things while telling yourself it was for them."

"Stop." A tear escaped his eye as he was forced to watch all of the terrible things he had done. Carlos had forgotten about the fact they were in a haunted house or that his wife was probably suffering at that very moment. They had found his fulcrum, his weak point. Now that it had been hit, the young man was falling apart.

"I'm sorry, Mom," he said, trying to console his crying mother while the younger version of himself simply walked past her.

"We should strive to be better, Carlos," Rosa had said to him, but Carlos didn't want to hear it. He hadn't noticed that he had been so drawn into the powers of the house that he had entered the body of his younger self.

"Leave me alone. It will all make sense when we make it out of here and get a better life," he responded to her. "Everything I am doing—"

"Is for us, right?" Rosa finished, looking like she was tired of that same old excuse. "This life you are living... it will catch up to you one day, Carlos," she said, walking away. "I just hope you are able to see the end of the tunnel you are striving so hard for us to reach. I hope we see it, too."

231

TOM COLEMAN

He was in tears. It had been so painful. He didn't like to confront the role his lifestyle and stubbornness had played in her demise.

"I'm… sorry." Carlos fell to the ground, crying, barely registering that he was inhabiting his younger body. "It's all my fault."

"You killed me," the image of Rosa said.

Carlos was so utterly transfixed, he thought it was really her. "It wasn't the rival gang to the one you joined; it was you. When you joined those guys and got into all that crap, you invited attacks on you, and by extension, on us."

He couldn't even counter what had been said because he'd believed it. Somewhere deep within him, he'd always housed blame for not heeding her warnings. He kept on going and moving forward but leaving his family behind.

"But by the time you came back for them," the ghoul whispered into his ear. For Carlos, it was as if he was hearing his innermost thoughts, "one of them was gone."

The room changed to the day he came home to find her lifeless body on the floor. "No, no, no, no—I don't want to see this! I don't wanna fucking see this!" Carlos closed his eyes, but it was as if his lids were transparent. Even with his eyes closed, he could see it. "Argh! Stop!" He was in the body of his younger self, watching like a passenger as he came home and yelled for his sister. He had heard they'd found out where he'd lived and attacked his home as payback for a series of problems the group he was in had caused them.

"There she is," the ghost said, as if satisfied. The entity stood beside Rosa's lifeless body as Carlos held her in his arms. There were bullet wounds all over her body. She'd been barraged by gunshots, probably from a drive-by.

"Mom wasn't around, was she?" the voice reverberated in his ear. "She was out trying to keep food on the table. Meanwhile, in your attempt to protect your family by joining the gang, you guaranteed its end. It... was... all... you."

"I'm... I'm so sorry. I didn't mean for this to happen. Please, come back!"

"You should pay for this. You have a happy life right now while she is in the dirt. You don't deserve happiness. She did, but you took that from her."

The darkness crept further into his psyche, and Carlos blamed himself. He should be dead. It should have been him. He was broken.

"Don't you want to see her and apologize for what you did to her?"

"Yes, I do. I really do."

"Then take this and come and meet me," Rosa said, smiling. She handed a knife to Carlos.

He gazed at the knife for a minute as if in a daze. "Okay."

CHAPTER SIX:
I CAN'T BELIEVE THIS

Christina yelled and screamed louder than she had ever screamed before. It was so painful having the needle in her eye that she fell to the floor, screaming as blood gushed out of it profusely.

"I thought this was not real," she screamed to herself.

The ghosts laughed. Christina thought she could hear nearly a thousand laughs.

She looked up, and with her working eye, saw several ghosts walking toward her. There were that many ghosts? All of them lived in the house? What exactly was this gnarly, scary dungeon masquerading as a house? "What is going on here? Why are there so many of you?"

"Join us and find out," one of the ghosts said, looking fierce. They hovered above the ground as they surrounded her.

Christina took a deep breath and thought. She had to open her mind to the fact that what she was experiencing was not real. The needle in her eye did not exist. Despite the excruciating pain, it was not real. None of it was. Sure, the ghosts had to be real, but the mindfuck was all in her head, and if it was directed by her own beliefs, that meant she could also control the outcome. She had the power, not them. Maybe she

TOM COLEMAN

was wrong, but Christina did not care. She was going to get out of there and find her husband or die trying.

She took a deep breath and shut her eyes, even the one with the needle in it. When she opened them back up, one word came out of her mouth: "Leave."

In an instant, the atmospheric doom and gloom, the darkness, and the ghosts disappeared, and she realized that she was still in the bedroom, as was Carlos.

Wait... Carlos? He was holding a knife and was about to stab himself.

"Carlos," Christina yelled, running over to him to stop him from stabbing himself. He was pretty strong, though, so the task proved difficult to accomplish. She kept yelling his name in an attempt to try to get him to stop his suicide attempt.

***

"What?" Carlos finally muttered, hearing a faint but familiar voice call his name from a distance. His hand gripped the knife tightly, but something was stopping him.

"You have to do it now, brother," Rosa said to him hastily.

"But that voice—"

"Do it," she yelled, looking a bit sinister as her corneas were turning red. "Suffer as we did! Become us! Become trapped!"

235

"This... isn't real, is it?" Carlos said, finally coming back to himself, morphing back into his adult body. He looked at himself, got some bearing on where he was, and dropped the knife.

"Carlos!"

The voice was louder this time, and he immediately pinpointed it as Christina's. He got up and looked around, trying to find her.

"You need to end it now," Rosa pressed. "We can be together, Carlos."

Carlos Hernandez closed his eyes and envisioned the great, kind, happy sister he knew. She would never have wanted him dead before he'd had a chance to live his life to the fullest.

"All Rosa wanted for me to be happy," Carlos said with an honest smile. He turned to gaze at the fake Rosa standing behind him and looking at him expectantly, waiting for him to kill himself. "You are an insult to her memory, demon." The veil cleared from his eyes. He'd faltered for a moment, but he was finally drawn back from the edge by his anchor: his wife.

"You can go now."

The demon slowly wilted away as soon as he'd said it, as did the construct around him. Facing him as soon as everything became clear was Christina, her hands cupping his cheeks while she stared at him with worry.

"Oh, thank God," she said the moment she noticed he was conscious again. "I was so—" Before Christina could finish what she was saying, Carlos held her tightly and kissed her. Without her, he would be dead.

"You saved me," he said after their lips had parted. "I would have been dead if you hadn't intervened."

"Well, I kind of owed you for the number of times you've saved me," she replied with a smile.

"We have to get out of here."

"Are you sure we can do that, Carlos? So far, we've been able to resist whatever's in this house, but something tells me it'll get worse when we leave this room. For starters, that large, dark, silhouette man could be outside."

"Yes, I am sure. It's just in our minds. He patrols out there to make us think we cannot escape. I'm sure the black goo stuff only affects us because we think it will. After the first dump, we were psychologically programmed to expect horrible things from it and fear it, and that gave it even more power."

"I guess you're right, but you know it's still gonna hurt, right?"

"I'm not scared," Carlos said to his wife with a smile, and he really wasn't. They had survived the worst and proven they could individually overcome the forces of this house. Together, they could help each other get past the obstacles no matter what they might be. As far as Carlos knew, the ghosts could not do any real damage to them, only influence them to damage themselves.

TOM COLEMAN

"We can do this together. I genuinely believe so; as long as we trust ourselves and one another, we can overcome anything." Carlos knew that Christina always felt safe with him, and she would trust his judgment.

"All right. Let's do it."

"Okay." They both took deep breaths, counted to three, and Carlos opened the door, but to his surprise, the Silhouette Man wasn't waiting there. He poked out his head cautiously, trying to check if it was a trick, but the coast was clear in the hallway.

"Let's make a run for it while we can," he said to her, and she nodded. They rushed out, but as they ran, the doors to the hall swung open. The Silhouette Man was in the creepy room with the doll, standing right next to it. The doll was seated on the body—or the skeleton, to be specific—of what they assumed had been a person. The other room looked empty and seemed generally brighter, but they didn't care and kept going to the end of the hallway so they could use the stairs.

"Why is no one chasing us?" Christina inquired, sounding a bit confused.

"Don't ask, honey—Just run!" As far as Carlos was concerned, they had to run first and ask questions later. They needed to go as fast as they could so they could leave and get the bloody suitcase. He was not even sure how to use the suitcase to banish the demons. He'd even burned the thing. A part of him believed the suitcase was intact or it would not have that much power. Maybe his assumptions had been way off, and the suitcase had nothing to do with the house. That

TOM COLEMAN

would mean they were better off running the moment they'd left the house rather than go back into the house. The worst part of it all was that he knew they'd have to still go back into the house and get into the attic so they could put the suitcase back where they'd found it. For some reason, however, Carlos felt as if he was forgetting something. He couldn't quite put his finger on it, but it was important.

"Carlos!" He was so deep in thought; he hadn't noticed that the stairs had completely disappeared. He would have fallen, possibly to his death, if it weren't for Christina, who had called his attention back to the situation at hand. He tried to stop, but he was running so fast that he was bound to fall if it weren't for Christina holding him back.

"Oh, shit. Thanks. That was a close one," he admitted.

Carlos finally knew why the demons hadn't chased them. He and his wife turned to see several ghosts facing them. There was an Army man, a set of twins who looked no more than eleven years old, a woman with messy hair, the skeleton with the doll, the Silhouette Man, and others. The same question that had been in his head all day came to the forefront again: what the hell was happening?

"We have to believe the stairs are actually there," Carlos said to her.

"Wait. What?"

The ghosts walked toward them slowly, making menacing noises.

They had to act fast. It was then or never.

"Yes. We have to take a leap of faith and believe that we are fine and the stairs are there. If we don't, things could get bad really quick."

"I'm not sure—"

"You just have to believe… in you and in me. The stairs are there… the stairs are there." Reciting this was as much for Carlos as it was for Christina.

The Silhouette Man had already opened his mouth to gush out some of his weird mucus at them. Even though they were prepared for it—or they believed they were—he would surely rather not have to go through that again. Even having the slightest doubt was enough to make the goo work. They both had to believe.

"Okay," Christina told him.

"Good. One…"

The ghosts raised their hands, reaching out for them.

"Two… three!"

They each placed a foot on where the stairs were supposed to be, and they fell.

"Fuck!" Carlos swore as he reflexively protected Christina, and they landed hard on the floor. He definitely had some broken ribs… either that or he had broken something else. Carlos already had a head injury, and now his body was messed up. Christina's leg was messed up and looked like it would no longer work.

"I'm sorry, baby. We have to get going and leave this place. We have to get to the door." Carlos dragged himself up and helped her to her feet. She limped a bit, but they knew they had to leave. Carlos did not know what they would do when they got to the suitcase, but one thing was for sure, there was no way he was going back into the building.

The ghouls hovered down, chasing them as they struggled to leave the house. They were both bleeding, but neither cared. It was do or die. Carlos wondered why the ghosts weren't moving any faster. It seemed as if they could appear anywhere they wanted in the house, but now they were moving incredibly slow.

He opened the door, and they went outside. It was evening and almost dark, but they didn't care about that. They went straight for the trash.

Carlos turned back to notice that the beings were stuck in the doorjamb. Why weren't they chasing them? He saw that ghost that had appeared as Rosa right outside of the house and even heard the guitar sounds.

He opened the trashcan and saw that the suitcase was intact. Both of them sighed in relief.

"Oh, thank God," Carlos said, reaching for the suitcase. He opened his eyes. Beside him, Christina also opened her eyes. All they could hear was laughter.

"What... what is happening?" Christina asked. "We were outside and reaching for the trash."

TOM COLEMAN

Slowly but surely, it donned on Carlos, who began laughing along with the weird laughter that echoed through the attic.

Yes, they were back in the attic.

"Why are you laughing? This isn't funny?" Christina sounded annoyed. "How did we get here?"

"I can't believe this," Carlos said. "I never went to work this morning. That was why it all felt so familiar. There were fewer people, and the sounds of the guitar were able to reach me at work. It was all so weird because I was in the house all along. This fucking house… the house used my memories of where I used to live and work before to create the fake reality. That was why and how everyone looked familiar or the same."

"What do you mean? I know you left."

"It was all in this house," he explained, still stunned at the fact. "We haven't left the house since we threw that suitcase away. It's been torture nonstop."

"Oh, God," Christina said in disbelief. Everything up until then had been nothing but sinking deeper and deeper into the hellish creation in the haunted house of doom. How the hell would they get out now?

"We were under the house's spell from the very start," he said, resting his head on his palm. "I just can't fucking believe this."

To be continued…

242

TOM COLEMAN

THE MASTER BUTCHER

(Based on a true story)

243

TOM COLEMAN

244

TOM COLEMAN

CHAPTER ONE: JUST AN ORDINARY GUY

As he walked past the droves of people in the bustling city, Armin Meiwes licked his lips. If only they knew how hungry he was to enact his dark fantasies. Just one. Only one would be enough.

Armin was a man of class, or he liked to think he was. There was no way he would attack any of those people or force them to indulge him in his acts. That being said, Armin wondered when the growing itch in his soul and mouth would be scratched. Nobody knew his secret, and he was okay with that.

Armin Meiwes worked for an IT company as your everyday computer technician. He never stood out, nor did he try to. He was cordial to his co-workers, and he tried to come and go as early as possible.

"Hey, good morning," Dave, the guy in the cubicle next to him, said after noticing his arrival. Dave was a tall African-American man with nice features. Armin always wondered why he had not gone into athletics or something physical since he had the right body for it. Dave seemed passionate about his work at the company, so Meiwes decided he had probably found his calling.

Armin was surprised to see Dave at that time. He never came to work that early—what was so special about that day?

TOM COLEMAN

"Why do you look so surprised, bruv?" Dave inquired, smirking. Armin assumed that Dave wanted to revel in the fact he had come in before him today.

"You don't usually come this early," Armin said, sitting in his seat.

Dave laughed, leaned back in his chair, and brought his hands together at the back of his head. "Now, why would you find it surprising that a hardworking, early riser like me would come early?" he said laxly.

Armin gave him a look as if to say, "Are you serious?"

Dave laughed again. He was a free-spirited who liked work and play in equal measure. "I am a dutiful employee in this prestigious establishment, after all. And also, Mr. Goodgeer gave me some extra work that I haven't finished yet, so I'm here tryna finish it before he arrives," Dave explained.

"Ah, there it is," Armin noted.

Dave rolled his eyes. "Anyways, did you watch the game last night? The…"

Dave knew that Armin didn't like sports, but he always talked about basketball, baseball, and football nonetheless. Armin mostly zoned out and did what he usually did when people talked about things about which he did not care: scan them. There was a particular albeit sickening reason he did this.

As Dave ranted on about the game—Armin couldn't care less to which sport he alluded to—his gaze was drawn to Dave's neck, and he wondered how it might taste. You see, Mr. Armin Meiwes had cannibalistic tendencies. He fantasized about

TOM COLEMAN

boring his sharp canines into human skin and tearing the flesh with his molars. Just the thought of it used to make him salivate, but that was before he had learned how to control his urges in front of people.

For a man as well-built as Dave Jeffreys, the meat would need more cooking time, unlike a woman's flesh. At least, that's what he thought. Would the eyes also be yummy, or should he avoid them entirely? Did he need to eat both Dave's outside and innards, or should he pick one? These were the questions roaming around in his mind as he studied Dave.

To an onlooker—Dave included—it might seem as if Armin was staring with such interest because he was intrigued by Dave's story, but that was far from the truth. Armin wanted to eat the man in front of him so badly, but he considered himself a good man, and he would not make anyone do anything they did not want to do. All the hungry man could do was lament about his situation and hope that he would get the chance to chow down on a person, as sick as that might sound.

After work that day, Armin rushed out of the office.

Dave, who regularly asked about why he was in the habit of leaving early, asked him yet again why he was in such a rush. "Dude, why do you keep doing that?"

"What do you mean?"

"Don't play dumb, man. You always rush off like you have a hot babe at home," Dave noted. "There's more to you than meets the eye, ain't there, bruv?"

"I have to go. See you tomorrow, Dave," Armin said, and he left. He knew why he had to get on time. The Internet continued to grow, and a lot of people could easily find one another to communicate their likes and desires. And when someone had the decidedly unpopular fetish for eating people, the Internet was the best place for him to find like-minded people due to the anonymity of the platform.

He tried to hold a smile as he waited for a cab. Armin Meiwes was so eager to talk about all the nasty things going on in his head; he began to tap his foot against the ground. "C'mon...c'mon...c'mon," he whispered under his breath as he waited until, at last, he was finally able to hail a cab and climb inside.

After paying his fare, Armin fled into his house, dropped his coat on the closet floor, and sat in front of his computer. He didn't care about the fact that he hadn't changed out of his work clothes yet. Armin didn't care about that. Instead, he booted up his computer, clasped his hands together, and gazed expectantly at the monitor.

A couple of minutes later and he was on the Dark Web, where he could talk to many people about different things. Armin had opened a number of accounts on a variety of forums for discussion where he could discuss his tastes. If he were ridiculed, he would leave the account and move to another. It was an effective outlet, but the troubled man ultimately did not get what he wanted. What he sought was people who loved eating others, or even better, being eaten themselves. How would he ever find that?

"Ugh," he groaned, getting up after having sat for hours. He stretched, grimacing at the pain before deciding to go out for a

TOM COLEMAN

walk. He was out of milk and needed to buy some at the convenience store nearby.

It was dark outside as Meiwes strolled down the road. On the way, he saw a lady standing on the corner under the streetlight. Since she was under the light, it was easy for him to see her features and hard for her to notice him. There were no other people around. She seemed focused on her phone, so he doubted she would notice him, even if she hadn't been in the light.

Armin noticed how incredibly beautiful the woman was, but not in a sexual or romantic way. Instead, he imagined how magnificent it would be to tear off the skin of a lady with skin as smooth as hers. Would it be best if he ate a skin as immaculate as hers raw? Skin like Dave's would need to be cooked first for maximum enjoyment, but hers would be soft and succulent. Simply biting, tearing, and chewing her flesh would be the ultimate raw experience.

Before Armin realized it, he had stopped walking and began staring at her. Thankfully, she still hadn't noticed due to being transfixed on her phone.

A part of him considered grabbing her and enacting his dark, sick desire, regardless of her willingness to take part in it.

No, wait! Armin cautioned himself. What if he asked her? Maybe she would be up for it?

Of course not. Was he crazy?

So many bargaining and primal thoughts invaded his mind, and he knew he had to leave before he was no longer able to remain a gentleman.

TOM COLEMAN

Armin took a deep breath, sighed, and walked past her without her even noticing him. As he did, he ground his teeth at not being able to partake in the glorious skin before him.

He bought the milk, and by the time he walked back, the woman was gone. He was partly happy and partly sad. He didn't have the temptation anymore, but man, that was some good skin.

The next couple of weeks were typical. Armin Meiwes went to work, acted like a normal human being, and returned home to unleash the desires he had buried in the online forums. Most forums and discussion groups were against the idea of cannibalism, but he tried to be an advocate for it, when there were negative responses from the general online populace. This continued for a while until Armin found the perfect place to actualize his dreams and fetishes: The Cannibal Café.

250

CHAPTER TWO: CANNIBAL CAFÉ

"Damn," Armin mused after reading the blog called "The Cannibal Café." He had gone through some of the posts there, and he realized it was the place for which he had been searching. The website was hard to find, which was understandable, but Armin was persistent, and once he had finally stumbled upon it, he was elated. The hard work he had put into his search would finally be rewarded as he set about chatting and sharing his fantasies to see how a conversation with a few cannibals—fully realized or aspiring—might go. He was happy the people on the other side of the monitor treated him like a normal person.

"So, there are others like me," he said, excited at the newfound community that accepted his deviant views.

Armin buried himself in "The Cannibal Café" to the point where he started arriving at work at the same time as the others and not earlier, though he still left as early as possible.

One day, after Armin had arrived late to work for the first time ever, Dave came over to talk to him about it. On that day, Armin had rushed into the large hall filled with busy people. Usually, there were scant people around due to the early hour. He made his way to his cubicle, where he was met by a scowling Dave. Dave never scowled.

"What?" Armin asked.

"Mr. Goodgeer asked about you."

Armin froze.

"Don't fret. I covered for you."

"Thank you," Armin said, relieved. The boss was not a lenient man.

"You can thank me by telling me what's going on with you."

"What do you mean?"

"Don't play dumb with me, man." Dave seemed irritated by Armin's deflection. "You've never been late. Then, all of a sudden, you are later than I have ever been. The time is nine o'clock, for God's sake, Armin."

"I'm sorry. I slept late." He'd slept late because he was busy chatting online on the blog late into the night. "I promise, I am fine. I've just been spending more time on the Internet these days." Armin knew that the best way to lie was to sprinkle in pieces of the truth, and that was the truth… at least partially.

Dave scrutinized his face and sighed. "Whatever, man. I'm not covering for you again."

Armin was silent. He had let his extra-curricular activities affect his work. He needed his job. People killed for a job like his. He had to wake up and handle his time well.

That night, Armin went home to converse with his "cannibal friends" for a while, but he was getting tired of the routine. The superficial conversations he'd made with like-minded strangers on the Internet just wasn't enough anymore. At first, Armin had been honored to chat with people who felt the same way as him about eating humans, but now, having engaged in these discussions night after night, he was bored, and he wanted more. Just talking about his needs and fantasies no longer cut it. Now that he had scratched the itch to find people who thought the same as him, it was time for the IT technician to go further, to take things up a notch. He had to experience the feel of chewing on someone's skin.

But no one would agree to that. How could he convince someone to go along without it sounding weird? Armin felt strongly that he could make them agree, but no matter how he tried convincing himself, he inevitably realizing it was impossible, but after thinking for a while longer, he came up with an idea.

Why couldn't he just ask them? Armin decided to set up an ad for whoever was interested in being eaten. He knew it was a stretch to expect people might respond in the affirmative, but it was the best he could do at that moment in time. He could only hope there was a kindred spirit out there who would be intrigued by the idea, the yin to his yang. Could there actually be anyone out there who would really agree to something like that? Someone who would be okay with having his skin chopped off and eaten?

Armin took a deep breath. He decided not to overthink it. The best thing he could do was to act and wait.

He posted an advertisement for a person willing to have his skin eaten. Armin was kind of nervous about taking that next step. It was far easier thanks to his anonymity online, but still, he was afraid and unsure. He'd never done anything like that before. What if he sent someone an offer and they tricked him?

Armin brushed it off, deciding to remain steadfast in his path. He could never forgive himself if he didn't try and stayed in his boring, everyday life instead. It was the best time for him to make a move, besides. Things had aligned at just the right time, which he felt was a sign.

He sent the offer, and he waited. His criteria were a well-built, eighteen- to thirty-year-old to be slaughtered and consumed." Meiwes knew he had to be blunt and straight to the point about the situation.

In the days after he'd sent the offer, he conversed with those who replied, trying to convince them it was a good idea. To his credit, Armin Meiwes never threatened anyone into partaking in his fantasy. If they backed out after talking about it with him, he let them be. There was no enjoyment in the experience if the other person resisted.

The longer it went on, the more conversations he had with people from "The Cannibal Café," the more annoyed he became. He was getting antsy with the discourse that never went anywhere. What was the point of people replying if they were not into it? Did they not read his offer? He was grumbling in front of his computer when he received a notification of a message from "The Café." He was usually eager to check to see if the person was willing to go along with being cut up and eaten, but now, after the discussions he'd had, he was a bit hesitant.

TOM COLEMAN

Nevertheless, he had nothing else to do, so he opened the message to see a response from username Brandes99. Upon reading it, Armin learned that the man's full name was Bernd Jürgen Armando Brandes. He was also highly interested in having parts of his body cut off so they could both partake in the pleasure. He left it in Armin's hands to gather the equipment needed to amputate a part of his body and take care of the medical aspect of the endeavor.

"Interesting," Armin said, his interest piqued. He answered Brandes99, telling him he had no problem procuring the surgical equipment necessary to go through with the operation. Armin was initially interested in eating someone alone because he didn't think the person would be interested in eating his own body. Now, though, he was glad that he would have a fellow cannibal with whom he could savor the experience.

After some back and forth, they agreed to each other's terms. Armin and Brandes would meet at Armin's house for the procedure and the dining experience afterward. The only thing left was to set the date to carry out the men's day of blood and gore.

255

TOM COLEMAN

CHAPTER THREE: OUT OF HAND

Armin was nervous. It was the day he was going to welcome his "guest." He had purchased all the materials needed for their transaction—at least, the ones he'd seen online. He'd picked up three containers of sleeping pills, a serrated saw, plaster, spirit bottles, iodine, white clothes, and a host of other necessary items. Brandes was to arrive shortly, and he had everything set up nicely. The operation would happen in the basement. He would cut off a part of Brandes's body, and they would partake in the ecstasy of eating it together.

There was a knock on the door, and Armin rushed to his feet, brushed off his shirt, and opened the door to see Mr. Brandes standing in front of him. He was a fairly tall, well-built man with a nervous smile. He seemed to be anxious, too, which made Armin feel a bit better—knowing he was not the only one nervous about what was to happen was assuring. Hopefully, the experience would prove a good gateway to his chopping more things off more bodies and being more comfortable in doing so.

"Hello," Armin said, moving to the side. "Come on in."

"Thank you," Brandes said with a smile, walking in. "You have a nice place."

"Nah. It's just quaint, but thanks for the compliment," Armin responded.

Brandes nodded. They sat, and an air of awkward silence filled the atmosphere. Armin felt as if he should be the one to lead the conversation since he had been the one to raise the proposal.

"So, why don't we get started, huh?" Armin said, finally breaking. "Would you like a drink or a meal before we start?"

"I plan to *be* the meal," Brandes remarked, causing both men to chuckle. It also put Armin a bit more at ease. It was nice that Brandes was also looking forward to tasting his skin.

"I have placed cameras around the house. I bought them just for this moment. I didn't want a handheld experience because that could be shaky," Meiwes explained to Brandes, who nodded his approval. He pointed to the one hanging from the living room ceiling. "So, where would you like to be cut? What part would you like us to dine on?"

"My dick." Armin wasn't sure he'd heard him correctly, and he blinked multiple times, trying to comport himself. Of all the parts of his body that could be eaten, he wanted to try his penis? Was he celibate or something? Had he had a vasectomy? The best thing for Armin was not to ask too many questions, lest his guest turn iffy. He needed to just appease him, so the man did not change his mind. Asking him about his personal life might make him emotional or cause him to back out of the operation.

257

TOM COLEMAN

"Well, okay," he said, getting up. "Shall we?"

Brandes smiled and got up as well.

The men went to the basement, where everything was ready and waiting. Brandes seemed to hesitate when he saw the bed on which his penis was about to be chopped off, as well as the saw.

"Don't worry. I got you sleeping pills for after the procedure. You'll have a good sleep," Armin explained, hoping to alleviate Brandes's fears.

"Oh, good, good," Brandes commented, appearing to settle. He climbed onto the bed, which had been covered by a rubber sheet.

Armin checked on the camera that had been placed right above the bed to see that it was still on. "I'm gonna have to tie you up so you'll stay still while I cut," Armin explained as Brandes got undressed. Just seeing the man's bare skin, the skin he was about to taste, made the IT man salivate.

"I understand," Brandes said, breathing heavily. The reality of what was going to happen next had finally settled in on the two men, and it was natural for them to feel diffident and scared. Armin had to be strong for the both of them. He summoned up the courage to tie his fellow conspirator to the bed, got some spirits, and rubbed it on the base of Mr. Brandes's penis. His heart beat fast as he was sure did that of the man he was about to cut.

"Close your eyes," Armin Meiwes instructed. "No matter what, don't look. I am here. I'll handle everything."

TOM COLEMAN

Brandes nodded and closed his eyes.

Armin took a deep breath. It was the moment of truth. All of his fantasies, discussions, and cravings had led him to that very moment. He had gone too far to back down now. To be honest, he didn't want to back down. He was doing what he always wanted to do. It was one thing to eat someone, but to cut them up and savor the experience with the person whose appendage he'd amputated? That was a rare camaraderie "normal" people would never get to experience. These were the twisted thoughts dancing through Mr. Meiwes's mind as he set about cutting off the dick.

Brandes, understandably, roared in pain. The blood splattered on the rubber sheets on the bed, on the floor, and even on Armin's face. He licked off the blood that hit his lip, savoring it as an appetizer before sampling the main dish: Mr. Brandes's dick.

"It's almost done! Just a little more," Armin assured Brandes, who wriggled in excruciating pain. Armin widened his eyes like never before. He was in total ecstasy as he moved the saw back and forth to sever Brandes's penis. With every sound of the tearing flesh and Brandes screeching in agony, Mr. Armin Meiwes felt more alive. It was the excitement for which he had been searching.

Armin removed the penis and used a cloth to cover the open wound. He placed the penis on a plate he'd stored nearby, along with forks and knives. "You'll be fine. I promise you'll be fine," Armin consoled the man who was still writhing in pain. He bandaged the cut area and removed the bindings holding Brandes down.

259

TOM COLEMAN

"Where is my dick? Where is the dick?" Brandes inquired frantically. He was still high on adrenaline, which was no big surprise, considering what happened.

"it's here. It's here." Armin brought him his dick and the two of them stared at it hungrily. Armin was surprised Mr. Brandes would be hungry after what he'd just gone through. Maybe it was because of the pain he experienced. Maybe he needed to eat his dick to know it had all been worth it.

"I'll cut it up for us," Armin said, getting a knife and slicing it into two. "Which end do you prefer?"

"The base. It's thicker," Brandes said. It was clear he was still experiencing severe pain.

Armin obliged, taking the tip end of the dick, and watching as Brandes ate the base. The men chewed on their respective pieces of Mr. Bernd Brandes's genitalia. Having someone there for them to watch each other as they cemented their identifies as cannibals—the feeling was indescribable for Armin Meiwes. He could not put it into words.

That was when the problem arose: the penis was hard to digest. Armin had not factored for that development. "It's too chewy," Armin admitted after they'd chomped on it for a few minutes.

"Y-yeah." Brandes seemed to be having trouble talking, probably due to the pain he felt in his nether region.

That was when Armin came up with an idea. "I'll go and cook the penis a bit. Why don't you rest while I do that?" he proposed. Since it had been his job to handle the procedures and the extra bits, it was also his job to make the "meat"

TOM COLEMAN

edible. Brandes had offered up a part of his body, and his penis, at that—the most valuable part—he had earned a rest.

"Here, have this," Armin said, handing him some pills and a glass of water. He had read online that fifteen pills should get him to sleep for the duration of the procedure without feeling any pain. Armin didn't know how true that was, but it was the best he do because asking a doctor such a question might arouse suspicion.

Brandes took the pills, and then he took five more.

"I'll take you to the bath. You can sleep there and relax. This place is already bloody," Armin noted.

"All right. Thanks," Brandes said. Armin carried him from the basement to the bathroom. He noticed the man was bleeding through the plaster, so after he'd settled him in the bathroom, he placed two more bandages on the wound after pouring iodine and spirits on it.

Brandes was asleep by then. They'd considered using the sleeping pills during the amputation, but they agreed that that way, the experience would be "more organic." Plus, if Brandes was awake through the pain, they could experience it together.

There was also a camera in the bathroom because Armin had anticipated Brandes might need a place to rest while he recuperated, and the bathtub seemed like a good place for it.

After checking on Brandes's pulse to assure he was still alive, Armin went back to cook the food and prepare a nice dish with the piece he'd taken from his cohort. Brandes

TOM COLEMAN

would be out for a long time, thanks to the sleeping pills, which meant he could take his time preparing the meal. He did, however, check on Brandes's condition every fifteen minutes.

After some time, Armin heard loud noises from the guest bathroom. That meant Brandes was awake. He left the kitchen and went to see Brandes, but he was met with shock. He was surprised to see Brandes on the ground, groaning, a trail of blood demarcating the path he had taken from the bathroom. He had lost that much blood?

Armin panicked. He went to the aid of his accomplice, trying to get him to stay conscious, but it was too late—Brandes had already lost too much blood.

"Help... m—" Brandes couldn't finish the statement, falling unconscious instead.

Armin had a choice to make: did he kill Brandes or not? The torn man battled with the decision. Mr. Brandes had not given permission to murder him. He had only given permission to cut off his dick. He could still get him to a hospital, maybe, but that would mean they could be caught and taken to jail, and he could not have that happen.

"I'm so sorry. You're gonna die anyway from blood loss, so I might as well end your misery," Armin said to an unconscious Brandes. Blood was everywhere and spreading...fast.

He went back to the kitchen to get a knife and lugged Brandes back to the bathroom. To say the bathroom was messy from the blood loss was an understatement.

TOM COLEMAN

"Fuck," Armin stated as he got him into the tub. He took a deep breath as he held the knife above his victim. In one swift, deep stab to the throat, Armin Meiwes killed Bernd Brandes. The blood gushed out like a running tap, spraying from Brandes's carotid artery and into the bathtub. More of it splattered on his face. And as he had done before, Armin tasted the man's blood.

"Wow!" A cacophony of emotions ran through Armin's mind: sadness, guilt, excitement. The adrenaline of taking a life had taken over, making him want to go even further.

Armin Meiwes hanged Bernd Brandes's lifeless body on a meat hook to prepare it for consumption. At that moment, Armin Meiwes was at his peak. He was confused as to how he felt—or rather, how he should have felt for what he had done—so he hid whatever he was feeling deep in his mind and simply carried on. It was the birth of a monster who would hunt for new victims while feeding on the old.

***

A year had passed, and Armin Meiwes was in a very different place. After having tried to get more people to offer up their bodies for his excitement, his newfound boldness had prompted a college student to report him to the police, who tracked his actions on "The Cannibal Café" when he solicited others to come to his house to be cut up and eaten. The police got his address. They searched his house and found the videos

263

TOM COLEMAN

of what he had done with and to Bernd Brandes. That, however, was not the most traumatic thing they discovered.

Armin Meiwes had fed on Bernd's body for ten months. He put the man's body parts into the freezer after dissection and slowly ate him, relishing the taste.

Now, the end of the cannibalistic monster that was Armin Meiwes had arrived.

Armin Meiwes sat in the penitentiary's cafeteria. He looked to his side to see a new inmate looking back at him. Armin got up and took his tray to sit at the man's side.

"You're him, right?" the inmate inquired with excitement.

Armin gazed at him in silence and went back to eating his veggies.

"I'm Marion. I see the rumors are true about your being a vegetarian because you're remorseful for your actions."

Armin continued to eat in silence.

"I wonder if you are really remorseful."

"I am," Armin finally said.

Marion laughed. "So, you mean to tell me that if you were set free to go out into the real world and you were given real flesh to eat, you wouldn't eat it?"

Armin did not answer him. Was it because he saw no need to engage with the newbie, or because, deep down, he

TOM COLEMAN

was still the cannibal who had chopped up and eaten the man he'd killed?

Only Armin Meiwes truly knows.

(Armin Meiwes is a real person, and this is a true story. He is a German, former computer repair technician who achieved international attention for killing and eating a voluntary victim in 2001, whom he had found via the Internet. After Meiwes and the victim jointly attempted to eat the victim's severed penis, Meiwes killed his victim and proceeded to eat a large amount of his flesh. He was arrested in December 2002. In January 2004, Meiwes was convicted of manslaughter and sentenced to eight years and six months in prison. In a retrial in May 2006, he was convicted of murder and sentenced to life imprisonment. Because of his acts, Meiwes is also known as the Rotenburg Cannibal or Der Metzgermeister (The Master Butcher). Today, he claims to be a vegetarian.)

265

TOM COLEMAN

TOM COLEMAN

YOU CAN`T ESCAPE

TOM COLEMAN

TOM COLEMAN

CHAPTER ONE: WHAT'S IN THE CLOSET?

Mary Crenshaw sighed as she looked around the house. It was a nice, quaint, three-bedroom apartment. Nothing fancy but definitely comfortable. She was happy they had gotten away and relocated to a new state. Now, in Orlando, Mary felt she and the kids were safe there. There was no way he would find them. She heard her kids giggling upstairs, and her worries disappeared. A smile formed on her face. Mary was at peace... well, as peaceful as someone like her could be.

All of her life, Mary had the sensation of being followed. Mary was thirty-two years old, and for as long as she could remember, there was always the feeling of being watched or followed by someone... or something. It was eerie, and she never liked it. That was why she got into running and kickboxing. She felt as if something might attack her at any moment, so Mary wanted to be prepared to fight back or escape.

She wondered if she were just trying to run away from her. Mary sighed. She was tired of running. He didn't give up, and he was someone who would keep searching for her as long as he lived. She knew him too well.

"Moooom, Sarah doesn't wanna give me my action toy again," one of her two kids, Brian, shouted to her from upstairs. Just hearing her kids bicker was music to her ears.

269

TOM COLEMAN

She wanted them to be happy and forget all of the horrible things they'd witnessed between her and Jonathan.

That night, Mary was putting Sarah to bed. Brian had already been put down. Brian insisted on sleeping in his sister's room until he was more accustomed to the place, to which the little girl begrudgingly agreed. Now, however, looking at the youngest of the family sleeping soundly, they couldn't help but feel at ease.

"Look at him, Mom," Sarah, who was eight, said. "Look how happy he is. I'm glad he doesn't have to suffer anymore."

Mary agreed. "I don't want you to think about the past anymore, okay, Sarah?" she said to her beloved daughter. "You are both safe now. We will start over with a happy life. I will protect us. Everything is fine."

"Mom," Sarah said. Mary heard the hesitation in her voice. The little girl still had residual fear after what she'd witnessed Jonathan do to her mother. Mary felt guilty for what her daughter had to go through. She was emotional, but she tried not to cry in front of her kid. If Sarah saw her crying, she might panic and not be at ease anymore.

The fear of Jonathan was strong. She knew it far too well. Mary also knew that Jonathan would chase them to the ends of the Earth, but the kids didn't need to know it.

She placed her palm on Sarah's hand. "Sarah, I am so, so sorry that you had to… I've failed you and Brian as a mother, but that all changes today."

Sarah frowned, surprising her mother. "How did you fail us, Mom?" she asked with her usual confidence. Sometimes, Mary forgot her daughter was just eight years old. Then again, having seen what she'd seen, considering what she'd been through, it didn't really surprise Mary that Sarah had to grow up fast. "Mom, you got your ass beat by a horrible husband and fath—"

"Language," Mary cautioned her daughter.

"Sorry. You know what I mean," the little girl said with a knowing look.

Mary sighed. "Shouldn't you be thinking more like girls your age?" she questioned.

Sarah laughed. "Mom, you're not the only one who believes she has to protect her loved ones, you know that, right?" That struck Mary deeply. Her kid had been forced to take on a motherly role at an incredibly young age. "Remember when I had to run to the convenience store at midnight to get bandages to tie up your stomach?"

Mary looked away and pressed her lips together.

"Or when I had to throw a stone from outside into the house to stop that man from beating you. It took his attention away from you so you could run away to your room." Mary noticed her daughter had stopped calling Jonathan "Dad." She liked that, but it was sad at the same time. She hoped that having such a bad male role model would not affect her daughter negatively, especially when it came to how she saw men.

"Or when—"

"Enough. I get it. Just stop, please." Mary couldn't hear anymore. She cupped her daughter's face and looked her in the eyes. "I know this might be hard to do, but I need you to just be an ordinary eight-year-old girl."

Sarah chuckled. "Come on, Mom. We both know that ship has sailed. We can't fix that." Her words broke her mother's heart. Was that how Sarah would be from then on, carrying the trauma with her? "If there is something you want to fix, you can finally start by calling someone to repair that weird closet."

"Closet," Mary corrected.

"Sure, Mom," she replied sarcastically. "I'm telling you: some weird noises come out of that thing."

Mary groaned. She glanced at the fancy closet she had bought for her kids. Brian had also complained about it, but she knew they were probably just whining.

"I'm serious. It's scaring me. Brian won't shut up about it, but in this area, I agree with him. You need to check it, Mom." She rolled her eyes, but Mary knew her kids wouldn't stop until she did what they wanted.

"Ugh, fine."

"Yaaaay," Sarah said in a low voice, trying not to wake Brian. She hugged her mother tightly. Mary loved these moments. It was the simple nights like these that she would always savor, partly because there had been so many chaotic nights. "Do you still have your headaches?" Mary had been having headaches, but she played them down. She particularly

272

TOM COLEMAN

had them when she was around Jonathan, most likely due to the stress of being around an animal like him.

"Actually, no. Ever since we escaped, my head has been free. I'm happy because I am with you two," she said to her daughter, withholding the fact that she still felt as if something was after her. Now, it was Jonathan, but she felt that way for a long time.

Sarah smiled. "Thank you, Mom, for everything."

"I love you so much."

"I love you too, Mom."

"I promise you: he will never find us." They detached from their hug, and Mary got up. She turned off the lamp, but not before taking one last look at her kids. This was the life she always dreamed of: having lovely kids and being a great mother to them. She had just... fallen for the wrong man. Regardless, her horrific experience had given her these two wonderful children for whom she would do anything.

***

Two days later, she had come home from work a bit earlier than expected, so the kids hadn't returned from school yet. A part of Mary wanted to have them home-schooled because of her paranoia, but both Sarah and Brian wanted the full school experience. She also wanted them to have a sense of normalcy, considering how bad the last few years had been, so Mary agreed to send them to the nearby school. She usually

273

went to pick them around three pm, having finished work thirty minutes earlier. This time, it was only one-twenty-four pm, meaning she had more time to rest or do whatever she wanted.

"I guess I could rest a bit." Mary mused, resting on the couch, but she had trouble sleeping, especially when she was alone. Too many flashbacks of being woken up by having her hair pulled for her to sleep well. She had grown slight bags under her eyes from not sleeping enough. Even after she'd run away from her hell, her trauma had followed her. At that moment, on the couch, she just couldn't fall asleep. Mary's heart beat faster as she wondered if he was standing there, next to her. The ghost that had followed her all her life was stronger than ever.

She opened her eyes, breathing heavily, looked around, and shivered.

Was he there?

"Fuck. My mind is just…" Mary took a deep breath, got up, and went up the stairs. She remembered that she wanted to call someone to check on the closet. For now, Mary chose to see what the fuss was for herself. There was no point in calling the carpenter if there was nothing wrong with the closet.

"Now, let's see what's wrong with this closet," Mary said after entering the kids' room. She noticed the closet was rattling, which was weird and made her cautious. What was that? She was paranoid and instances such as this did not help to curtail her fears. Did this have to do with Jonathan? she asked herself.

TOM COLEMAN

No, that was crazy.

She was just too scarred from her experience with the man. Mary held the handle to open the closet, took a deep breath, and whipped the door open, bracing herself for whatever was to come.

"What the hell?" To her surprise, there was nothing there but her kids' clothes. "I really need to get some sleep," Mary said. She was upset at herself for even considering that the closet might be... weird.

She did, however, notice that some of Brian's clothes were unkempt. "That boy. When he comes back, I'll make sure he arranges his cl..." She lost her train of thought after noticing some grass at the bottom of the closet. Mary squatted to scrutinized the plant matter on the floor of the wooden structure closet. She looked closer to noticed that it was a weird type of grass.

"What is going on?" she wondered. She didn't know much about grasses, but she knew it was definitely not from around there, at least, to the best of her knowledge. She was new to Florida, after all.

"Probably fell off of Brian's clothes or something." Mary brushed it away and was about to close the closet door when a second thought came to mind: why not check if there is any more grass inside the closet? She remained static for the next ten seconds, trying to decide if she should check.

"Ah, fuck it," she said. She poked her head into the closet and landed on the floor with a thump.

TOM COLEMAN

***

Mary got up, feeling a bit sore. She looked around to see that she was in a room, one that was definitely not in her house, and she wondered where, exactly, she was. Another thing she noticed was the antique materials in the room. As a lover of antique pieces, Mary, recognized the place belonged to someone who was very interested in old furniture, light bulbs, and even architecture.

"What's going on?" she asked herself, confused as to what was happening. It took her a bit longer than she would have anticipated, but it finally hit her that she had just gone through the wardrobe and come out the other side.

"Oh, my God." Mary couldn't believe it. Her kids had been right after all, but she was sure that even her kids couldn't see this coming. Who would have ever thought there'd be a portal in a closet that led to… wherever she was?

She heard a scream coming from outside of the room. Was there a problem? She could tell the person who'd screamed was a woman, and she had flashbacks to when she'd screamed while suffering at Jonathan's hands. She froze. A part of her considered going back into the closet, and hopefully, get back to her kids' room, but her curiosity was strong at that moment.

Mary went to the door, about to open it, but she decided to look around first and found a small penknife. One thing she'd learned from being in an abusive relationship: always to have a weapon with which to defend yourself. She turned back to the

TOM COLEMAN

door and glanced at the calendar on the wall as she passed it. Mary hadn't noticed the calendar before.

"Wait…that can't be right." Defiant, Mary moved closer to the calendar to get a better look because she could not believe her eyes.

The calendar said it was the nineteenth of January, 1977. Fifty-four years in the past from the date she'd entered the closet.

TOM COLEMAN

CHAPTER TWO: CHAOS

Mary was still having trouble understanding what she saw.

"It's probably old," she said, trying to dismiss it, but deep down, she knew that nobody kept calendars for fifty years. Her situation felt dangerous. Maybe going back through the closet was the safer option. Mary heard the faint scream again. She recognized it as being from a girl, and she acted almost instinctively. The girl might need help. She could be stuck somewhere, or something bad could be happening to her. Mary knew how much she wanted a person to come to her aid when she'd been in physical and emotional pain, so she rushed out of the room, closing the door behind her as silently as she could.

Mary considered calling out to the girl who was screaming, but she chose not to. Something in her gut told her to be cautious, so she tip-toed through the wooden hallway as best she could.

It wasn't hard to find the source of the yells and pleas.

It was only after Mary had left the room that she realized she was on the upper floor. She hadn't thought to check the window, which—thinking back—she probably should have been done. At least, she'd have a better understanding of where she was.

278

TOM COLEMAN

As Mary got closer, she realized that there was more than one person screaming. She reached the door to the room the women were in, and she peeked through the keyhole, shocked to her core by what she saw. There was a girl with her hands tied up over her head. She was so scared it brought back unwanted memories. Mary almost vomited on the spot at the sight of the woman. That look of abject fear on her face— Mary knew it incredibly well.

She staggered backward, making an involuntary sound. Upon realizing she'd messed up, she ran to hide behind a cabinet nearby.

Mary cursed herself when she heard the door to the room open. The worst thing she could do now was to try to get another peek or even move. She just had to stay still until whomever the man was went back inside.

After what felt like an eternity, the door closed. It was only then she noticed she'd been holding her breath.

Mary exhaled, happy to be out in the clear—at least, for the time being. The next thing was to save those women. They were definitely there against their will, and she wanted to save them from their oppressor.

She left her hiding place to see a man standing in front of her with a menacing glare. She startled, stumbled to the floor, and yelped. Here, she thought she'd outsmarted the man, but he had been the one to outsmart her.

Mary took a good look at the man, and she couldn't believe what she saw.

279

TOM COLEMAN

"Jonathan?" It was him. Definitely him. Either that or someone who was the spitting image of him that had existed fifty years ago. His blond hair and green eyes were a distinctive feature of the maniac who'd tormented her for a huge chunk of her life. He had the charming smile and eloquent diction to deceive girls—and people in general—into thinking he was a decent human being. If only they knew the monster behind that thick façade of apparent charm.

"Who the hell is that?" he inquired. Even his voice had an uncanny resemblance to Jonathan's. "And who the hell are you? Why are you dressed like that? Where did you come from?" There was a coldness to his glare that hinted she might be tortured or killed if she did not provide him with a plausible answer and fast. It would be better for her if she lied assertively than be tentative and tell him about her true situation.

"I…" the problem was that she couldn't think of a plausible lie.

He definitely locked his doors and windows if he was going to do stuff like that, and she did not have a sensible explanation for the way she was dressed. Did she even know how people dressed back in the seventies?

Mary sighed, thinking she might be dreaming. Maybe she'd wandered off to sleep on the couch, and this was all a big, bad dream.

"Look, I—"

TOM COLEMAN

A powerful and vicious slap brought her quickly back to reality. It was no fucking dream. The guy who looked like Jonathan was not playing at all. "I won't ask again," he added.

She observed that his knuckles were bloody. Had he punched those women? She guessed the man wasn't just similar to Jonathan when it came to looks.

"I don't know how I got here," she said, deciding to be honest. "I just found myself here. I'm not even from this timeline."

That seemed to pique the man's interest. "Timeline? What do you mean?" he asked. "Nah, never mind. You're most likely lying."

"I swear to God, I am not." Mary had to be as persuasive as possible. "Please, just let me go. I just want to get back to my kids."

"You have kids? That makes things interesting," he said, smiling. "How many?"

"T-two,"

The disappointment on his face was evident. "Fuck, I only kidnap from three and above," he said to himself, bringing his palm to his forehead. What the fuck did he mean by that?

Mary needed to escape and quickly, at that. She already knew what her best plan would be: run back through the closet. The man did not seem to know about the closet from where she had come, so she could just make a run for it and destroy the closet when she came out on the other side.

281

TOM COLEMAN

The main problem, however, was the man right in front of her. He didn't even look at her as he asked the questions.

"I wanna fucking know how you got into this house! My home!" He was getting agitated.

Mary heard the girls' voices screaming for help, and it set him off. He held Mary by the hair, and she could not help but feel déjà vu, given the number of times this had happened to her when she was with Jonathan. Mary groaned at the pain.

"You don't wanna answer me, huh? I'm gonna show you what happens to people who disobey me." He dragged her into the room.

She had to wait for the exact right time to stab the man and make a run for it. Mary wouldn't be able to save the girls, and she felt bad about it, but the situation was way beyond her. Besides, her first priority was her children, and she had to leave to be with them. To do that, however, she had to be alive.

The man threw her into a "dungeon"—at least, that was how she saw it: a dungeon of hell. She saw three women there. One of them kept sobbing, another one looked mentally broken, and the third was the one she'd seen through the keyhole. Mary was terrified of him and had bruises all over her hands and face.

"I need you to understand the kind of animal I am," he growled and gave Mary a huge backhand slap—Mary likened it to a punch—and it sent her to the ground. She was still conscious, but she had to act unconsciously, and she remained on the ground until she realized the horrific thing that was about to happen.

"Please, not again," the lady begged.

Was he?

Oh, God, no.

She could not make a run for it when another woman was suffering what she had suffered several times at the hands of her ex-boyfriend.

"Two kids is never enough. I only go after three and above, and you have four kids, don't you, Rhonda?".

Mary had to move. She needed to find the strength to stand up to the monster. She had the strength to run away, only this time she was going to have to face the monster and her trauma head-on. "Enough," she said to herself, getting up and charging at the psychopath, full speed.

CHAPTER THREE: YOU CAN'T ESCAPE

Mary ran at him as fast as she could. He was so focused on Rhonda, in front of him, that he did not notice Mary dodge her attack. She stabbed him between his ribs, causing him to fall and moan in pain.

She twisted the knife, pushing it deeply into him before pulling it out, figuring he would bleed out and die, doing the world a favor in the process.

Mary went to the woman which she just saved from Jonathan, but he punched her in the side of her head so hard, everything went black for a moment. When her consciousness slowly returned, it was to insults being thrown at her. Now was no time to worry about others. She did not have enough power to save them. The man was too strong. Mary knew from her own experience that she was much better at running than fighting. She was afraid, and she was neither good enough nor strong enough.

She remembered her kids, and it gave her the adrenaline necessary to push herself up from the floor and race out of the room.

"Get back here, bitch," she heard him call from behind her. "You can't escape me! You can't fucking escape!"

Her head was throbbing, but Mary did not care—her kids needed her. As she ran, Mary remembered those three words, the exact same words Jonathan said to her when she tried to run away from him.

Was the man his father or something?

Enough of that, Mary thought. She had to clear her head and run as fast as she could.

Mary reached the room with the closet, still hearing the man yell at her. She noticed the windows in the room were barred—this guy was really a sicko!

She rushed the closet, and just as she had begun to climb in, Mary was pulled back.

It was him. His eyes had a menacing glare with which she was very familiar.

Mary kicked him in the face, sending him stumbling back. She climbed back into the, closed the doors behind her, and the next thing she knew, she was falling back into her kids' room. She quickly closed the closet behind her and grabbed a hammer from the corner of the room. She had told Brian repeatedly to stop playing with something as dangerous as a hammer, but now, Mary was grateful because her son find out where she hid the hammer and put it in his room.

She took a deep breath and bashed the closet over and over again. Mary didn't care about the clothes or whatever else might be inside. All she knew was that she had to destroy the thing. Her heart beat faster, and she wondered if her assailant would come through the closet after her, so she ran downstairs as fast as she could to get some kerosene. She ran back with a

TOM COLEMAN

pack of matches and poured some kerosene on the now broken closet. Mary was still reeling from what had happened to her and she was not about to leave anything to chance. She lit a match and threw it on the broken closet, setting it on fire. When she was done, she ran to the kitchen to retrieve the fire extinguisher from under the sink, and used it to put out the fire. to put out the fire.

Only after the closet had been burned to nothing more than a pile of ash did Mary allow herself to breathe. She panted heavily, still in shock while looking at all other stuff that was destroyed from fire, the floor, carpet and walls.

What the hell was that?

A time portal?

Did those things actually exist?

Once she'd finally caught her breath, she went downstairs to check her phone for the time. Upon reaching the living room, her phone rang. She picked it up to see that her ordeal hadn't lasted as long as she thought.

The number of the caller was unknown, but she picked it up anyway, hoping to get her mind off what had just occurred.

"You. Can't. Escape." The three words sent shivers down to her very core. The voice was that of the man she had just encountered.

"Leave me alone."

" I will always find you."

TOM COLEMAN

Mary heard it coming from the phone, but she also heard it coming from behind her. She was scared to turn around. Her knees were weak.

If it was really Jonathan behind her, she wasn't ready to face that reality.

"Turn around. I want to see the fear in your eyes, my wife," the voice continued.

Mary cut the connection and tried to run, but he knew her too well. He placed his leg in her path, and she tripped over it and stumbled to the ground.

"Do you have any idea how long I have waited to have this conversation with you, Mary?"

She looked up to see it really was Jonathan. He was wearing this sickening smile as he walked toward her. "After you stabbed me all those years ago, I tried to run after you, but when I entered the closet, something was wrong."

Mary couldn't believe it. Was he saying that he was—

No, that couldn't be right.

"Oh, the look on your stupid face is priceless." Jonathan laughed. "Remember this injury you asked me about when we first met? You were twenty-one at the time, right?"

It was slowly becoming clear to Mary what was going on, but she still didn't want to believe it. "What are you saying exactly, Jonathan?"

"Wait—Where are the kids?"

TOM COLEMAN

Mary snapped. She still had her penknife with her, having pulled it out of the Jonathan from the past.

It was him. Based on what he was saying, that had been *him*.

"Stay the hell away from my kids."

Jonathan looked at her, confused. "Your kids? You mean to say you made them alone?"

"Were you the man I stabbed in 1977?" She tried to put up a strong front, but to be honest, Mary was terrified.

"Yeah, but something happened when I entered the closet in which you escaped, and I got transported to another time: 2006. I had a score to settle with you, so I searched for you until I found you. You experienced time out of order. Until I figured that out, I never even knew time travel was possible."

"Jesus." She was flabbergasted. "What happened to those women? Are you a serial killer?"

"I guess you could use that term. I have a particular type, though. The mothers... they have to learn."

"Is that why you never told me about your mother or father or family?"

"Yes, of course. I wanted you to fall in love with me. I followed you from your teenage years to now. I had to learn the new stuff and way things worked in this era, but that wasn't too hard. I've managed to kill a lot of people, too, and evade the police while doing so."

"Are you saying that you kept killing, even when we were together?"

"Definitely." He licked his lips. "

"You… are a true animal," she said, trying to stay composed. "A monster."

"You have no idea how long I waited. I needed you to have three kids before I killed you. It's better that way. It hits the parallels well. Women are worthless once they become mothers. They forget their kids and beat them and turn them into broken individuals."

Mary sensed his insanity had been borne from an unstable childhood, but that was no reason or excuse. He was a serial rapist and murderer, and now, he had targeted her. He needed to die.

"I just needed you to have one more kid for me and then I would have been justified in ending your stupid life. Beating you up was just to cool my anger for sending me to a different time. How did you manage that, by the way?"

It must have happened when she'd broken the closet then burned it. Mary had no intention of explaining to him, however. She was planning on killing the guy, here and now.

"Shut the fuck up!" Mary yelled as she lunged at Jonathan.

He was paying attention, and he dodged her swipe and swung a punch at her.

She spat in his face and hit him in the neck.

TOM COLEMAN

Jonathan coughed as he clutched his neck, and he moved backward, trying to regain his balance.

"You... fucking... b—"

Mary wasn't going to let him finish. All her fears— when she thought she was being watched, when she was taking care of her kids, when she'd endured beatings from the monster, and now, finding out he was a serial rapist and killer. She thought it was only her, but there had been other women, as well.

"I ran before, leaving those women behind, but this time, I won't run." She tackled him and tried to stab him in the chest, but a huge blow on her nose hit her hard. Mary was about to fall backward, but then she didn't. She had been hit so many times that she was used to it.

Jonathan grabbed the hand holding the penknife.

"I will end you," he growled. What he didn't see was the hammer behind her back.

She pulled it out and bashed him over the head with it. The claw bored deep into his skull.

He looked shocked.

Mary looked him dead in the eyes and said, "This is for them, for Sarah and Brian, and me."

TOM COLEMAN

THE CURSE OF HERNANDEZ PART FOUR

291

TOM COLEMAN

292

TOM COLEMAN

CHAPTER SEVEN: HOPE

Carlos sighed. He looked at the ceiling, exhausted. All he wanted was to leave that house, but in his exhaustion, a part of him was resigned to simply wait for the demons or ghouls or whatever they were to take his life. He could not take it anymore. Whatever the house was, it was too much for him, but being tricked into thinking they had left the house… that had been the breaking point.

"It's the hope that kills you, isn't it, babe?" his wife said to him. Carlos had almost forgotten she was by his side. He turned to face her. She was smiling, her eyes still filled with hope. How could she be so optimistic in their hopeless situation? They were in the attic, the hotbed of scary shit in the house, so why was she relaxed?

Carlos felt a hand creep into his, and he was scared at first, but then he looked to see it was her warmth soothing him.

"It's just me," she said after noticing his fears.

"How can you be so… not broken?" He needed to know. Someone could not be that amazing. Christina was almost always happy, upbeat, and optimistic, but this? No way. He needed to understand how and why she was not as

293

dejected as him. "Even if you aren't exhausted, at least be scared. They could kill us at any moment."

"Are you scared?" she asked with a smile. Was this a dream? Is that why she was smiling that much? Carlos asked himself these questions because he could not for the life of him understand how Christina was not as distraught as he was if not more.

"Well... no."

"Why not?" Christina asked. It struck Carlos as an interesting question. He had been scared a moment ago—why wasn't he still terrified?

"I'm terrified," Christina added, and Carlos was shocked. "I know it doesn't look like it, but I am shaking in my boots." She leaned closer to him and rested her head on his shoulder. "But you know what gives me hope and keeps me from giving up? You know why I am scared?" She squeezed his hand even tighter. "The answer is simple: you."

"I don't know if I am strong enough to give you hope. I'm not even sure I have any hope left in me, and if there is a little left, it'll be gone soon."

"Don't say that." Christina gave him a stern look. He could see that she wasn't a fan of his current behavior, but he didn't have any fight left in him. Carlos knew that wasn't completely true. As long as he had her by his side, there was no way he would lose the will. A part of him just wished he could just give up.

He'd been waiting for the ghosts to arrive, but there was no sign of them yet. Maybe they were already there and

TOM COLEMAN

watching him and Christina, cackling all the while. Carlos just wanted the pain to end, and by pain, he didn't mean only the physical, but the psychological. Maybe his brain was just scorched after all the attacks it endured since they'd entered that stupid house. He wasn't even as mad at the house now as he had been earlier, which was telling about his mental state.

"Gosh," Carlos said, resting his forehead on his palm. He was close to tears. "I just can't… I'm… enough…" He couldn't formulate the words.

Christina held him close as he rested his head on her bosom, trying to compose himself.

"I know. I know," she said, smoothing his hair, "but we can't die like this. There is still too much for us to do together for me to let all that go. If they are going to kill us, they will have to do it with us fighting to the end. At least, we'll be together, right? What could trump that?"

"Being alive together?" Carlos replied, and they both chuckled. It was good that he could still smile in a situation like that. He raised his head and looked at her. Christina lit up like a lamp in the dark, showing him the way when he was lost.

"I love you so much," he confessed as he regularly did to his wife.

She smiled. "I love you, too."

"Well, isn't that cute?" a voice said, butting into their conversation. It was a woman with spiky hair. From what Carlos could tell, her hair was more unkempt than spikey. She was smiling from ear to ear… literally. Her eyes were completely white, unlike when he'd seen her before, and Carlos wondered if the place had somehow enhanced her demonic capabilities.

They knew it was the end. The fear came back. However, Carlos welcomed the fear this time because it meant he wanted to live. Being scared of death was a good thing; it meant you wanted to be alive.

" You're not going to kill us. Bring it on.," Christina said, clutching tightly to Carlos.

"It's okay, Christina," Carlos murmured. "I can't believe I forgot they can't really harm us physically."

"You are what you believe you are," the ghost said, sitting down to face them. In an instant, they were surrounded by what looked like an inordinate number of ghosts.

"Why… why are you doing this to us?" Christina asked.

"We aren't doing anything to you," the woman ghost said. "You are doing this to yourselves."

"What the hell does that even mean?"

"You'll see soon." The ghosts laughed creepily.

Carlos and Christina frowned. They looked around, confused. Carlos still did not understand a single thing about the house. It was hard to understand, and the more he thought about it, the less Carlos understood about what was going on there. He did, however, know some unmistakable truths. First, the ghosts really had a foothold after the suitcase had been opened and thrown away. Next, the house fed on their memories, using them to torment them. Also, neither the ghosts nor the house could harm them physically, as far as he knew. Lastly, the only way he knew to stop the mess was to leave the house and get the suitcase, which was impossible at that very moment.

"I still don't understand why you are all here. You are ghosts, aren't you? Shouldn't you be at peace in the afterlife or something?" Christina's question indicated she wasn't quite sure of how things worked with regard to what happened when someone died, either, but she was curious as to why the house was like that. Carlos concurred. The demons were horrific creatures, but what made them that way? Why were they so hellbent on inflicting pain on like that?

"Come and play with us," one of the ghosts said.

"You can't leave," another voice stated.

"Come!"

"Come!"

"Here!"

"Over here!" Everyone called them as if they were snacks to be devoured.

The couple held each other's hands tightly and prepared for the worst.

"Remember, Christina," Carlos said, taking swallowing the lump building at the back of his throat as he awaited their attack. "Whatever happens, we can take it—"

TOM COLEMAN

"As long as we are together," she said, finishing his statement. Carlos was glad to know they were on the same page.

"Yes, my love. As long as we are together, we c—"

***

Christina opened her eyes. She was in a field of many eggs. Christina had no idea what was in the eggs, and she was not curious to find out. She knew it was yet another illusion and that their real bodies were still in the attic. She also had to keep in mind that her husband was probably having his own attack and trying to defend himself to get back to her. The ghosts would do anything in their power to keep them from leaving the house, but now that they knew more about the limitations, maybe they could fight and escape.

"Your attempts won't work on me anymore," Christina said to the air. She could not see anything but the eggs far into the horizon.

One of the eggs started to crack. This gave her pause, but Christina knew she had to stay still and remain calm. She watched as the egg cracked open, and from it came a little child, a girl, wearing a dress.

"What the fuck?" Christina was taken aback by the fact that it was a girl, no more than five years old. "Wh... what... why are you... what is this?"

298

TOM COLEMAN

The girl was slimy after coming out, but her face was clean. She stared at Christina, and the words that came out of her mouth horrified the woman to her core: "Hi, Mommy."

Mommy? Christina was confused. Why would the little girl think she was her mother? This attack did not seem like it was from Christina's memories because she did not have any children.

"Who are you?"

"Don't you recognize me, Mommy?" the girl asked, a crazed look in her eyes. "You don't deserve me, Mommy. You killed Susan—why do you think you do deserve to have us?"

"Us?" Christina was starting to get a bit rattled. She could tell what part of her psyche this horror was coming from, and she did not like it. Christina had wanted a family all of her life. She wanted to be a great parent and marry a man who would be a great parent, as well, because her parents hadn't been the best.

"Yes, Mommy—us," the girl said as the other eggs began to crack open.

"Oh, God," Christina said, realizing what was about to happen. "Get out of my head! Leave me be," she screamed, getting scared. Children of all racial backgrounds with different features came out of the eggs. They all looked scared and deformed in some way.

"This is what everything that comes out of your womb will be like, Mommy."

"No."

TOM COLEMAN

"Because you do not deserve a normal child. We will all be as disfigured like Susan was after you hit her," they said in unison.

"Nooo!" Christina screamed. She turned and ran, but the creepy kids chased her. Some of them had enlarged. Others had one eye and a gaping black hole where the other should be. Christina did not want those "things" anywhere near her.

"All hope is lost, Mommy. Come and play with us, Mommy. We will chase and consume you, Mommy," they recited between laughs. "Give up!"

"Why? Why? Why? Why? Why?" she asked, confused at how the house was always able to hit where it really hurt. Christina had always feared she would not be a good enough mother because she had not been raised by a good mother, but being slapped right in her face by that reality in such a revolting way was enough to make her—or anybody, for that matter—crack.

"Mommy!" she heard a particularly screechy voice say from behind her. Christina did not look back. Instead, she kept running. She ran as fast as she could.

"Play with us, Mommy." One of the children, a boy, grabbed hold of his leg, causing her to tumble to the ground. In no time, the menagerie of ghastly kids had jumped on top of her, laughing and making incoherent sounds.

Amid the noise, Christina was able to make out a clear voice: "You didn't love us. You can never love children because you a killer of children." The voice grew louder and sterner, its words boring deep into Christina's psyche. She was about to have a panic attack. Christina could see nothing but darkness as the bodies kept piling up on top of her. The slime on their skin rubbed against her face and body, and the smell was atrocious. She could barely breathe, and for a time, she considered giving up.

Maybe they were right. Maybe the house could see deeply into her and know she would be a horrible mother. What right did she have to be happy with kids when she had deprived a family of theirs, causing a family of three to turn into an individual of one? Did she really think karma wouldn't eventually catch up with her?

"I... I..." A part of her wanted to throw in the towel, but then Christina remembered the conversation she'd had with her husband, but the man she'd married and had always seen as a pinnacle of solidity was breaking down before her eyes. She supported him and gave him the strength he needed to carry on.

"I'd be a hypocrite if I didn't do the same," Christina said, giving herself the power to keep moving forward. She knew there was no chance she could overpower so many children to push them off of her, but she didn't have to. It was all a dream.

Christina used to think that knowing this was the solution, but it was only half of it. Overcoming her fear and guilt was the only way she would truly defeat these nightmares. She knew that now, and that was the key thing that just might get them out of there alive.

"I am a good person who has done bad things. I am not perfect, but no one is," the lady said to herself, calm as can be. She took deep breaths to soothe herself, nullifying the panic attack. "I will be a good mother and have good children. I

TOM COLEMAN

can't give up now because of this." Christina could only imagine what Carlos might do if he came back from his nightmare to find she had given up. He would most likely lose himself to the house.

Instead of fighting the waves of children on top of her, Christina gave in, sucked herself into the floor, and came out on the other side.

She was back in the attic.

TOM COLEMAN

CHAPTER EIGHT: ESCAPE

Carlos turned to see his wife had passed out on the floor. The ghosts had probably put her inside another illusion. He was worried, but he also knew she could not handle it herself. His job now was to hold his ground, no matter what they did to him.

He could no longer see the ghosts, and Carlos wondered where had they gone. He decided to pick up Christina and make a run for it, but—

Wait!

What if this was a nightmare sequence in itself? It had happened before, when he thought he had gone to work, but in reality, he hadn't left the house.

The Silhouette Man appeared in front of him. "It's easier to believe an illusion when you want it to be real, isn't it?" He was the one illusion Carlos legitimately feared due to his past experience with the fiend.

"Your tricks won't work on me anymore," Carlos said to the quiet, mysterious figure who was standing roughly two meters away from him. If he were to be honest, Carlos would rather do without the pain coming from that thing's black liquid, but if that were the only way to escape, he would endure it.

TOM COLEMAN

"This isn't real," Carlos said, calming his nerves. In a flash, the atmosphere changed, and Carlos knew that he had escaped whatever illusion he had been in. The real attic was exactly the same as it had been before the veil had cleared, but Carlos could feel the difference. This was reality, and the Silhouette Man was between him and the exit. Carlos knew it would be hard enough getting away if he was alone, but with his wife? Carlos was definitely not willing to risk her like that. The fact that she was unconscious made it impossible for him to take her with him. His best course of action was to go outside, suffer it alone, and come back with the suitcase. She was in her own illusion, so he could go and be back before Christina had even noticed he was gone... hopefully.

"You'd better wake up, baby," Carlos whispered to his beloved. He needed her to defeat whatever mental demons she was facing and come back to him. He also had to endure whatever came his way to get the suitcase so he could also get back to her.

"I don't suppose you would be kind enough to let me leave with my wife?"

The Silhouette Man responded by opening his mouth wide—wider than before.

Carlos sighed, bracing himself. "Worth a shot.

"Christina, I'll see you when I get back," he said and ran straight for the Silhouette Man, whose liquid landed on him. So much came from the ghost's mouth, and with so much force, it sent Carlos back a few steps.

TOM COLEMAN

He felt instant pain. Had he imagined it, or was the pain greater than before? Carlos swore. He could barely move.

The Silhouette Man stood in front of him as he writhed on the floor. His insides felt as if they were burning up because they were full of acid.

Carlos knew his main obstacle: the nature of pain. The problem with pain was that it was in the mind as much as it was in the body. People think pain is mostly physical, but some people in the world don't feel or register pain in the mind or body. If a person injures his foot but does not register it in his mind, his body will continue to deteriorate, and the person won't seek treatment. Carlos knew this applied to his situation, as well. The fact that he could feel and register the pain meant it would always be real for him. Given his memories, it was easier to detach from the illusion because there would not be physical repercussions, but The Silhouette Man was different. His pain ground its way deep into the very marrow of a person until he couldn't help but give in to the pain and accept it as a reality.

Carlos Hernandez was not, however, ready to let the ghost win. He struggled while dragging himself past the Silhouette Man. He knew the ghost could not actually inflict physical harm on him, but it felt as if he was already in an immense amount of pain. Carlos knew he had to keep going, no matter what. Stopping was not an option; he had a wife to save, a future to preserve, and a house to defeat.

"Mooove!" Carlos crawled right through the Silhouette Man. "Stand up!" He yelled, struggling to get up while crawling. Carlos could see the exit, and he knew the ladder would lead him down. Honestly, with the pain he felt, it would be impossible to climb down. He knew the only thing he could do was fall. That would also hurt, and it wouldn't be just an illusion. It would be real. That, coupled with the hurt he'd still feel after what the Silhouette Man had done to him, would be unbearable.

As Carlos reached the exit, and the acid in him spread to his brain. He found it hard to see clearly now that the pain had seeped into him. Even though he knew it was all a lie, Carlos could have sworn the acid was melting his bones and corroding some of his organs. It was hell.

The attacked man pushed himself down from the attic and to the floor below it. He landed with a loud thump and groaned. It was all too much—had he reached his limit?

"Someone… help," Carlos yelled, unable to stand. From the way it felt, his shoulder might be dislocated. His body was still tearing itself up from the inside, or that was how it felt. His head throbbed as well. He was bleeding from the forehead.

"Is… this… it?" He wondered if this was his nadir, the final blow in the series of hits he had endured since he'd entered the house. His body had given way, and he could no longer fathom the pain. He wanted to blackout, but he also wanted to fight. His mind was growing numb, and for a split second, Carlos entered a state of calm. It was quiet within that calm. The pain was the only thing left. Carlos Hernandez's mind wondered about all the possible things that could happen to him if he died or let the house take over.

TOM COLEMAN

"Mother… Christina… Rosa," these words left his mouth just as his eyes were about to close. "Family." An image of the people he loved appeared inside his mind— Mother with her worried but warm look; Rosa and her cute smile; and Christina, brandishing her beaming smile.

"I have no business letting it stop here." Carlos got up, much to his own surprise. The pain had gotten lighter for some reason, or maybe it was his mental resolve that had strengthened. He was bleeding from the head and had a dislocated shoulder, and that didn't account for whatever internal damage that had taken place.

The ghosts appeared in front of him as he walked away, but he had tunnel vision and barely registered them. Carlos finally understood the house. He had the power. Since everything happening to him was dependent upon his mental state, he was the real ruler of anything involving him.

"You're just tools being used by this horrible house. I don't even hate you anymore," he said, dragged himself through the cloud of ghosts. No matter how much they made scary faces, no matter what they said, Carlos did not care.

"*I am leaving this house with my wife,*" he said, refusing to allow his conviction to waver.

The Silhouette Man spit out a large amount of black mucus on Carlos from behind. The amount was so great that it carried Carlos through the hallway and down the stairs to the ground floor. By the time Carlos had landed, his skin was corroded, and he could not hear due to the irritation and anguish he felt.

TOM COLEMAN

There was mucus in his mouth, and he coughed out. The black fluid was all over his body. Standing up should have been impossible. Carlos didn't mind dying, but he knew his only real injuries the dislocated shoulder and his throbbing forehead.

"What did I do to deserve this?" he asked, taking a moment to calm down and let the pain in. The more he fought the mucus, the more painful it became, so there was no point in fighting.

Carlos took a deep breath, got up, and continued his slow drag to the door. He could see a bit now in one eye after getting used to the pain, so he was able to watch as the lights flickered and the ghosts surrounded him yet again.

"Why can't you just let me fucking go?" He let his frustration get the better of him, and the mucus inside him roasted him further. Carlos fell to the ground and screamed in terror as the mucus turned into gasoline that lit and set him on fire.

Carlos could only muster a groan as the fire burned viciously. Immolation was statistically the worst way to die, and he was seeing exactly why first hand. The pain was unimaginable, but Carlos knew it wouldn't kill him. It was hard to concentrate while on fire, but he had to calm down so they wouldn't win. This house was going all out with its attacks as he neared the exit.

"Just give in," one ghost said.

"It must hurt so," another one said.

TOM COLEMAN

Carlos's skin suppurated, even though he knew it really wasn't. His tongue and eyes gave the sensation of splitting open, slowly and excruciatingly. At that point, it would be hard to convince him his body was not completely aflame, but he had to convince himself.

"It's... fake!" Carlos struggled to speak through his scorched lips. "All... lies!" He fought until his conviction slowly crept back into his psyche. The burning man felt the heat of the flames cool as his mind and heart cooled. He knew he had to stay calm and be at ease, which was easier said than done, considering the situation.

The fire reduced as it cooled, and Carlos heard several voices, most of which he could not make out. They sounded as if they were complaining, maybe because he'd finally overcome the mucus.

He focused on the ghosts around him, and he could tell they were shocked. Some seemed even... happy? What the hell? Why were they smiling? Was that another trick? They kept quiet and paved the way for him to leave, but then the house reacted.

"Is it angry?" Carlos wondered as the doors banged and everything shook. He couldn't wait for the flames on him to completely die out before leaving the house. The house was angry, and he had to leave.

Still on fire, Carlos Hernandez dragged himself as quickly as he could, considering the huge amount of pain he endured. All that rested on his mind was the door before him. The rumbling around him was as irrelevant as the demons. As

309

TOM COLEMAN

far as Carlos was concerned, everything would be better once he'd left the house.

Carlos opened the door. The hurt he felt forcing the door open was inexplicable.

The house was fought him as it tried to stop him from opening the door and leaving.

"C'mon… give me a breeeeeeaak," He said while forcing the door open. Tears leaked from his eyes, thanks to his pain, but it was worth it. The door opened, and Carlos Hernandez fell across the threshold. The fire went out, and the pain disappeared save that in his shoulder and head. Carlos laid on the ground, face down, not wanting to get up. All he wanted to do was rest.

"But I can't," he said, struggling to get up. His legs shook vigorously as he struggled to maintain balance though he was on his last legs.

Just how many ghosts were in that house? How long had the house been torturing people? Were the ghosts people who had lived there? These questions and more bothered Carlos.

He brushed that to the back of his mind and carried on to the trash can. Carlos felt he should have been dead ten times over. His blood covered part of his eyes and his left shoulder, and he used his right hand to supported it to minimize the pain.

Carlos Hernandez reached the trash and opened it with great difficulty. He was tired and sore. He groaned while opening it and fell to the floor the moment he flipped it open.

TOM COLEMAN

"If I survive this, I'm gonna need some sick therapy," he mused, but Carlos knew that nobody would ever believe such a story. How did one live after an experience like that? He could not think about that now—he had to get the suitcase and go back to the house to save his wife.

Carlos got up and checked to see if the suitcase was still there or if it had burned. To his relief, it was perfectly intact. If the suitcase had been burned to a crisp, he didn't know what he would have done.

He reached in and used all of his power to pull out the suitcase and fell to the ground. Frustrated, Carlos punched the ground. "Fuck! Just how much pain can a man fucking take?" Carlos screamed. He understood that shouting wouldn't solve anything, and he tried again. This time, Carlos succeeded in dragging out the suitcase. The easy part was now done; but now he was facing the hard part.

"Here we go again," Carlos said, rushing back into the hell from which he had just escaped.

He heard a loud scream from the attic—it was Christina.

"She's awake!" Part of him was glad she had overcome her nightmare, but it was not a good scream, and that was what worried him.

He ran back into that haunted house of horrors to try to put an end to the hellish home.

(To be continued…)

TOM COLEMAN

TOM COLEMAN

POSSESSED

313

TOM COLEMAN

TOM COLEMAN

CHAPTER ONE: RUNNING

Ruth Mercer waited impatiently in the area. It had been a while since she had seen him, and after what had happened, she was even more worried. Frank had refused to see her for the past three months, and this bothered her. All she wanted was for him to be better, and she cared about him a lot.

The doctor walked over to her, and she got up quickly. "Is everything okay, doctor?" she asked, clutching her bag.

The doctor smiled at her, and this managed to relieve some of her initial fears. "He is fine. He almost overdosed, though. We are still confused as to how he was able to get his hands on the drugs he used."

"You guys have to find out how this happened." Ruth was pissed. They should have done their job in keeping him restrained or keeping the drugs out of his reach.

"We will, Mrs. Mercer."

"Please, do," she said. "Can I see him?"

"Sure. Follow me."

Ruth hurried to see Frank, partly wanting to berate the shit out of him but mostly just wanting to hug her kid brother.

***

Franklin Mercer was trying to stay calm. He was still weak from the drugs he'd taken, but he was conscious. His hand was cuffed to the iron side of the bed. He knew they would never understand. They'd all think he was crazy, anyway. Maybe the warden would finally get annoyed and send him to a psychiatric hospital, not that it would solve the problem. He would rather die there than go back to being haunted by the thing that had haunted him for most of his life. His life was a waste now; the Smiling Lady made sure of it. He could not get better, and he had destroyed the few relationships he'd had with friends or family—whatever was left of his family. All that was left was for him to die. At least, in death, he would not be haunted anymore. Frank just wanted to rest, once and for all.

The door opened, and Dr. Chin—or as Frank liked to address him, Dr. Douchebag—came into the room. A guard was watching him inside the rehab facility's med bay, and Frank was grateful for that. The last thing he needed was to be left alone. He knew what happened when he was alone.

"Hey, Dr. Doucheb..." his voice trailed off, and his eyes widened when he saw Ruth enter the room. She looked scared for him, and that was more painful than any physical pain he had ever suffered. She was the only person in

316

TOM COLEMAN

the world who still tried to reach out to him, no matter what he did or said. He never wanted to disappoint her, but he knew that was precisely what he would do, so Frank tried to push her away and had said hurtful things many times, but nothing did the trick. Even when she got angry and stormed away, Ruth always came back.

"Ruth…" He didn't know what to say.

"Can you give us a moment alone, please?"

Just hearing the word made his heart tense up. He never wanted to be alone. He'd suffered enough, needing the drugs just to keep the demons away. Frank didn't want to scare his sister, however, so he tried to remain calm.

"Sure, Mrs. Mercer," Dr. Chin said, and he left with the guard.

There was silence. Neither of them spoke for what felt like an eternity, and it was killing Frank. He closed his eyes, trying to avoid her gaze.

"Why?" she said. He heard the quivering in her voice from that one word. Frank opened his eyes and looked at her. She was shedding tears, and it broke him.

"I can't even apologize because I know you're tired of hearing it," he remarked.

Ruth sat down on the chair next to his bed and placed her hand on his.

317

"I know you never said I was lying when I told you about my... issues, ever since Mom and Dad died, but you also never said you believed me."

"Is that what you want me to do? If I say I believe you, will you stop trying to kill yourself?" He heard her getting a bit irritated. What he'd said had not come out the way he'd wanted it to. He didn't mean for it to sound like he was blaming her. "I always wanted to ask you this, but I was afraid of how you might answer, but am I not enough to make you want to live?"

"You have always been enough, Ruth," he replied swiftly. "I am still amazed that after everything I have done, you are still here. I'm sure Derrick isn't too fond of your still coming here."

"He is frustrated, I'll admit, but he does worry about you. I think he is more concerned about how my distressing over you has affected my mental health."

The worst thing Frank could think of being was a burden, and that was precisely what he was. "I know I said apologizing was pointless, but I am sorry for being the worst brother ever."

"I will always love you and never leave you. Please, all I ask is that you don't leave me, too." That hit close to home for Frank. He had never thought of it that way. To him, she never needed him, and he was a negative in her life. He was the one afraid of being left alone by her. That was also his greatest fear: loneliness.

Then, he heard the sound, that screeching sound similar to a metal chair being dragged against the floor. He squinted his eyes and pressed his lips together at the sound.

Ruth must've picked up on what that meant after seeing him go through it several times, beginning around the time their parents had died. "I'm here, Frank. I am with you. She won't come near you when I am here, whatever that Smiling Lady is."

He was no longer focused on Ruth. The drugs were wearing off, and he knew she was coming. Frank was becoming fully sober again, and from the corner of the room, he heard that screeching sound, which was actually her sinister laugh. A tall figure with weird limb proportions, it was the face of that spirit that always caused Frank's fear to seep in. The smile on the face of the disfigured woman with long, black hair was wide and bloody as if her mouth had been slit open on the sides.

"I...I..." He had trouble breathing. What was she going to do to him? He always either did what she wanted, took drugs, or ran away whenever she came around. That was his coping mechanism.

"Listen to me, Frank," Ruth said to her brother, slapping him lightly on the face to get him to listen. "You have to calm down. As long as I am here, you know that nothing will happen. You need to get better. Whatever these visions are that you see, they could be the remnants of the drugs, or it could really be the ghost you always speak of, but it doesn't

TOM COLEMAN

matter. Those things do not have power over you unless you allow them to.

"Breathe, okay? In and out." It was not the first time Ruth had coached him on his breathing. He'd almost suffocated once when he hadn't realized he was holding his breath because of the Smiling Lady.

"In… and out. You remember, right?" Ruth smiled, trying to calm him down and put his mind at ease.

Frank remembered how it went, so he followed her instructions. His sequential breathing mimicking hers brought him back to a sense of normalcy—the young man's version of normalcy, anyway, which was being an addict, which wasn't really normal.

"You're fine, now."

Frank gazed back at where the Smiling Lady was, but she was gone. "No, I'm not," he said, tired and exhausted from life.

Ruth frowned at him. "Why do you have to keep fucking blaming yourself for everything without trying to get better?" she snapped.

"You think I'm not trying? You just don't understand!" Frank was angry that he was so helpless and at the mercy of a stronger power. He didn't want to be like that, but it was the reality he was forced to face, having been haunted by ghosts all of his life and having to distract himself with all sorts of things instead of facing his problem. "After the accident, I started seeing her everywhere. I tried… I really did, but I just could not and still can't. She just won't go away. She whispers into my ear at night, constantly reinforcing the fact that she will never leave." He was getting teary-eyed, relaying how he felt.

"I have no friends. My only family member who cares about me and is willing to put up with my bullshit is doing so to the detriment of her own mental health and relationships. All of my goals washed down the drain when the Smiling Lady came into my life. I can't keep living like this." He held her hand tightly and looked at her pleadingly. "Please, let me die." Frank could see that his sister was shocked and appalled at the plea, but he did not care. He would not survive another night with his demons.

"No," she said calmly, and he sighed. "Have you ever considered actually facing this minacious Smiling Lady instead of running away from her all your life?" she asked. "Running from your problems will not do anything. You are just prolonging your pain… and mine." Frank knew it was the truth, even though a part of him hated it. The Mercer siblings were inseparable. He knew that Ruth was sad and annoyed that they had to endure her brother's issues, which were beyond his control, though he was at fault.

And Frank? He was sad and annoyed at himself and the fact that she always absorbed his pain alongside him. Even though Ruth would never understand the sheer horror of being haunted from your early teenage years to full-fledged

TOM COLEMAN

adulthood, she was still his sister, and she felt her own version of the pain.

TOM COLEMAN

CHAPTER TWO: TRAUMA

Ruth left because she had something important to do, but she was not happy, as evidenced by the silent treatment she'd given him. Right now, there was almost nothing left in Frank. He couldn't afford to be tortured anymore. He dreaded the night because he knew what came with it, but soon, the night inevitably came.

Frank Mercer laid on his bed. His roommate was fast asleep, but Frank found it hard to sleep. Whenever he slept, he had nightmares about the day of the car crash. That had been the day he'd made the worst mistake of his life.

He heard a sound and jumped to a sitting position. It was dark—as was the procedure in the facility—so Frank really could not see much. He could put on the lights, but Frank knew better by then.

"There's no point," he said as if talking to someone. "You'll just render the bulbs useless until you are done messing with me." What Ruth had said about confronting his demons remained at the back of his mind. He had been thinking about it all day. The reason he feared facing the Smiling Lady before was that he did not want to die. He wanted to keep fighting, but he was afraid the demon wanted to kill him. Now, though, he had no qualms about dying, so he might as well go out fighting, right?

"Just come out," he said, trying to summon the courage.

He held his breath, and everything went completely silent. Even the sound of the fan had stopped, though it continued to move. There was also a stench in the air he hadn't smelled before. Every time the Smiling Lady attacked, there was something new that hadn't been present the time before. This time, it was the smell.

"What the hell?" he murmured to himself, trying to endure the smell. In a flash, Frank's head landed on the floor with a thud as if he'd been pushed. He got up, squinting from the pain.

"If you're gonna fucking kill me, why don't you do it? I am not scared of death anymore!"

His roommate slept like a log, so Frank wasn't surprised he hadn't been woken up yet.

Frank saw the glow of the Smiling Lady's aura at the door. It was as if she were telling him to follow her. Frank no longer cared. He might as well let her finish him.

He made his way out of the room and into the dour, empty hallway. For some reason, Frank saw parallels between himself and the empty hallway. His soul was filled with ennui, maybe because the long-lasting creature had been

TOM COLEMAN

feeding on anything good he'd ever had. It just took and took and took.

"And now, you're gonna take me," he said, getting chills from the cold air surrounding him. The smell returned, and the younger Mercer sibling closed his eyes. Was this going to be the time he finally dies? Frank wondered. He opened his eyes to see the Smiling Lady standing opposite him in the hallway.

"I'm not running anymore." He tried to look certain, but deep down, he was diffident and frightened by the idea of dying. The Smiling Lady obviously knew this since she had soaked deep into his psyche.

To his horror, the ghoul ran at him at an insane speed, covering him with its aura and enveloping him in a black shroud. The next thing he saw was his childhood home. Frank was perplexed as he watched a younger version of him and Ruth playing around the house.

"Ruth," he said with a grin, noting how happy she was.

"Ruth! Stop letting your brother sway you to roam about the house." He'd recognize that voice anywhere and anytime.

Mom came down the stairs with a disapproving look on her face, but as soon as he saw her, her face began to melt.

TOM COLEMAN

"What... what is this?" he asked, watching in disgust as the image of his mother became disfigured as it melted to the ground.

The environment changed, and he was in a blood-laden bathroom. In the corner of the room was the Smiling Lady. That smile... the way blood exuded from the torn edges of her lips was eerie and unsettling.

"What do you want from me?" Frank yelled. "Please, just let me go. You got me to cause their deaths, and you have been tormenting me ever since. I thought you were gonna fucking end me, but instead, you are just... what the fuck are you even doing? "

The screech in the bathroom grew so loud it caused Frank to fall to the floor, clutching his ears. He screamed in agony as his earbuds bled from the sheer force of the sound. Amid the painful scream, he heard the Smiling Lady speak to him. It was not the first time it had happened, but it didn't happen often, either. "You... set... me... free," the demoness ground her terrible voice into his brain. "You... belong... to... me. "

Frank yelled in agony. He prayed for a helper—anyone... anybody... anything: drugs, Ruth, Mom, Dad. "Please, just let me go, " Frank begged as the voice tore into him... and then it stopped.

Frank panted as if he had just run a mile, but he was grateful the pain had stopped. He opened his eyes to see

326

TOM COLEMAN

that he was in a field. On further inspection, he realized it was not a field; it was his childhood backyard.

Frank got up and noticed a boy playing with a voodoo doll. He knew what it was, and he did not want to see it. "Why are you doing this?" he inquired. "Get me out of here!" The boy was him. Young Frank spoke to the doll. Behind the doll was the Smiling Lady. She had been talking to him ever since he'd found the voodoo doll in the basement of the house they'd moved into.

"You told me it was going to keep us safe when they drove me to the dentist's appointment," Frank muttered. His exhaustion was evident in his eyes. "I thought it was true, so…"

Now, Frank was in the car, seated next to his younger self in the back seat. Ruth had not followed them because there had been no need to, and she'd wanted to watch Disney Channel, besides.

"I was just a kid."

He watched as his younger self said the incantations that horrific ghost had told him to say for good luck.

"And then it happened."

Frank was standing outside, now; the bashed-up car remained in the distance as paramedics put his young self

327

TOM COLEMAN

on a stretcher and into the ambulance as the fiend cackled in that screech while standing next to his parents' covered bodies.

He sat on the floor, back in the hallway. Frank had blocked out the details of how they'd died because it was too painful, but the more he watched, the more he remembered. At that moment in time, he was a broken man.

Frank did not want to see any more mental or emotional attacks from the Smiling Lady, so he got up and ran away, trying to get as far away from her as possible. He heard the sadistic, weird laughter from the monster as he ran as fast as he could to escape a fate worse than death.

CHAPTER THREE: FREEDOM

"Somebody... help... I don't want to be alone right now," Frank yelled to anyone who might listen. Maybe one of the guards would help him. Could he find some drugs? The stench was getting stronger, a telling sign that Frank needed to find someone, and quickly.

Luckily for him, one of the guards, a huge man who Frank knew by the name of Cooger, found him. "What the hell is wrong with you, man?" the guy asked, clearly annoyed and tired of what he believed to be Frank's shenanigans. "We are trying to sleep. Why are you doing this?"

"Can I sleep with you?"

"Huh? What the fuck?"

"No, not that! I mean, can I sleep in the room with you?" Frank kept checking his back to see if she had caught up with him because the stench had gotten really bad; the Smiling Lady was nearby.

"Why the hell would I agree to that?" Cooger looked confused. "One, it's against the rules. Two, I can't trust you, considering all the stunts you keep pulling or the claims you keep making. And three, it's just weird, man."

Frank heard the screeching. He was already covering his ears due to the sound. "Look, we have to go." He looked up to find Cooger, who was holding his ears as well. "Wait—you can hear that screeching sound?"

"Of course, man, it's loud as fuck," Cooger said. "And what's that smell?"

"Oh, thank God," Frank exclaimed. He had waited so long for another person to tell him he was not crazy, that the things he was seeing, hearing, and smelling were not schizophrenic or in his mind, but a demonic entity attacking him. "Dude, you have no idea how—"

He shut up the moment Cooger's head split in two. Cooger gasped and staggered backward as blood gushed out of the lower half of the man's head, and his upper half fell to the floor beside him. Behind him was the menacing, ghoulish monster that had been the festering thorn in Frank's side.

"Fuck, fuck, fuck," he yelled, backing away from her. That was when it hit him— she could attack people all this time?

"Wait… so, all these years, you could have killed my sister when I ran to her so I wouldn't be alone? You could have attacked her husband, my former friends, and so many others. Why didn't you?"

The screeching sound hit him hard again, and he fell to the floor, crying as the Smiling Lady cackled. The

TOM COLEMAN

pain was excruciating, but his mind was more focused on trying to figure out why she had not attacked anyone else until then. Had she just been torturing him all this time? Yes, that was it. Torture. Demons are nothing more than demons. They exist to do evil, and for the Smiling Lady, evil meant making everyone—including himself—think he was crazy.

"She did all of that just to alienate them from me, driving me further into solitude while the bitch fed on my loneliness... probably getting stronger." Frank was pissed, but he was more scared than pissed. Now that he knew she could kill people and affect other corporeal beings besides him, the scared man paused his screaming for help. He did not want others to die, but he also knew that had been why the maniacal being had killed Cooger. The Smiling Lady wanted him to know that she could kill anyone, and therefore, stop him from calling others.

"To hell with that," he yelled as he ran. "Somebody, help me, please!" Frank yelled this over and over as he ran away. He heard some of the doors in the corridor open, but he did not wait to see who they were because he wanted to get to the phone to call his sister to get him out of that place. Now that Frank had realized the entity could do whatever it wanted, there was no point even trying to fight. He had to just run.

"Frank, what the hell is happening?" one of his acquaintances at the rehab center, Jerry, called to him as he ran. Frank was about to tell him the truth, but he understood how ridiculous it would sound. Someone was dead, and he blamed a demon? He'd been the only one at the scene, and he was mentally unstable. Was the Smiling Lady trying to send him to jail? A psychiatric hospital? Rehab was not enough?

"Someone killed Cooger and is attacking us! Run, scream, and wake the others," he yelled before running again.

"Wait… where are—" Frank didn't wait for Jerry to finish his sentence. He just kept running until he found a landline.

"Perfect," he said, lifting the receiver and typing out Ruth's phone number. "C'mon, c'mon, c'mon, c'mon… " he repeated, tapping his foot on the floor impatiently.

"Hello?" Ruth said, having answered the phone.

Frank breathed a sigh of relief. "Oh, thank God," he said. He exhaled deeply. "Ruth, I know I am a burden and whatever, but I need you to please come and get me out of here. Things are out of control—"

"What do you mean out of control?" she asked calmly. He had expected her to be worried or freaked out, but he surmised he'd probably just woken her.

"The Smiling Lady is here again, and she literally just killed someone. I don't know why she did that after all these years, but—"

TOM COLEMAN

"Do you want her to go?" Ruth said, cutting him off.

He frowned. Did she not hear what he'd said? "Huh?"

"I said, do you want her to go?"

"Uh… yes?"

"Then give her your soul."

"Wait… what?" Frank was not sure he'd heard his sister correctly.

"Give… her… your… soul." The voice on the phone morphed from that of his sister's to the screeching, haunting voice that had terrorized him for most of his life, sending shivers down Frank's spine. He heard the breathing and the stench right behind him. Frank did not want to turn around—the fear of what he might see was too great for him to bear—so he tried to run, but the demon's claws slashed his back, and he fell to the floor.

Franklin Mercer was in pain. He crawled on the floor as the Smiling Lady cackled at him trying to make his escape. Hearing the architect of his failure laugh at him after all that had been done to him turned his desperation to rage.

"Enough." Frank got up. His sister had always told him to face the monsters in his nightmares head-on, and yesterday, she had told him to do the same to the Smiling

TOM COLEMAN

Lady. He'd never been able to do that, even when he thought he was doing it, and he wondered why that was the case.

"Because I thought you had power over me," he said to the demonic entity as he got to his feet. Frank was pretty banged up, but for the first time in his life, he faced the Smiling Lady, looked her in the eye, and smiled.

"You don't have any power here," he said, walking toward the demon, who stared at him with that disgusting smile. "All you are is a parasite. You've infected my mind and made me think I was mentally ill. That I was crazy. That I was worthless. That's how you feed on people— you find innocent minds and poison them until their psyche is a conducive place for you to live, just like a dirty bathroom."

The Smiling Lady screamed loudly at him as if to say she did not like the way he was talking to her. Her mouth opened for the first time, revealing the serrated teeth and black goo in her mouth. Frank was disgusted by the sight, but oddly enough, he was not scared.

"Look at you," he said, still walking toward her. "You're a hideous, gnarly creature, straight from the depths of hell. You have no power in the land of the living. I have the power, so you made me feel weak, and you confused me into thinking you had the fucking power." He spoke with such confidence it sent the Smiling Lady staggering backward.

Frank had a lot of pain from the claws that had torn his back. He was bleeding, too, and his mind had been so fucked up to incredible levels over the years that a part of him just wanted to die. Even if he cast the demon away, here and now, what would it change? Maybe he was already too broken for it to matter, so he could—

Wait.

No!

The Smiling Lady was trying to seep her way into his mind yet again!

"Get out of my heaaaaad," he screamed at her.

The ghost screeched and was blown back by a powerful gust of wind.

"You see? That is all you can do—infect and lie and destroy. You made me think I needed you and feared you. I've wasted half of my life in pain and misery because of you. But now? Now it all ends."

"Hey, Frank—where are you, man?" The minute Frank heard Jerry's voice, he knew what was going to happen. Fear filled his mind, knowing what the demon could do to the guy.

The fear only emboldened the Smiling Lady. By the time Jerry had turned the corner to the hallway where Frank and his demon were, the Smiling Lady had her claws around his neck. Her dark aura seemed to envelop every portion of his being. It was a threat.

335

TOM COLEMAN

"You want me to let you in?" Frank heard her whispering in his head. He had denied her entry all of these years despite all she'd done to him. Sure, the demoness had accrued much power, but he still had not let her in, and they both knew why.

"I still have my sister," he said out loud.

"Dude, what the hell is going on?" Jerry managed to ask. The demon's sharp claws were around his neck, and he was bleeding lightly. Jerry was looking at the Smiling Lady, and he was as scared as fuck.

"Don't be afraid." Frank tried calming him down. "It will soon be over." It was almost surprising how calm and free he felt at that moment.

"My sister kept me anchored when I was so close to your dragging me over the edge." Frank gazed into the face of the arbiter of his pain. "And now, I am strong enough to push you off the cliff on my own."

The Smiling Lady screamed at the top of her lungs. The screech burst the glass and cracked the walls around them. It was its last stand, but it would not be enough. She tried to kill her hostage but could not.

"You still don't get it, huh?" Frank was at peace. "It is not you who has the power anymore. In fact, you never had the power… you just made me think you did.

"You have done enough. Now it is time to leave the land of the living for those who are still alive."

Frank held out his palm and faced it at the entity as it wailed and screamed. "Be gone," he said.

The demon seemed to peel away, bit by bit, and Franklin Mercer did not take his eye off of it. He looked right at the Smiling Lady, watching as she wailed and screeched from the pain. She withered away, but the pain that had been inflicted upon him was still with him. Frank fell to the floor, sitting down and panting heavily.

He felt happy. He was finally at peace. "I guess I can live my life now." He smiled. "Mom… Dad—I'm sorry, but I feel like I was able to avenge you guys."

"Ruth, sis, I'm coming home." With that statement, Franklin Mercer closed his eyes and passed out.

TOM COLEMAN

TOM COLEMAN

THE ROSE KILLER

339

TOM COLEMAN

340

TOM COLEMAN

CHAPTER ONE:

The alarm rang yet again, annoying Matt. He groaned, slammed it as hard as he could with his hand to stop it from ringing. It fell to the ground, partly broken. Too late. He was already awake.

Matt glanced at the alarm. "Shit," he cursed. That had been the fifth alarm clock he'd bought in the past three months. He'd been spent recently, due to the new investigation over the serial killer, The Rose Killer. The notorious individual had been on a tear in the city for the past five months, taking seven victims. Matt Knowles, being the promising detective coming up the ranks in the precinct, had been placed on the case. He'd handled murders before but never a sequential murderer. To make matters worse, the Rose Killer was incredibly meticulous.

"Another fucking one," Matt complained, "and another early morning trying to catch that fucker." He'd been waking up earlier than usual and sleeping later, thanks to the case. Being the obsessive hunter he was, Matt felt extra enthusiasm when it came to apprehending the evasive murderer.

341

TOM COLEMAN

"Well, gotta go to work nonetheless. No point in crying about it now." He knew the sooner he'd caught this fucker, the sooner he would return to normalcy.

Matt placed his feet on the floor while still sitting on the bed. His body ached. It only did that when he had not gotten enough sleep. It had been like that for three months now.

The phone rang. Matt rolled his eyes. There was only one person who could be calling now.

"Fuck," Matt said. He picked up the phone. "What is it, Cardozo?"

"There's been another body," Cardozo informed. Matt was already tired. "The same M.O. You should get here as soon as possible."

"Where is here? You haven't even given me the location yet."

"It's in front of the precinct."

"What?" Matt was shocked. "I'm on my way."

The young man got up from his bed, had a quick shower, and headed for the precinct. Unlike most police officers, Matt lived uptown in a lavish part of the city. His father was a rich mogul, but instead of carrying on with the

TOM COLEMAN

family legacy, Matt had only one passion. After many fights, his father had finally agreed to leave him alone and let him to decide what he wanted to do with his life.. His father had given him his portion of the wealth when he'd turned 18—as he had with all the children—and Matt had used a lot of it to invest in real estate, which had paid off for him in dividends.

As he drove through his neighborhood, Matt noticed how empty the streets were. It was still pretty early, but he should have seen some rich folks jogging or the odd car here and there. People were scared. The threat posed by the killer had really seeped into the fiber of the community's being.

"And that's on me," Matt mused with a frown, referring to the fact that he had to carry the load of finding the maniac on his shoulders.

He drove to the precinct, which was situated in midtown, and got out of his car. There were too many cars on the street that early, so it was clear that word of what happened had gotten around. Matt decided to use a medium-priced car whenever he went to work so as not to seem like a pompous rich boy.

Matt went into the precinct to meet the man who had been forced upon him as a partner, Miguel Cardozo.

"Where is it?" he asked.

TOM COLEMAN

Cardozo nodded in the direction of the body.

Matt turned to see a young man without a face. It was definitely The Rose Killer's modus operandi. He bashed the faces of his victims beyond recognition, then placed a couple of roses on the concave area of their faces. "Fuck," Matt said. "How did he get it inside?"

"It was originally right in front of the precinct, but even that is worrisome," Cardozo explained. "We brought him inside be—"

"Why the heck did you do that?"

"Can you let me finish before jumping the gun?" his partner retorted. Matt rolled his eyes again. It helped to calm him down. "Good." Cardozo was used to Matt's tantrums, but he seemed pretty pissed off that morning. "The body came with a letter."

"Where is it?"

"I handed it to forensics after reading it. Don't worry; I wore gloves."

"All right. Are you gonna keep me in limbo, or are you gonna tell me what the bloody letter said?"

"You and your rotten mouth," Cardozo noted before telling him the contents of the letter. "The letter said,

TOM COLEMAN

'Hello, Detectives Knowles and Cardozo. This body is a gift to you and your police department. You have to take it inside the precinct within the next twenty minutes, or I will kill a hostage that I have here with me. I want you to feel powerless and understand that you cannot catch me. I want you to know that I can drop these bodies anywhere and at any time I like. To show how great I am, I will perform a nice spectacle soon. I'll be sure to keep you posted. Thanks, Mr. Rose.'"

"The fact that you've memorized the letter is almost as shocking as the crap the loser said in it," Matt remarked. He tried to sound casual, but he was pissed. The killer was toying with them. What was this talk about a spectacle? What was the guy planning? All the detectives at the precinct were concerned, and rightly so. He was sure they were all thinking the same thing: how could the killer have done this right in front of their precinct?

"You know I have an insanely good memory. Anyway, we can now confirm he is a guy. The sicko has even accepted the name of Rose. It's interesting, though, that he didn't refer to himself as a killer, opting instead for Mr. Rose. Do you have any idea what he means by spectacle?"

"It could mean a host of things, but the fact he called himself Mr. Rose is telling. How would he know if we brought the body into the precinct?"

"It would mean he either works here in some capacity or that he has ties to someone who works here." The men glanced suspiciously at their fellow officers.

345

TOM COLEMAN

"Were you the one who found the letter and the body," Matt asked, "or was it someone else?"

"I already know what you're thinking," Cardozo replied. "It was me. I told no one about it. Of course, I couldn't hide the body, but I could hide the letter and give it to forensics discretely. I've filled Chief in on everything over the phone."

"And I was just going to say that we have to tell Chief about the letter," Matt said. "Why haven't forensics taken the body yet?"

"I wanted them to hold off until you saw it in its original state."

Matt understood why, and he turned to the body to inspect it closer. He heard the other cops' murmurs. The uncertainty and doubt surrounding the case and their current situation was palpable.

"Get to work. Do your voodoo stuff."

"Oh, shut up," Matt, haughty as ever, sniped at his partner. He tried to focus on the other parts of the body, considering that the head was unrecognizable, and he noticed indentures on the man's neck. There was no redness on the neck, so he hadn't been strangled. The slight, wound-like marks on his neck looked like they were from someone's nails, particularly someone with long nails.

TOM COLEMAN

"We need to go to the control room for the cameras," Cardozo said to Matt.

"Good idea." Matt had already been thinking about it, but he needed to analyze the body well first.

"Uh, are you coming?"

"You go without me. I need to concentrate."

"All right." Cardozo left, heading for the Control Room to check on the cameras and ask the cameramen if they'd seen anything when the killer had dropped the body.

Matt checked the body further, trying to zoom in on any inconsistencies. He noticed a ring on the man's ring finger, alluding to the possibility that he was married. They'd have to do an autopsy to see if anything stuck out. There was nothing else to be done, and Matt knew that.

"Excuse me, Knowles," a female voice he recognized said from behind him.

Matt smiled. "I guess forensics has finally arrived," he mused. He turned to face Abby Cole, one of the forensic analysts.

"Yes, so could you please excuse us so we can get the body out of here and do our jobs?" she asked in her usual sweet manner.

347

TOM COLEMAN

"Do as you wish, Abby." He liked calling her by her first name even though she'd complained it was unprofessional. "I'll come by later to ask what you've found."

Matt walked out of the building to check out the area in front of the precinct. Cardozo hadn't told him the exact location of where the body had been found, but that didn't stop him from finding the area—officers walking in and out of the precinct kept dodging one particular spot.

"Bingo," he chimed.

The Rose Killer's statement was bothering him, especially the stuff about the spectacle. The sicko had not bothered to contact the police before—did that mean they had a part to play in the success of the spectacle, or was he just so confident that the cops wouldn't be able to stop him, even if they knew what was about to happen? It was enough to piss Detective Knowles off. "Fucker," he muttered, "I'm gonna catch you if it's the last thing I do, and it's gonna be before you can do whatever shitty spectacle this is."

Matt saw the chief of the department, Jeremiah Cruz, drive into his reserved parking space. He got out of the car and walked toward the precinct. As expected, he was greeted on his way by more than one officer. Matt detected a slight annoyance on his face.

"Knowles, come with me," Chief Cruz said once he'd spotted Matt. "Where is your partner?"

TOM COLEMAN

"Good morning, Chief. He's checking the cameras and questioning the cameramen if they saw anything."

"All right. Tell him to come right here when he finishes with them."

"Sure thing, Chief." Matt took out his phone and texted his partner to come to the chief's office when he was done with the cameras.

The two men went past the other police officers on their way to Chief Cruz's office. Once there, Matt closed the door behind them.

Cruz sat down and took a deep breath. "Knowles," his tone already conveyed the seriousness of the situation, "what do you need to catch this son of a bitch?"

"Honestly? I need him to mess up, just a bit," Matt admitted. "The guy hasn't made a single mistake yet. At least, we are sure he is a man, so that's good. He also doesn't see himself as a killer. He used Mr. Rose in his letter instead of The Rose Killer, the name the media gave him."

"So, how do you get him to make a mistake? You're the genius, kiddo. Use that insanely smart brain of yours to find a way to draw him out, 'cos the public is already antsy. They are starting to blame us because they have no one else to blame. We have to give them something… anything."

Matt knew that Chief wasn't being harsh; he was just being realistic. Things would only get worse if they were unable to catch the killer, but the man didn't leave any clues that could be traced back to him. The only thing known was that he used blunt force weapons like hammers or mallets. Occasionally, he uses a knife to kill his victims. The list of victims consisted of both men and women, so it would be hard to find a type to use to track him to draw him out.

"Wait!" Matt had that look he always does when he gets an idea, and this pleased Chief Cruz.

"What is it, Wonder Boy?"

"I think I know how to draw him out."

"Tell me."

"It'll be better if I showed you," Matt said with a smirk.

Cruz groaned like he always did before he accused Matt of being a showman. "Just don't go overboard. Remember, this is a serious case."

"Sure thing, Chief."

"When do you plan on drawing him out?"

TOM COLEMAN

"The press conference is tomorrow, right? I assume info of The Rose Killer has already been leaked to the press. If it hadn't yet, then it will be tomorrow morning." Matt replied, smiling broadly. "I'll handle the press conference tomorrow. It'll really rattle him and cause him to make a rash move."

"How do you know that?"

"Because he is the competitive type," Matt responded. "Trust me, Chief."

Cruz sighed and waved him off. "Do whatever you want. Just be ready to take the blame if it all goes to shit."

"Sure. Got it," Matt said, leaving the man's office. Matt had a really solid plan he felt would lure the bastard out, but would it work? Would it be enough?

CHAPTER TWO

Later that night, Matt finally got home. He had been working all day, trying to find a way to place security cameras around the precinct. The camera tapes Cardozo had been able to get, as well as other ones around the area, had spotted a truck nearby that had dropped off the dead body before speeding away. They were able to follow them for a few miles on the cameras, and Cardozo was following up by tracking the car.

Mat went into his large mansion and went straight for the bar. He let out a sigh after landing on his sofa, happy to finally rest. Matt had already sensed the danger—he heard some weird noise and assumed there was someone else in his house.

He took out his gun slowly, the one he'd hooked to the inner part of his sofa on the side, underneath the fur. Matt removed the safety; he was ready to fire.

"I know that you know I'm here," a voice said from a dark corner of the room.

"How did you get into my place? The security system is pretty tight."

"I'm pretty good with stuff like that."

TOM COLEMAN

"So, I can start searching for all the I.T. guys in the city, Rose Killer?"

"Why would you think I am the Rose Killer?" The man's voice was distorted, which Matt attributed to some sort of voice scrambler. It lent itself further to the man's claim of being good with devices. Was he, in fact, The Rose Killer? Who was the man?

"Even if you did, you wouldn't find me."

Matt got up casually and pointed the gun at the darkness. He could not see who was there, but he could hear the man's voice emanating from the corner.

"And I am Mr. Rose, not the Rose Killer."

Matt had been right in his assessment—the man didn't like being called The Rose Killer.

"So, Rose Killer," he said, ignoring the man's wishes, "what is this spectacle you speak of?"

"I am not a killer. I am merely an instrument to show the depravity of this world."

"Oh, here we go. The lame villain speech on how they are the good guy." Matt rolled his eyes.

TOM COLEMAN

"For that, I will make sure you suffer, too," the voice said in a vicious tone. He was clearly angry.

"Dude, you think entering my mansion is enough to get me? Why don't you come out of that place you're hiding, and let's see who really is the boss? Can you take me down?" Matt knew he was getting under his skin. Now was the time to get that bastard who was stupid enough to come into his home.

The voice scoffed, "I didn't know what I would think when I finally met you. I used to watch you from afar, and you seemed like the embodiment of everything I hated in this twisted society. I'll give you a chance to stop the spectacle. I want to see what a pompous, pampered brat can do in the face of real adversity."

"So, that's what this is about—the rich?" Matt was tired of hearing attacks on the rich. He was rich, yet he'd chosen a job that was definitely not something rich or well-to-do people chose to do. Not every rich person was an asshole.

"Look, just come out so I can arrest you. I've had too many sleepless nights to let you go."

"Why don't you come and make me?" The way he'd phrased it let Matt know the man was prepared if he tried to go after him. It meant that the best thing for Matt to do was simply to kill him. The worst thing that could happen would be for him to fall into whatever plan this stranger had for him.

TOM COLEMAN

"Enough of this."

"I haven't even told you about the way I can help you stop the spectacle, yet. You sh—"

Matt fired several bullets in the direction of the voice, interrupting his statement. He lowered his gun and ran to the corner to turn on the lights. "Fuck," he said when he saw it was coming from a voice transmitter. The guy had never been there. Maybe that was why he'd been so confident. Now, though, Matt had been given a lifeline. If they could track the source of the transmission, they could pinpoint where it had come from. It might not be the killer's base, but it was still something.

Matt called Cardozo, who picked up the phone on the first ring.

"Hey, I was just about to call you. I was able to track the van to an abandoned building in the slums. Bystanders said they saw a man come out of it and go into the building, but when we checked, there was nothing. We are still search—"

"He infiltrated my house," Matt cut him off.

"Who?"

"The Rose Killer. He left a transmitter and talked to me via it."

"How the fuck did he know where you were staying?"

"Well, my dad is pretty popular, and I wasn't really secretive about where I was staying, so anyone could figure it out, to be honest," Matt answered. "What's shocking is how he was able to get in. I even got upgrades to my system less than a month ago, thinking it would make me extra secure. He seems to have a great affinity for tech and stuff like that, so that may narrow our search a bit."

"What did he say?"

"He talked about giving me a chance to stop the spectacle and incessantly denied being a killer. What a psycho. He also has an intense hatred for those in power, as well as the rich."

"That would mean we're looking for someone in the middle- to lower-class, which would support the fact that the bus was dumped in the slums," Cardozo opined. "Whatever this spectacle is, it could be an attack on the wealthiest in society."

"But something doesn't make sense," Matt disagreed with his partner's assessment. "All his victims were middle-class individuals. They were average people."

"No, think about it for a sec—none of them were particularly upper-middle-class if you know what I mean.

TOM COLEMAN

Cole told us about the latest victim. He was the manager at a Walmart. Not a huge paying job, but definitely one of the better ones, considering the economic climate right now."

"Fair enough. He would also want to go after people who could be easily reached and killed," Matt concurred. "So, does that mean the spectacle will involve an attack against those in power?"

"It seems likely. That would be a good assessment," Cardozo agreed. "We have to contact as many politicians or the rich and powerful as we can before whatever he's planned comes to fruition."

"From the way he talked, it seemed like he was going to act soon. I'll give my speech pretty early tomorrow, and since the news outlets already got wind of the latest murder, I'll have to respond, so yeah."

"All right. Get some sleep. Tomorrow is going to be a helluva day."

"I bet," Matt said, and the call cut out.

TOM COLEMAN

CHAPTER THREE

Matt looked at the reporters and journalists with their cameras, pens, and papers. They stared at him anxiously until he was ready to step into the limelight to give his eagerly anticipated address to the press. Thankfully, they did not know about The Rose Killer's letter. He had arrived later than he'd wanted because some florist company had a big sale, and the roads were jammed with delivery trucks sending flowers downtown. Had they changed the date for Valentine's Day? Regardless, he couldn't care less what was going on down in the slums. Speaking of the slums, the police had spent some time there combing the abandoned building but found nothing.

"You ready?" Cardozo asked, and Matt nodded. He just wanted to get it over with and get back to tracking the killer. Something was about to happen, something big. The suspense felt unhealthy. A part of him wanted the serial killer to just do what he wanted so it could be done with, though he knew that was unreasonable as a lot of people were bound to die because of it. This was his best chance to draw out the animal and get him to play on his terms.

"Yeah," Matt replied, "let's go." He left Cardozo and headed for the podium. The moment they saw him step on, the journalists all began talking at the top of their lungs, each one trying to outtalk the person beside them.

358

TOM COLEMAN

Seeing the rowdy lot of individuals vying for the chance to get in the first word disappointed Matt.

"Okay, let's begin."

Somewhere in the lower downtown area of the city, Mr. James Rooser lived in a rusty one-room apartment. He was just trying to get by and provide for his family as well as he could until his failure as a provider had led him down a path of alcoholism. Now, he was a shadow of his former self, and all he did was lay on his couch and wallow in self-pity. The door rang, and he groaned.

"Sarah," he called for his daughter to open the door since he was too lazy to do so himself. "Sarah, where the fuck are you?"

After another knock, Mr. Rooser finally got up to open the door, but when he did, no one was there. All that was on the front stoop was a gift basket filled with roses.

"What the hell?" he said, carrying it in and looking at what was inside.

Back in front of the precinct, everyone waited in anticipation for Matt Knowles to make his speech.

TOM COLEMAN

"Before any of you start with a barrage of questions, I have a few things to say to and about The Rose Killer," Matt began his speech. "The man known as The Rose Killer took another life last night and delivered it to our doorstep. However, this was not The Rose Killer."

Murmurs filled the crowd. They either whispered to one another or asked him questions yet again, which only served to irritate the detective.

"He was an impostor that wants so badly to be the Rose Killer he tried to copy his work, and in doing so, gave himself away. The media does not know this because we did not release the autopsy reports as well as the letter accompanying the body, but the modus operandi does not fit the original Rose Killer. In the message, the killer referred to himself as Mr. Rose, as if trying to differentiate himself from The Rose Killer. The serial killer known as The Rose Killer never confronted the police directly. From these facts and more that we cannot share, we can only come to the conclusion that this latest murder was enacted by a fame-seeking follower who is impressionable but frankly, stupid." Everything Matt had just said was a lie. He wasn't lying all the way, though. The letter was not in line with what the killer had done in the past, and he had referred to himself as Mr. Rose in the letter. Nevertheless, the autopsy had revealed that it was, in fact, the same person who had killed the other victims that had taken the life of this one as well. The killer would be annoyed at this inaccuracy and lash out, which is what Matt was counting on. The crowd was shocked but enthusiastic for more answers, but Matt was surely not going to let them speak.

"Our intel has also led us to believe there might be an attack on the wealthy sometime soon. The killer seems to have a big grudge against those who are at the top of the money chain in our great city."

"Is that so?" a man said from the other side of the road. Matt recognized him a bit, but he could not pinpoint from where he knew him. The man looked angry and annoyed. "You dare lie about me like that? You fucking bastard—you called me an impostor?"

"Matt, he works in the control room," Cardozo whispered into his ear.

Matt finally saw the whole picture. That was how the guy had known so much about devices and I.T. and how he had been able to plant the speaker.

"Ah, so you were one of the guys who came to upgrade my security system, weren't you?" The media watched as Matt bantered with the Rose Killer, their puzzled expressions letting on that they had no idea what was going on.

"As expected, rich elitists like you would never notice nobodies like me. Today, however, you will. The spectacle will show you just how pointless it all is," the man continued.

"His name is Victor Rochas," Cardozo whispered to Matt. "Thirty-one years old. Single. That's all we have on him now. We're trying to get more info."

"I wasn't going to reveal myself, but you really got under my skin, I must admit," Victor lamented, chuckling. "After coming this far, who would have thought that I'd fall prey to my own emotions first."

"Happens to the best of us, Victor."

His face perked up at the mention of his name.

Matt believed he had Victor right where he wanted him. He supposed Victor thought the same.

"Nice one. I wish I had gone with Cardozo to question you about the cameras. Then, maybe I would have noticed how sketchy you were," Matt said. "Anyway, the jig is up, asshole. You aren't getting anywhere near the governor or whomever you're after.

Victor smiled, and for the first time, Matt was nervous.

"You still don't get it," Victor said. He laughed. It sounded maniacal. "I told you I would give you the chance to stop the spectacle, and do you know why? It's because I knew you wouldn't be able to."

"What the fuck are you talking—" The detective's words were drowned out by a loud explosion. It wasn't just one. They came from over the city. Matt knew it was the spectacle, but the explosions hadn't come from either uptown or the suburbs. They were right there in midtown and downtown, close to the slums.

"What did you do?" Matt inquired.

"Guards, arrest him!" Chief Cruz ordered, finally finding his voice.

The officers tackled Mr. Victor Rochas, pinning him to the ground.

Matt ran from his podium and into the press, pushing them violently aside as they scattered, probably frightened from the bombings.

Cuffed and on his feet, Victor continued to laugh.

He grabbed Victor by his shirt. "What. The fuck. Did. You. Do?" Matt growled.

Victor simply laughed. "Did you all, by any chance, see roses being delivered throughout the downtown?"

Matt could not believe it.

TOM COLEMAN

"The target wasn't the rich. It was the poor. When two elephants fight, the grass suffers. In the end, those at the bottom always suffer, and those at the top keep moving on."

"Is that what this was all about, proving how pointless it is trying to be a cop or changing the system?" Matt had never been more enraged in his life. "Look around you! People are dying! People like you! You killed them!"

"I started killing people one by one randomly and when everything was set, I was finally able to show them my spectacle." Victor looked relieved, but all Matt saw was a deranged psychopath. "There were bombs placed in each of the gift baskets, set to blow up thirty minutes after they were picked up from the flower shop that my dead wife used to own. I am doing this because of her. No one cared when she got killed by two punks that felt like robbing a flower shop, and killing her because she put up a fight. No one cared then and I don't care now."

"What if they weren't able to deliver them within those thirty fucking minutes?"

"The drivers would die, then," Victor responded calmly. "Delivery guys are also lower-class. Did you even care when you saw them making the deliveries? Did you wonder what was going on? No, you didn't because people like you don't see our world. You don—" A hard punch to the nose shut him up. Matt followed it with another, and then another.

The world around the two men went up in flames. Matt Knowles did not care about any of that. All he wanted was to beat the bastard to death.

He was eventually held back by his fellow officers, but he kept trying to reach the man that had destroyed all he stood for.

Two hundred and thirty-one people died that day.

TOM COLEMAN

TOM COLEMAN

THE CURSE OF HERNANDEZ
PART FIVE

367

TOM COLEMAN

368

TOM COLEMAN

CHAPTER NINE:
THE WINDOW AND THE
SUITCASE

Christina opened her eyes. She could tell she was back in the attic. Christina looked around, but she couldn't see her husband, and it made her worried. Did that mean she was still in a dream? Christina could never be too sure, but her gut told her it was not an illusionary construct.

"I don't have the luxury of being overly sure," she noted to herself, getting to her feet. A part of her was telling her to scream, but she knew the risks. To be honest, the ghosts would already know she was awake, so she might as well scream for her husband. Christina kept in mind that she could still be in an illusion, so she had to tread carefully.

"Carlos," she yelled, but there was no answer. What was going on? Christina always asked herself that question, but then again, she was also in a situation where she needed to ask herself that. The tired woman had no idea what was happening or where her husband was, and that was disconcerting. She tried making her way outside, but her parents were blocking her way.

"So, this is an illusion, huh?" she surmised.

TOM COLEMAN

"Not really, *hija*," her father said. Christina reasoned that this was only a representation of her parents, constructed by her subconscious mind. Her memories of them weren't good, so she knew this was going to be stressful. The best thing was to ignore them and look for her husband, so she continued walking on to the attic's exit.

"Remember how much of a stubborn child you were?"

Don't take the bait, she told herself, don't take the bait. It was the only thought on Christina's mind as she struggled to walk away.

"You did so many bad things, and we let you get away with it. You know why? Because we loved you. That is what you do when you love your children; you protect them at all costs."

"Is that how your parents raised you?" she turned and screamed back at them, rather reflexively. They seemed shocked at her outburst, just as they would whenever she had gone on one of her temper tantrums as a kid.

Christina scoffed, almost amused at their lack of awareness. "You don't still get it,"she said, baffled at the people who had brought her into the world. "You still don't bloody get it. You do something so terrible and inconsiderate, but when I get angry, you both gasp and act all fucking shocked." Christina didn't care if it wasn't really them. She had forgotten they were an illusion, and she had fully immersed herself. There were so many things she wanted to say to her parents that she might never get to, so she felt as if she might as well let it all out.

TOM COLEMAN

"You're both pathetic. Sure, I was a troublesome kid, but why the hell do you think I was troubled? I did anything I could to get your attention, any one of you or both, if possible. Isn't it sad that you only cared about me when I did something bad?" She kept on with her rant, her parents watching with slight surprise as Christina blasted them. "You just never cared. Sometimes, I wonder why you even had a kid if all you were going to do was work and not be at home, leaving me with nannies or alone."

She was tired, but she still had the strength to spare. There was still so much she wished to say. Christina hated her parents so much, and there were a lot of unresolved matters festering in her heart and mind. "Why did God have to give me worthless parents like you?" she kept going. Christina just wanted to hurt them, to make them feel anything: anger, sadness, disappointment. It was as if she were a young girl again, trying to spur a reaction from her parents, but it didn't work. They seemed a bit startled, but other than that, both of her parents remained calm.

"You never were the daughter we wanted," her father said, his typical frown plastered on his face below his thick mustache, the one she always hated because it made him look like the quintessential villain in the Mexican books her mother used to read her. Now, it was Christina's turn to be lambasted. Since she knew it was all in her mind, Christina was fully aware that it was all just a projection of her insecurities when it came to how her parents saw her.

"Why did we have to give birth to such a horrible and lousy child?" her mom added. Her father looked angry most of the time, even when he wasn't, but her mother

371

TOM COLEMAN

had an aloof look. To Christina, the only thing worse than a negative expression was disinterest, and the word disinterest summed up her mother pretty well.

"You never did any chores because we had the maids to do them. The least you could do was just shut up and be a good little girl, but you couldn't even do that." It was not what she wanted to hear. She had wanted an apology, some kind of closure. Was this the house's doing?

Her parents continued, exposing Christina to the worst possible things stored in the deep crevices of her mind.

"You know, we are manifestations of your mind?"

"Stop." Christina walked backward, trying to put some distance between herself and them.

"Which means we are merely saying what you already think. You know that you were and are a terrible daughter," her mother continued.

"Just stop." Tears streamed from her eyes.

"You blame us for your mistakes to avoid your shortcomings." The revelation of how Christina saw herself and how she felt her parents saw her as was too much to bear. She had thought that she couldn't be caught off-guard again after the trauma of Susan, but oh, how wrong she was.

"Stop," Christina yelled, covering her ears with her hands and closing her eyes. After a few seconds, she opened them to a squint, but her mother and father were there

TOM COLEMAN

and only a few feet away. The house shook in a phenomenon she had never experienced before, but it was not enough to take her mind away from the verbal shellacking she was enduring at the hands of her parents.

"We wished you'd have died in that car accident so you could have saved us the trouble of having to save your ungrateful ass, yet again," her dad said, scowling even more than usual.

Christina screamed as loudly as she could. She tried to push her father away, but she simply passed through him instead. She turned around, only to be attacked by her mother.

"What kind of child can't even die right? We were so happy when you finally decided to cut ties with us. It saved us the ire of our peers and friends seeing us as bad parents. You left us, and things got so much better," Mrs. Solis explained, her deadpan look clear as day. "Why do you think we haven't tried to reach out to you, Tina? We have the resources to track you. Surely, if we wanted to be with you or see you again to patch things up, we could have done that, couldn't we?"

Christina clutched her head as she screamed and cried. This was bad... really bad. Was that how her parents really felt? Had their lives gotten better after she'd left?

"You, your mother, and I all know why we have not contacted you." Dad stepped in again. "You are a disease that sickens everything it touches, a poison that will destroy the life of the poor man who was unfortunate enough to marry you." Was she really a disease, after all?

TOM COLEMAN

"You don't even know where he is right now. That alone should tell you how disgustingly toxic you are. He is probably dead, and it is all your fault. You have never been loved, not by a single person on this Earth, not even Carlos."

Christina could not stop screaming. She covered her ears again, but it wasn't working. The sound seemed to pass through her parents, and she fell to the ground, begging her parents to stop.

***

Carlos rushed quickly back into the house, suitcase in hand. The moment he entered, a vase flew in his direction, almost hitting him squarely on the head. He was able to evade it by the skin of his teeth.

"The house is alive?" Carlos had always known the house was a sentient being in its own right, but he never thought of the house itself, nor did he consider that the components of the house could move independently. He guessed it was its final attempt to stop him from getting the suitcase to the attic. He ran as fast as he could to the stairs, but the chandelier at the entrance came loose, fell, and landed right in front of him.

"Shit," Carlos yelled, dodging it by jumping sideways and landing in an unorthodox fashion. His eyes were wide open now—the house was not playing, not that it was playing before, but shit just got real. Getting to the attic was going to be a hell of a task. Carlos also noticed the ghosts were

TOM COLEMAN

nowhere to be found. For the first time, Carlos really considered the relationship between the ghosts and the haunted house. He thought they might be working in tandem, that the ghosts and the house were one and the same, or, at the very least, a matched set.

"What the hell is this?" Where were the ghosts? This would be the perfect time for them to get him. The man got up from the floor of the rattling house to notice there were so many things in the air, flying about. He had never seen anything like that in his entire life. The house was not normal. How the hell did a house get so... maniacal?

"If there is a God, please, help my wife. Save Christina," he prayed. Now that things had gotten so out of hand, all he had was hope.

He ran to the living room while running away from the flying glasses and other objects. Carlos had a broken shoulder, a bleeding head, and now, an entire houseful of flying objects.

Carlos entered the living room, wondering why he thought it would be better than the hallway entrance. The books on the table were floating, and the television flew from where it was and came right at him. It hit him hard, but he was able to block it as best as he could. The impact of the television sent him flying a bit, and he landed painfully on the floor. He groaned and grimaced, pushing the television away from him.

He was on his last legs. How many times had he thought he was at his end and wanted to give up? Regardless, he couldn't let now be one of those times. He heard ominous swirling noises around him as he writhed on the floor. The

375

TOM COLEMAN

pain was too great, and he prayed the agony would come to an end. Why couldn't he just die? Would that be so bad? It was all just too much. The television had bruised his sternum, and he felt a considerable amount of pain there. He chalked it up to yet another issue in a growing list of problems he had accumulated.

Something clicked for Carlos: was he insane? Had he forgotten that his wife was in danger? He had heard her scream, hadn't he? If so, why was he sitting there whining? Carlos did not care that things were flying around. The only thing that mattered to him was Christina. If she died, he would really give up because she was the only thing keeping him going whenever he wanted to give up.

"It's not how many times you fall down or wanna quit, but how many times you fight the urge to give up," Carlos said, espousing words of encouragement to himself as he struggled to get up. He was spent, but it was the time for him to push his body to the limits. He managed to get up, his knees shaking. He hurt everywhere. Something hit him on the back of the head. He squinted. Things were flying about, so he had to be careful. Carlos kept going, even though everything was flying everywhere. He held his broken shoulder with his other hand, trying to minimize the pain. His weakened arm was also the one carrying the suitcase. Carlos would rather have used his strong arm, but he was busy using it to clear the way from the items flying around the house. He wasn't moving very fast, which meant he was an easy target, but Carlos Hernandez had already resolved to take all of the hits. The ones he could dodge, he would, especially some of the bigger things flying about. Thankfully, he hadn't gone into the kitchen, or a knife might have entered his skull by then.

TOM COLEMAN

He made his way slowly but steadily back to the stairs, being hit by all sorts of things as he went on. As he climbed the stairs, the steps beneath him slowly tore apart. "You've got to be joking," he said in disbelief, quickly picking up his pace as he mounted the stairs. He climbed as fast as he could, but his leg got stuck in one of the steps. He groaned while struggling to extricate his leg from the spot on which it was stuck. All around him, things were coming apart; Carlos knew he had to hurry.

Carlos broke free with one final push. He did not take a moment to celebrate because there was so much danger around him. The fearful man made his way upstairs, being hit by clothes coming from the bedrooms on the upper floor.

He finally reached the hallway where the ceiling route to the attic was. He could hear screaming, but he did not know who it was. The voices sounded familiar, like something he had recently heard, but he did not know to whom the voices belonged. Carlos dragged on, nevertheless.

The walls were crumbling, and sand poured from their innards. Upon getting closer to the entrance, Carlos remembered he hadn't used the ladder when going down. This time, he wouldn't make the same mistake.

"The attic," he murmured, "it always felt different." He felt a dark essence exuding from the bedrooms as he walked past them to the ladder. It got more potent the closer he went. To him, it was as if the attic were the epicenter of it all, and he gained a newfound confidence that what he was going to do would resolve everything. Then again, what if it didn't? Carlos

377

TOM COLEMAN

did not even want to entertain that idea. It would work. It had to.

The sand pouring from the walls in had reached his ankles, and Carlos finally recognized a voice, that of his wife, Christina. She was screaming, from what he could tell, maybe even begging. Something was seriously wrong.

"Christina, I'm coming. Just hang in there, " he shouted, hoping she would hear him.

Carlos reached the ladder and struggled to climb up. He now heard voices whispering in his ear in the nebulous manner of the house. What was, however, strange was that the words he was hearing were ones of encouragement.

"Do it… do it," a voice whispered in his ear as he tried to find the strength to climb to the attic—using his worn-out legs and half-working arms had proven more difficult than he'd anticipated.

"Help us," said another voice.

"Set us free," yet another said.

Carlos climbed, moaning in agony with every push of his arm, spurred by the crackle of his dislocated bones as they rubbed against one another, coinciding with an excruciating level of hurt. When he finally reached the top, he saw Christina there, yelling at nothing. She looked petrified, but there was nobody else there.

The moment he entered the attic, the rumbling reduced significantly. It really was a special place, but Carlos thought it

TOM COLEMAN

would be worse in the attic since he was sure it was the origin of the ghosts.

"Christina!" Carlos ran to her and shook her vehemently. Her eyes were closed, but it was apparent that she was incredibly scared of something. "Christina, are you all right?"

"Tell them to go away," she screamed over and over. From what Carlos could ascertain, she was suffering from another of the house's nightmare illusions, but where had the ghosts gone?

"Snap out of it, Christina," he said to her, trying to get her back to reality. "It's me, Carlos."

"C-Car... Carlos?"

"Hey. Hey, sweetie, it's me. I'm here," Carlos said, making sure she was fully conscious of her surroundings.

"Where are my parents?"

"So, that is who you saw." He wanted her to explain more, but the voices in his head spoke again.

"Hurry," they said sternly. "It's coming!"

Carlos finally realized to whom the voices belonged: the ghosts. But it made no sense that they were trying to help him. Was it a trap? No, it did not seem like it. Irrespective of what they said, Carlos knew he had to put an end to it.

The attic began to crack, and he could see the grains of sand already falling from the nooks and crannies.

TOM COLEMAN

"We'll talk later," Carlos said. "We have to put this back where we found it."

"You were there the one who found it. Where was that, Carlos?" Christina inquired.

Carlos was too tired to move, but he did not want to show it because they were almost at the finish line. No way was he going to lose strength now. In spite of what he had said, Carlos fell to the ground, exhausted. The combination of pain and strain was just too much for him, and losing the amount of blood he had was not helping matters either.

***

"Carlos? Carlos. Oh, my God." Christina was worried. She was mentally worn out, but Carlos looked much worse. It was like his mental and physical wellbeing had both taken a hit.

"Just over there. Right in front of the window." He pointed to where he had found the box, and she knew what she had to do.

The wind howled, blowing vigorously in the attic. That wasn't normal, especially considering the window was closed. Christina surmised that the house must be really upset, and it was fighting back. She put the suitcase where it should be, but the wind kept shifting it to another part of the attic.

"The wind is taking it away," she informed her husband.

TOM COLEMAN

"What do you mean," Carlos managed to reply, raising his voice to overcome the sound of the howling wind. "It should be correct. That's exactly where I found it."

"Are you sure this is precisely how you saw the suitcase?" she asked.

Sand suddenly poured from the walls, knocking her back, and Christina hit the ground head first. She was unsure if she had a concussion, but the fall had made her dizzy. The sand was getting worse, so they needed an answer and fast.

"Wait… yes," Carlos said as if he'd remembered something. "The window! It was covered when I came here." The sand engulfed Carlos, too, and this worried her. Christina, however, knew she did not have the time to worry about him right then—she had to finish the job. A medium-sized piece of cloth on the floor in the corner of the room, so the young lady fought her way through the bombardment of sand, stretching, arching, and trying with all her might, spitting out sand and getting some of it in her eyes until she had reached it.

As she went for the window, Christina had something akin to an out-of-body experience. It was as if all the evil in the world had passed through her in an effort to scare her from covering the window. Christina was scared—no, terrified—but she knew it was the only way they could survive. She found her inner strength and pushed through, hooking the cloth over the window frame by tucking it behind the frame.

Christina Hernandez no longer knew where her husband was. She did not even know if covering the window up would work. What she did know was that they had both done their best to end the crazy house of horrors.

381

TOM COLEMAN

"Go back to hell, bitch," Christina said as she tucked the final edge of the cloth behind the window frame.

The chaos ended, and everything went white.

TOM COLEMAN

CHAPTER TEN: OUR STORY

Carlos Hernandez opened his eyes to see white space as far as the eye could see. There were no landscapes, environmental or household. He was the only thing to fill the white void.

A hand grabbed his hand. When he looked to his side, he saw Christina, and he was shocked that she was there with him.

"Oh, thank God, Christina," Carlos said. He grabbed his woman and hugged her tightly.

She returned the action. "I am so happy you are here with me," she said, overjoyed. A slow dread set in, and they looked at each other cautiously yet knowingly. Neither of them wanted to say it, though both of them knew it had to be asked.

"Are we dead?" Carlos inquired.

"I don't know."

"You were able to cover the window, right?"

"Yeah," she said.

"The ghosts told me that I forgot the window," he explained. "We wouldn't have done it without them."

"Wait—the ghosts... helped you? Helped us?"

"Yes," a woman with messy hair said. "Yes, we did." It was then that Carlos noticed there were people around them. Carlos had already recognized some of them, but the same could not be said for his wife.

"Who… who are these people?" she asked Carlos, looking a bit scared. Who could blame her after the torrid time she had had?

"A woman with messy hair," he said, pointing at a female with spiky hair who was smiling at them. "A young girl with a creepy-looking doll." The girl looked shy, and she wasn't smiling. She hid behind another individual whom Carlos assumed might be her father or a father figure.

"A huge man." Carlos gestured at the largest person standing before them. He was burly in build, but he had a welcoming face. "The Silhouette Man."

"Oh, my God," she said once things had clicked for her. "You're all ghosts."

They nodded.

"You were the ones tormenting us all the while." Christina frowned.

"Wait, Christina," Carlos said, trying to calm her down. Even though he did not understand the full scope of what was happening, he knew they were not their enemies.

"What do you mean by wait?" she complained. "Those demons attacked us and made our lives a living hell."

"We didn't," the woman with incredibly messy hair said.

TOM COLEMAN

"What do you mean? You didn't?"

"The house did."

"What exactly is this house?" Carlos asked. "What is happening here?"

"I guess we will tell you... our story," they said in unison.

"Now that we are set free, we have full control over our realities and can share them with you," one of the ghosts, a man with an army uniform, said. The environment changed, and he showed Carlos a scene depicting the army man when he had first entered the house. It was definitely not in the computer age, and that begged the question of just how long the house been around. The features of the house were definitely old, but they had since been updated to fit the times.

"I came here after the war to settle down, thinking that I would be free from the demons I faced in war," he explained to Carlos and Christina as the three of them watched the man's story unfold. They watched as he stumbled upon the chest and the covered window.

"Back then, it was just a box with papers inside," he said, shaking his head and looking distraught. "I opened it, not thinking much of it. I didn't even throw it out or touch it again. I just closed it after I saw the weird language, then kept it somewhere in the attic. I removed the cover on the window, too." Carlos saw everything he described.

"Just that... little mistake..." The man broke down crying. Carlos understood his pain after watching what happened next. The poor man started seeing the people he had

TOM COLEMAN

killed during the war while in his bed. The illusions got worse and worse until he could take it no longer. He tried to leave the house but was unable to. A soldier like him back then must have killed many people during World War II, and he might have even done some morally questionable things or killed people he did not want to, all in the name of war. Carlos knew how much he carried his own rough childhood with him and the people he had hurt, and he could not imagine how this man must have felt.

"Eventually, I had to let the nightmares end," the man explained as Carlos watched him hang himself. "But instead of dying, a strange phenomenon occurred.

"We found out that anyone who dies in this house and falls prey to the attacks without figuring out how to stop them would remain trapped in this house forever," the woman with spikey hair said, taking over, and the scenery switched to her time spent in the house.

"One by one, we all opened the suitcase and saw the papers. We also uncovered the window. None of us even thought that could be the reason for our troubles. I took medication to try to stop it to no avail. In the end, it was all pointless." Carlos saw how a beautiful woman devolved slowly into madness and insanity after being haunted by the Silhouette Man. She had pulled her hair so many times out of frustration that her hair became messy and spikey, and that was how she died.

The ghost reached out to Christina, touching her on the shoulder. Once she made contact, Christina's face softened, and Carlos knew she could see her at last. "I'm

Heather," she said. "I'm sorry for the part I played in your experiences. This twisted house uses me like a doll. Well, used—not anymore."

"I have been here with my doll for a while now… along with Daddy," the little girl with the creepy doll said, taking over from Heather.

"How? You, too? It came for you? You're just a little girl." Tears flowed down Christina's cheeks as the shy little girl spoke.

"Daddy and I were happy. He bought me nice presents like this doll I got for my birthday," she said as they watched. "And then one day, bad things started happening."

Christina turned green when she saw how the girl had died, and Carlos wondered if she was about to throw up. "I can't watch this." Carlos hoped she'd look away. Considering her past, watching little girls getting killed was most likely triggering, but it was her story. The ghosts had suffered enough. The only thing they asked for was to be heard and acknowledged. They had to open their eyes and see the girl's plight.

The girl had been drowned by her father right before he slit his throat. She struggled for air as he forced her head into the bucket of water. It was, perhaps, the most gruesome death they had to watch.

Carlos looked at the ghost of the girl's father. No matter how bad they felt, it was nothing compared to what the man had felt for what he had done to his daughter, even as a ghost.

TOM COLEMAN

"To drive a man to kill his own daughter…" Carlos said quietly.

"I didn't even have my doll with me. I left it in my room."

Carlos remembered seeing the doll in one of the rooms on his first day in the house.

"Mine was back in 1922," The Silhouette Man said. That old? Carlos could not believe it. "I died by mistakenly poisoning myself with arsenic. The house tricked me, using illusions to confuse my mind. Ever since then, I have had to spit out the poison."

"The weird fluid you spat out whenever you saw us," Carlos confirmed.

The man nodded. "I died in the dark, with only my silhouette visible to me in the mirror as I coughed out blood."

They were all very sad stories, making him hate the house even more.

"We are now free from this haunted house. Thank you and farewell," they said as they faded away.

"You were the first to defeat the house, so all the poor souls held in its grasp are now free," the Silhouette Man, who was the last to go, said. "My name is Jeremiah. Please, remember me. Please, remember us."

As their essence melted away, the reality of the house set in. They were in the attic of a rugged old house.

"Let's leave this goddamn house, then burn every inch of it to the ground," Carlos said, still reeling. He took one last look at the suitcase and the window that had brought so much pain to so many people, and Carlos and Christina Hernandez left the attic and then the house.

The realtors, the property, and even their health—all of that could wait. Right now, after pouring fuel onto every inch of the bloody murder house, Carlos Hernandez held the match, his wife by his side. He took a deep breath, threw it into the entrance, and watched the house of horrors wail, scream, and burn to a crisp. What a satisfying sight it was to watch the root of all evil burn. Who better to watch it with than the one he loved?

THE END

TOM COLEMAN

TOM COLEMAN

JOIN OUR COMMUNITY

We are gathering all people with a passion for Horror and Thrillers in our special group. If you want to be in and connect with us, join our group :)

Join here:

https://www.facebook.com/groups/541739063097831/

TOM COLEMAN

HONEST REVIEW REQUEST

Dear reader, if you liked my book and want me to keep on writing, please go online and leave an honest review.

Your review means a lot to me, and it will encourage me to surprise you with more books and stories.

TOM COLEMAN

THANK YOU!

TOM COLEMAN